Sizzlin' 7s

A JAKE LEGGS NOVEL

WM. E. BOBB

Copyright © 2021 Wm. E. Bobb
All rights reserved
First Edition

PAGE PUBLISHING, INC.
Conneaut Lake, PA

First originally published by Page Publishing 2021

This is a work of fiction. That means I made it all up. All the characters, places and events portrayed in this book are products of the author's fertile imagination or are used fictitiously and are entirely coincidental.

ISBN 978-1-6624-2929-3 (pbk)
ISBN 978-1-6624-2930-9 (digital)

Printed in the United States of America

PROLOGUE

The pickpocket didn't know it yet, but he didn't have worry about his overdue electric bill, or anything else for that matter.

He'd just lifted a wallet from a kindly looking grandfather type playing the dollar Sizzling Seven slots. In the bathroom stall, he was astounded to find forty-nine one-hundred-dollar bills along with a half-dozen top-end credit cards. He stuffed the bills in one pocket, the credit cards in another, dropped the wallet behind the toilet, and walked out. He knew a guy that would give him another twelve hundred for the cards. He couldn't believe his luck.

Unfortunately for him, the old gentleman whose wallet he just discarded was indeed a grandfather, but he was anything but kind.

He was the head of the Phoenix Mob.

1

When I got back to my room at the Riverside Casino, the message light was blinking. I was in Laughlin, Nevada, on involuntary temporary exile. This was imposed upon me for a little misadventure in Flagstaff, where I had been living peacefully until a shitstorm landed in my lap. The man generally considered to be the next chief of police there—Detective Sgt. T. Tom—had personally given me the order over drinks two weeks ago. If I had to be exiled, what the hell, Laughlin wasn't so bad. Like Br'er Rabbit said, "Throw *me* into the briar patch."

Me being Jake Leggs, pushing fifty, in good shape, erstwhile finder, most times contractor, sometimes fixer. My job description is a little vague. I do what I do. I don't have a résumé. I don't carry a gun, but I have friends that do. People that need my services know where to find me.

Lately, I didn't want to be found, so I ignored the flashing red light on the phone and decided on a shower to wash the cigarette smoke off me. I didn't smoke, but it seemed everybody else in the casino owned stock in R. J. Reynolds.

I was drying off when there was a knock at the door. I figured it was housekeeping, so I yelled, "I don't need service today! Thank you!"

The knocking began again.

Oh…what the hell was I thinking?

"Yo no necessito servicio ahora. Gracias!" I tried.

Knock, knock, knock.

With a sigh, I wrapped the towel around my waist and went to answer the door. And to my surprise, it was Leo, probably the last person I expected to find at my door. Leo was Tony's butler.

Tony was the head of the mob in Phoenix.

I'd accidentally landed a deck and roofing job at Tony's cabin in the pines a couple of years back. One thing led to another, and before I knew it, he'd had me do a few things that didn't have anything to do with construction. By the time I'd figured out who he was, it was too late.

"Tony wants to see you. Put some clothes on," Leo said, brushing by me and into the room.

I started to protest, but I knew it was futile. *When the king summons...*

Leo studied the room while I got dressed. I was putting on my shoes when he said, "Where's the broad?"

"What broad?" I responded. Answering a question with a question was always a stall tactic so I could have time to think. I did it all the time with Leo.

"Oh, please, Jake. Don't insult my intelligence. The big-tittied DEA agent you checked in with two weeks ago. The one that looks like Marilyn Monroe with an attitude. Ring a bell?"

Tony was one of the reasons I was in exile, so I should have known he'd be keeping tabs on me, to monitor the fallout, if nothing else.

"Oh, that one. She used me, abused me, then abandoned me when she was finished," I said with a smile.

Leo smiled back, lifted his coat to the side so I could see his holster, and said, "Get used to it. Let's go."

2

We got to Harrah's casino up the hill five minutes later. Leo pulled up to valet parking and tossed the key to the attendant as I hurried to catch up with him. We walked to the elevators and took one to the twenty-fifth floor in silence. Tony's suite was at the end of the hallway, with a chunky guy standing guard by the door. He opened the door as we approached.

The suite was spacious with a panoramic view of the Colorado River below and the mountains in the distance. Tony and Francine, his wife of sixty long-suffering years, were sitting on a couch watching the huge wall-mounted flat-screen TV. It was tuned to a cooking show. Figures. She loved to cook. Francine was the reason Tony looked like he was carrying a boulder for a belly. He needed new knees every five years. He'd probably need a new heart soon too, if they could find the original.

Leo was already helping Tony to his feet when Francine saw me. If she was surprised to see me, she didn't show it. She waved and went back to watching Rachael rustling up some rigatoni. Tony came over and hugged me like I was his long-lost son, whispering in my ear, "Let's go in the bedroom and talk."

When the king summons...

I followed Tony into a bedroom the size of my two-room suite at the Riverside. Leo closed the door behind us. That worried me, so I sat in the chair closest to the door. Like old girlfriends, old habits die hard.

Tony sat on the corner of his California king-sized bed. He took a couple of minutes to catch his breath while gazing out the window. I kept my mouth shut and waited.

"I got a little problem," he finally said, still looking out the window at the river.

I immediately translated that to mean *Jake's got a little problem.*

Jesus. I'd just forked over two hundred grand to this guy two weeks ago for some logistical support on a problem that *he'd* gotten me into. I *knew* it—he wanted more. I didn't have it. I'd already given it away. If somebody had told me a month ago that I could blow a million bucks in three days, I'd have asked them what they were smoking. Now I knew better.

I threw my arms up in surrender. "Look, Tony, if you want more than the two, I gotta tell you, I don't have it."

First, confusion crossed his face, followed by surprise, and then he laughed softly. Tony didn't laugh very often.

"No, Jake. I still owe you. This is something else."

Whew…

"I had my wallet lifted in the casino. I want you to return it to me and find the asshole that did it."

Excuse me?

I was flabbergasted. As usual, my mouth moved before my brain engaged. "You gotta be kidding me, Tony. How the fuck am I supposed to do that? This is your backyard. Use your *own* guys. You got more resources than me." By this time, I was standing up and waving my arms. I did not want to have anything to do with this. I was already on probation—sort of—and this smelled like screwing the pooch. *Muy malo.* Bad.

Tony watched me with a smile until I ran out of steam and sat down.

"The answer to your question is yes. Normally I would handle this in-house…" he said.

In-house? Like, normally I'd have Leo kill him?

"But in this case, I can't. It's delicate."

That's when I knew I was in serious trouble. I put my hands up to my face and rubbed it as I tend to do when I was in deep shit.

"Why me?" I thought out loud apparently, because Tony answered me.

"Because you're uniquely positioned to do so."

The last time I'd heard those words spoken, it hadn't turned out well for the recipient. He was in jail, and Jesus would be on the streets before he was. Nevertheless, my curiosity was piqued, so I had to ask.

"And why is that?"

His smile got even bigger, as if he got the joke and I didn't.

"Because you're a nobody," Tony said with a laugh.

Hell, I knew that. *When the king laughs...* I laughed along with him.

3

Tony looked at me like my father did sometimes. Father to son. Baseball came to mind. I could almost hear the announcer over the PA system.

"The pitcher has got the signal. Here comes the windup…" What I mean is that nobody I know, knows *you*," he said.

"And it's a…fast ball, right down the middle."

"Nobody knows I'm traveling. Losing the wallet is a major inconvenience for me. I don't care about the money—close to five grand—but the credit cards are a concern. I want them back, and I don't care what it takes. I can't use my own people because I'm not supposed to be here."

I couldn't help myself. "If you don't mind me asking, why the hell *are* you here?"

"We're on our way to LA to see the kids. We stopped here for the night. Francine doesn't like for me to gamble, but she loves Keno. Thinks it's bingo but with bigger balls," he said with a smile. "I gave her a grand and off she went. I sent my guy to keep an eye on her, and I walked next door to Tres Palms. I played the dollar slots to kill some time."

Kill some time. That was funny. Knowing Tony, that was the one thing he couldn't terminate.

"That's when some shithead lifted my wallet. I didn't even feel it." He looked at me, smiling again for only the third time I'd ever seen him do so. "I don't care about the money. The cards are the thing."

"Why don't you just cancel the cards?" I asked as a formality.

Something else was in play here, I thought, but I had to be sure.

Tony's smile disappeared. "That's not an option. You have some contacts here. Use them. I want that plastic back. If you can't recover it, I want to know who had it last."

Now that I was sure Tony wasn't going to jack me up or kill me, I said what any red-blooded American would.

"What's in it for me?"

"How about the two hundred grand you just paid me, plus a tip."

The door to the bedroom opened, and Leo walked in with an aluminum briefcase. He set it on the lampstand next to me and snapped the locks on it, opening it.

There, in front of me, were five one-pound bundles of hundred-dollar bills, vacuumed packed. I recognized four I'd already given him by the marks I'd made before handing them over to him last time we met. At forty-eight thousand dollars per pound, I could play the ponies for at least a couple of years. I was impressed.

"That'll do," I said, reaching my hand across to Tony.

I should have known I was shaking hands with the devil.

4

After unsuccessfully attempting to pry more information from Tony about why the credit cards were so important, I told him I'd be in touch and left.

I took a cab back to the Riverside and had the manager put the briefcase in the hotel safe. I was tempted to dip into it on the ride over, but I knew I'd have to give it back if I couldn't retrieve Tony's cards. I didn't even want to think of the consequences of that.

After leaving the manager's office, I stepped into the Loser's Lounge. Tom, my favorite bartender there, put a longneck Coors in front of me when I sat down.

As I sipped my beer, I thought about my assignment. Someone had lifted Tony's wallet. He'd lost close to five grand, but he wasn't concerned about that. He'd lost a half-dozen credit cards, and he *was* concerned about that. Concerned enough to pay me a quarter million dollars to get them back. He said he couldn't cancel them. What the hell was *that* all about? They were obviously something other than credit cards, but what? Laughlin was about halfway to LA, so maybe he really was going there, but it wasn't to shop or see his kids. That was total bullshit.

Some of what he had told me sounded credible enough. Francine loved Keno as much as shopping, so she had undoubtedly prevailed upon him to stop off here and break up the long trip. Laughlin was relatively free of mob involvement, so it wasn't likely he'd be recognized here. After checking in, Francine went down to play Keno. So that his wife wouldn't see him gambling, he had walked next door to Tres Palms to play the slots. Okay, I could see it.

Tony had probably been merely a target of opportunity for a thief with a death wish.

I finished my beer and signaled for another. As Tom handed it to me, I asked him, "How often do you hear about pickpockets here?"

Tom laughed. "Are you kidding me? Almost never. The last one was a couple of years ago. The security guys accidentally dropped a cinder block on his hands, several times, before they turned him over to the cops. Word gets around. But then again, some people might not report it for whatever reason. Why?"

That told me either the thief was just passing through and didn't know the local ground rules, or he was desperate enough to take a chance. I hoped it was the latter.

"Just curious," I said, paid my tab, and wandered out onto the casino floor.

I sat down at a blackjack table that had a young good-looking dealer. She promptly relieved me of a hundred bucks while I concentrated on her cleavage instead of my cards. Some people might call that lechery. I preferred to think of it as formulating a plan of action.

I tipped her a ten, got up, and left the casino.

5

The night was still young, and it was warm outside, so I decided to walk to the Tres Palms casino. It was only about a mile away, and I hadn't walked today. I gave up jogging decades ago. I noticed there were a lot of older couples—salt and peppers, I call them—doing the same thing in companionable silence.

I was a people watcher. I think I could tell how long a couple had been married just by looking at them together. The more they looked alike, the longer they've been married. If they looked like twins, they've been married forever. Fifty years, minimum.

They always looked happy, and they always waved. I wished *I* was that happy right now. I didn't have a clue how to go about this.

A thought came to me—that wasn't entirely true. I remembered that Mike O'Shanahan, a Flagstaff cop I used to know, had moved to Laughlin after retiring. Everybody called him Shane. We'd fished together a few times and still kept in touch.

The last time I talked to him, he said he worked at the Palms, but he didn't tell me any more than that. I figured, what the hell, even if he was a part-time security guard, it was a start. Besides, I wanted to see where it all went down.

Once there, I wandered around until I found the one-dollar Sizzling Sevens slot machines. There were five them in a row next to a carousel of five-dollar machines. I put a twenty in the end one. That gave me six pulls at max play. You only got the jackpot if you bet the max, which was three bucks a pull, so you always bet the max.

SIZZLIN' 7S

At one pull every five seconds, I was done before I could even order a drink. I cashed out my remaining two bucks and went looking for a waitress.

I found one standing next to Shane at the cash-out window. He looked like he'd lost some weight, dyed his hair, and had a real tailor. I was impressed.

His eyes tracked me before I got close. He said something to the waitress, and she moved off before could I catch her. His eyes smiled, but not his mouth. He didn't even try to look surprised to see me and had his hand out to greet me.

"Well, well, well. Look what the javelinas dragged in. Jake, how are you?" He seemed genuinely happy to see me, which was good. Because I had a favor to ask of him. He still could do his innocent look. "What the hell are you doing here?"

I figured he'd already heard by now. He had two brothers and niece still on the force back in Flagstaff. I told him the truth.

"Sarge ran me out of town, temporarily."

"Yeah, I heard." He was finally smiling. "Sarge called me. Said you might be floating to the surface soon and to keep an eye out for you. Of course, I don't think he meant that in a bad way." By this time, he couldn't help laughing.

I laughed along with him. He was a good enough guy, and I'd never had a problem with him.

The waitress showed up out of nowhere and handed me a Coors. I guess he told her what I drank.

I handed her a ten. Service was everything.

"I need a favor," I said to Shane as soon as she skipped away.

"Surprise, surprise." He was still laughing. "Let's go into my office."

I guess Sarge must have told him why I was in exile.

As I followed him through a door and down a set of stairs to a labyrinth of offices clustered around a video command center, I realized that Shane was not just a security guard in a nice suit.

We entered a large office overlooking the nerve center of the casino. He sat down behind a large desk and said, "Have a seat, Jake. What can I do for you?"

I sat down in the plush leather chair in front of his desk and looked around, then back at him. "Damn, Shane. Does this mean we can't go fishing anymore?"

He was enjoying himself. "Cool, huh? Hell yeah, we can go fishing. Only now we don't have to use that piece of shit you call a boat. I got a real one. Hey, you remember that time on the Colorado above Lee's Ferry when we ran out of gas?"

"How could I forget? I remember me rowing and you giving orders. If we'd have missed the dock at the ferry, we'd have been dog meat," I said, laughing. "And speaking of which, I've got a client who is gonna be dog meat if his wife finds out that not only was he here, he managed to lose not only his money but his wallet and all his credit cards as well."

Shane smiled. "Yeah, I can see where that might be a problem."

He reached over and punched a button on a console built into the desk. "Marlene, didn't somebody turn in a wallet a couple hours ago?"

I didn't hear the response. It must have come through his earbud. He nodded. "Let me have it."

When he turned to me, I said, "Marlene?" I knew that was his wife's name. "Your secretary is named Marlene too? That must get confusing."

"Not really," he replied as the door opened and his wife came in with the wallet.

You could have knocked me over with a feather. "Your wife is your secretary?"

"Hell yeah," she said as she tossed the wallet to Shane. "You don't really think I'd let him hang out in a casino all day without me, do you? It was part of the deal." She gave Shane a sweet smile, then turned to me.

"Do me a favor, Jake. Take him fishing. He's looking too good. He needs to be roughed up a little bit." She patted me on the shoulder and sashayed out of the room.

Salt and pepper with spice. No doubt about it, she was coming along very nicely herself and could sashay with the best of them.

I watched her go and turned to Shane. "Damn."

"Tell me about it. The new tits, face-lift, ass lift, and liposuction cost me a fortune." He turned his attention to the wallet, which took about three seconds.

"William Smith," he said, reading from a driver's license. "Cute." He threw the wallet on the desk and handed me the driver's license. "That's all that was in it. Is that your client?"

The face on the photo was so blurry as to be unrecognizable. Fake name, address, everything.

Tony, Tony, Tony…

I looked at it and started hedging. "Hard to tell."

"He's not one of ours, so I had Marlene check the other casinos. Do you know how many Bill Smiths are registered at the major ones? Over fifty. If it's his, he can claim it. I'm sorry if he lost any money, but there's nothing we can do about that."

William Smith was never coming to get his license.

"Maybe there is," I said. "You've got cameras everywhere, right.?"

"Everywhere except the bathrooms. Why?"

"Can you pull up some video of a bank of slots from a couple hours ago?"

"Sure. Which ones?" he asked.

"The Sizzling Sevens. By the five-dollar carousel."

He got up and headed for the door. "Come with me."

6

I followed him into the control center. He tapped a woman sitting in front of a bank of monitors. She got up, and he took her seat.

He started the tape from three hours ago, then fast-forwarded until I said, "Stop."

I saw Tony standing in front of the same machine I'd just played.

"Back up," I said. "Now regular speed."

We watched for about ten minutes and nothing happened. Tony had pushed the chair aside and stood playing the machine.

"Okay, stop. Can you go back, look to the left and right?" I asked.

"Sure." He zipped back to the start and panned right. Just a few older women walked by. He backed up and panned left. A man was standing about twenty feet away with a cup of coffee, watching Tony.

"Stop. Can you zoom in and copy that face?"

"No problem," he said, typing in a command. The printer spit out a copy.

I was pretty sure what I was going to see next. "Now go back to the old guy and fast-forward until you see another figure, then stop."

It didn't take long. Seventeen minutes in, another figure brushed by. Shane backed it up and ran it slow motion, zooming in. He had to do it a couple of times until we saw the pick. Tony didn't even turn around. He acted like he didn't feel a thing.

"What do you think?" Shane asked.

SIZZLIN' 7S

I think that pickpocket is a dead man. "I don't know. It's hard to tell if that was even my guy," I said, grabbing the photo of the coffee drinker from the copier. "I'll show this to him, see if he remembers anything."

Shane wasn't buying it, but he let it slide for now. He went back to the video of Tony playing the slots. "You know, that old guy looks kind of familiar. I just can't place the face."

Oops. Time to go.

I got up to leave. "Thanks, Shane. I'll let you know if I turn up anything," I said as I headed for the door. He waved and went back to studying the screen. I didn't want to be around when he finally figured out who the old guy was.

I grabbed the first cab sitting in the portico. "Do you know where the Tiki Lounge is?" I asked the cabbie, who looked like he was from a country that liked really thick mustaches. He nodded vigorously. We drove over the bridge, turned right on 95, and headed into Bullhead City in silence. I had no real plan, and I didn't want to hang out in one of the casinos.

The Tiki Lounge was a dive owned and run by a crusty eighty-four-year-old lady named Ruby, who also cleaned the place in the morning. She was a tough old bird—a relic—and I admired the hell out her. When I was in town, which was every three months or so, that's where I hung out. I'd been there a half dozen times in the last two weeks.

Ruby had moved here fifty years ago with her husband. They bought the bar, and he promptly dropped dead of a heat stroke the first summer. This was before air-conditioning. If you've ever been to Bullhead City in July, you'll know what I'm talking about.

She didn't let that stop her. After a half century, she'd seen it all, done it all, and knew everybody. She wasn't shy about sharing her knowledge either.

Halfway there, the cabbie—who looked Pakistani, and I noticed from his displayed license was named Mohammed—asked me, "Will you be needing me to take you back?"

Why are all cab drivers from the Middle East?

"Can you wait, Mohammed?"

He turned around and smiled. "Everybody calls me Mo. And yes, I'll wait as long as you want me too."

I gave him a fifty and climbed out of the cab.

The bar was dim and smoky. I gave my eyes a moment to adjust, then spotted a seat near the cash register. That's where Ruby hung out.

I nodded to her when she spotted me. I really didn't want any more alcohol, but I needed a reason to be there. Ruby glided back with my Coors and leaned across the bar.

"You look a little jittery, Jake. What have you been up to?" she whispered in a whiskey voice. She may be old, but her eyes glittered like a young woman's. She was a hoot.

"No good. As hard as I try, I can't seem to say no," I replied truthfully.

She started laughing too, but it quickly turned into a hack. I hoped she wasn't going to drop dead on me.

She grabbed a bar napkin to wipe her chin when she finally got herself under control. "Get used to it. I've had that problem for seventy years." She cackled.

That was the second time today somebody told me to get used to it.

I pulled the picture of the coffee man out of my back pocket and showed it to Ruby. "You know this guy?" I asked her.

She looked at it for so long, I thought she was having a senior moment. I was about to snap my fingers in front of her face when she grunted and handed the picture back.

"Yup. That's Dudley."

I should have been surprised, but I wasn't. If the guy was local, Ruby would be the one to know. She was my best shot. If I didn't score here, the chances were that the coffee man was just passing through, and I was screwed. For once, things seemed to be falling into place. This was almost too easy. *That should have been my first clue.* I was elated.

"So what did he do?" She wasn't dumb. She knew I wasn't looking for Dudley to give him money.

For some reason, my instincts told me I needed to back up. "Skip trace."

"I'm not surprised. He's always struck me as shifty," she said with a shake of her head. "He comes in here every now and then. Bounces from here to Vegas and back." She straightened up and rubbed her lower back.

I needed a last name. "Dudley who?"

"Don't know. But he always comes in here with a couple local guys. His cousins. I know them, and they're no great shakes either. Trailer trash."

"When was the last time you saw him?"

"Hell, you just missed him. He met his two running buddies here, bought drinks for everybody, and left."

Well, shit.

"You don't where he lives, by any chance?" I asked, taking a shot in the dark.

"Nope." Her eyes were twinkling again. "But I know where you can find him."

Hot damn. "Where?"

"I overheard them talking about going to Pussy Willows, that titty bar that just opened next to the Home Depot," she informed me with a wicked grin. "Talk about smart marketing. I wish I'd thought about that."

She probably already had, but it was forty years too soon.

Dropping a twenty, I reached across the bar and kissed her hand. Her smile was radiant.

I scooted my ass out the door and jumped into the cab. "Pussy Willows," I told Mo.

7

Pussy Willows was located in a building across from the Home Depot.

It used to be a bustling real estate office before the housing market tanked. Now the windows were blacked out, except for the neon beer signs.

The place was run by a forty-something-year-old woman named—you guessed it—Willow. She ran a clean place, didn't allow drugs, and anything the girls did, they did on their own time. The cops rarely had to be called here, and that's just the way she liked it. I don't frequent the place because I don't normally have to pay to see naked women, but Willow and I have been in more than a few poker games together, and we were friends.

When Mo pulled up to the front door, I said, "You got a cell phone?"

He grinned. "Doesn't everybody in America?"

"Write down your number on a card," I told him, pulling out my wallet. "I want you to wait for me across the street in the Home Depot parking lot. I don't know how long this will take, but here's another fifty. I'll give you another when I call you."

Mo obviously couldn't believe his good fortune. He muttered something that sounded like Turkish. For him, this was shaping up to be not only a profitable night, but a lot more interesting than his usual casino-to-casino runs.

He had no idea.

SIZZLIN' 7S

When I walked into the place, it took me awhile for my eyes to adjust to the lighting inside. Willow caught sight of me, came over, and gave me a hug.

"Well, Jake, this is a surprise. And to what do I owe the honor?"

"I'm looking for a guy. No big deal," I told her as I grabbed a table in the corner, away from the action.

She patted me on the knee. "What'll you have?"

"Coors, if you got it."

She was back in a flash with my beer. "On the house," she said and went back to tending bar.

I turned my attention to the rest of the bar. A topless woman was bumping and grinding energetically on an elevated stage in the center of the room. Her smile was a professional's, and she was putting on a good performance, losing pieces of fur at regular intervals from her lithe body. The good ole boys were eating it up. A dozen men watched from seats around the platform, and they didn't care if she smiled or not.

Locating Dudley and his two pals was easy. They were the loudest and drunkest of the bunch, throwing dollar bills and crude comments at the stripper.

It looked like they were going to be here for a while, so I settled in for the evening. It wasn't like anybody was waiting for me at home. I was probably going to have to double down with Mo.

I nursed my beers and waved off lap dances for another two hours, until the boys finally ran out of steam, got up, and staggered out the door.

I called Mo and told him to come pick me up at the bar.

Dudley and his two pals gave each other high fives in the parking lot like they'd accomplished something other than getting stinking drunk, offending everyone, and throwing their money away. After a couple of minutes of that bullshit, his two cousins got in a pickup, Dudley climbed into an old Camaro next to it, and off they went.

Mo had the cab in front of me before they got out of the parking lot.

I got in beside him. Pointing at Dudley's Camaro, I said, "Follow that car." I'd always wanted to say that.

Mo grinned. "Yes, sir. I assume you do not wish for him to know he is being followed?"

I smiled back at him. "You assume correctly."

Mo did an excellent job of tailing Dudley, all the while humming the theme song from *Goldfinger*. I pulled out two more hundreds and laid them on the dash. His smile got even bigger. He thanked me and Allah in Turkish, I think.

We headed south out of town, toward Needles, across the river in California. There wasn't much traffic, so Mo stayed back quite a ways. After about ten miles, Dudley's brake lights flared, and he turned left onto a dirt and gravel road. No turn signal.

"Turn off your headlights and go slow," I said. The moon was full, so it was easy to see the road. "Make the turn, then let's see what happens."

There was a lot of nothing out here, only desert scrub brush and cactus, and except for a few dips, flat as a pancake. The dirt road continued east, straight as an arrow.

A half mile ahead, Dudley's brake lights came on again, and the car turned to the right, the headlights coming to rest on single-wide trailer with a small front porch.

Mo didn't need any instructions from me. He approached slowly while I rolled down my window. Dudley had exited his car, leaving the door open and country western music blaring from the radio. There wasn't much chance of him hearing the crunching of our tires on the gravel.

Mo stopped about a hundred yards away and put the cab into park. Dudley had staggered his way to the front door and was trying unsuccessfully to get his key into the lock. It took him almost a minute before he succeeded, finally pushing open the front door…and blew himself to hell and the trailer to smithereens.

The huge fireball sent all four walls and the roof of the trailer in different directions, and it threw Dudley onto the hood of his car, fifty feet away.

"Fuck!" I yelled and ducked as the pressure wave hit us. Damn good thing I'd rolled down the window or I'd be wearing it on my face. Mo had his hands up over his head and said something in Turkish that sounded like a prayer. Debris rained down all around us.

I jumped out of the cab and ran over to the Camaro. Dudley was sprawled face up on the hood with eyes open. But he wasn't breathing, and his head was twisted at an odd angle. Not to mention his hair was gone and his clothes were smoking.

He was dead, bigger than shit.

I realized I didn't have much time, so I dragged him off the hood and onto the ground in front of the car headlights, which were miraculously still working. Checking his front pockets and finding nothing but loose change, I rolled him over and found a wallet in one back pocket and a wad of hundreds in the other. I stuck them in my jacket and rolled him back over just to make sure he was dead. The head didn't roll with him.

Yup. He was dead.

I ran around to the driver's side door, which was still open. The dome light was on. I didn't want to touch anything, but a quick visual scan of the seats, dash, console, and floorboard revealed nothing that looked like credit cards.

I hauled ass back to the cab, which Mo had had the presence of mind to turn around, and hopped in beside him. He was moving before I could shut the door.

I saw that he was sweating profusely, and his eyes were huge. He was still muttering in Turkish or Arabic.

"Head back to town," I told him unnecessarily. He was already making the turn onto the highway and turning on his lights. We were so far out of town it would be some time before the fireball was reported and before the first responders were on their way.

Mo put the cruise control on fifty-five, kept his eyes on the road, and tried to control his breathing. He had been enjoying our little adventure, but now it was turning out to be lot more dangerous than he had expected.

Me too. *What the hell had just happened?*

Obviously, Dudley's trailer had exploded, killing him. But was it an accident, like a gas leak? Or murder? I was leaning toward murder. I pulled Dudley's wallet out my jacket and turned on the dome light. In it, I found his driver's license, some dirty pictures, and cards from a number of Las Vegas casinos. No credit cards. No plastic of any sort.

Well, shit.

I stuck the wallet back in my pocket and pulled out the wad of money—mostly hundreds—and counted it. A little over three grand. Dudley had managed to burn through almost two thousand bucks in eight hours or so.

I turned to see Mo staring at the money. His eyes were even bigger, if that was possible. I counted out five hundred and handed it to him. He thought about it for about two seconds and took the money. His grin was back. He was decompressing. He thanked Allah. I came to recognize the phrase as "Thank God" in his primary language. Akbar something or other.

"Needless to say, none of this ever happened," I told him.

"I have no idea what you are referring to, sir," he replied, turning his attention back to the road and still smiling.

We were almost back into town when the first cop car and fire truck blew by in the other direction. Mo gave them a cursory look in the rearview mirror before going back to humming *Goldfinger.*

As we approached the Laughlin bridge, he said, "Are you a policeman or are you a criminal, sir?" while negotiating the turn, as calmly as if asking, "Where are you from?" like any cabbie would.

"Neither," I replied, and that seemed to be the answer he wanted to hear.

I had him drop me off at the Edgewater Casino. I told him I'd be in touch and walked toward the front door.

8

In the reflection of the glass doors, I saw Mo drive off.

Essentially, Mo didn't know my name, where I was from, or where I was staying. And technically, he wasn't guilty of anything other than giving a fare a ride in his cab. I was comfortable with that, and I think he was too. If he kept his mouth shut, we'd probably be okay.

I continued through the doors and into the casino.

The Edgewater was one of the oldest casinos and seemed more like an old lady's bingo parlor. Nickel shots for the blue hairs. Laidback. I love the place.

I didn't know my mother was a gambler until after she died. Her favorite casino was the Edgewater. I think she might still be here, like a ghost. Sometimes I wander through here wondering which machines she liked. It's kind of like a connection, and I enjoy it. For about five minutes.

Then I was out the back door, headed uphill to the Harrah's Hotel and Casino. To see Tony.

Another walk, and time to think was just what I needed right now. The river walkway was perfect and calming at the same time. Dudley's demise could have accidental, but I didn't think so. If it wasn't, the question was why. And by whom?

The why was apparent: Dudley stole Tony's cards and the money.

The who was more complicated. Could be Tony, could be one of Tony's rivals, could be a pissed-off girlfriend, could be anybody.

I didn't think it was Tony, not that I wouldn't put it past him to kill a guy that stole from him, but he didn't know about Dudley yet. How could he?

My gut feeling was that one of Tony's enemies had picked up on an opportunity. A local thief had some plastic to sell. Maybe he'd already sold it and the buyer then eliminated him. I hadn't found the cards, so it was possible that they were still in play.

Since Tony had paid me an obscene amount of money to find the guy who stole his wallet, I felt an obligation to report that I had achieved that goal. I had the wallet. But then he would ask if I had recovered the credit cards or knew where they were. After I told him no, his butler would kill me.

It all came down to the plastic, the credit cards. What was so special about the cards? Something niggled at the back of my mind. It took a minute, but then I knew what it might be. They weren't credit cards.

They were data cards. I'd read something about it in a recent issue of *Scientific American*.

They *looked* like credit cards, but they held something far more valuable. They held information. Essentially a thumb drive that looked like a credit card, allowing the user to access and transmit data, including bank codes and password—practically anything—in encrypted form.

If my suspicions were correct, Tony hadn't lied to me, but he hadn't exactly been up front either.

After a refreshing fifteen-minute walk up the hill, I walked through the doors at Harrah's. I made my way to the tower elevator, passing two Sizzling Seven machines that were calling out to me. It could have been tinnitus, but I knew what Odysseus went through with the sirens.

Unfortunately, I had no mast handy to lash myself to, so I promised them I'd be back later, if I was still alive.

The ride to the twenty-fifth floor was uneventful. It got eventful as soon as I walked out of the elevator. Two no-neck peckerwoods grabbed me and dragged my ass into a room next to the elevator, and before I knew it, I was face-first against a wall. Rough hands assaulted not only my space but my privates as well. Once he was satisfied I wasn't armed, I was escorted into the suite's main room. Leo was waiting.

Tony was watching the exercise channel, the one with all the broads with perky tits and tight asses selling the latest variant of a rubber band. Francine must have been down the hall in another room.

Leo pulled out a chair for me next to Tony and turned down the sound down on the huge flat screen. I sat down and kept my mouth shut. I was still pissed off about the sexual assault thing, but I decided to let it go and concentrate on trying to walk out of there alive.

Tony gave me his undivided attention as I sat quietly. Nobody said a word for a full minute.

Finally, Leo said, "Would you like something to drink?"

"A beer would be great, Leo," I replied. "It's been a long night, and yes, I am a mite thirsty."

Tony's mouth didn't smile, but his eyes did.

"Okay, Jake," Tony said as Leo went to get me a beer. "You've had your fun with Leo. What's the deal?"

Translated, that meant, *Did you find the fuck-wad that robbed me, then kill him and get my shit back?*

I decided to go with the good news first.

"The man that lifted your wallet was named Dudley Conor," I said, tossing Dudley's wallet to Tony. "His driver's license was the only thing in it other than this." I laid the remaining hundred-dollar bills on the table in front of him. I thought William Smith might catch the irony of a license being the only thing in a wallet. I'd kept the business cards and the dirty pictures of Dudley's girlfriends.

Tony didn't even look at the wallet or the money. "You said *was.*"

Leo took that moment to deliver me a Coors. I heard him step back and then felt, more than heard him, pull his automatic from the pancake holster on his hip. I knew it was pointed at the back of my head. A .22 most likely, perfect for executions. The bullet penetrated the skull, did a Cuisinart on the brain, and there was no exit wound. Made cleanup a snap.

"He's dead now. He didn't have the cards on him or in his vehicle," I said to Tony, looking him in the eye.

Tony looked up at Leo. I swear to God, I heard the safety click off. The gun was ready to fire.

"But I *think* I might know who has it," I hastened to add.

I heard the rustle that leather made when metal pushed against it. Leo had put his piece away. I was going to get to drink my beer and explain to Tony what I thought was going on here.

And ask a few questions of my own.

9

Interrogating the head of the mob was like doing an oral examination on a cobra. You had to be *very, very* careful how you go about it. I took a healthy swallow of my Coors while I thought about how to proceed. There were some things I needed to clarify, but I didn't want to know too much. Some people would say you can never have too much information. I beg to differ. In this case, it could make me dead.

I began by telling Tony what I knew. "I was able to identify Conor through video cameras at the Tres Palms casino." That wasn't entirely true, but the less he knew about my methods, the better. "Acting on a tip, I located him and followed him to his residence. Unfortunately, he was killed in an explosion when he got there. I don't think it was accidental."

If Tony was surprised by that, he didn't show it.

"I was able to search his person and his vehicle before I was forced to leave the scene. What you have in front of you is what I found. If the cards were in his residence, they're toast now."

I waited for a response. When none was forthcoming, I continued, "On the premise that he somehow disposed of the cards before I caught up to him, I am shifting my efforts to his associates. In that respect, I should have more for you tomorrow."

I thought my report sounded almost professional.

Tony leaned back and closed his eyes. When he didn't ask any questions, I decided it was time to ask some more of my own.

"Have you ever seen this Conor before?" I inquired.

He shook his head, his eyes still closed.

"Do you think he could be associated with any of your competitors?" By that, I meant any other syndicates, but he knew what I meant.

He opened his eyes, picked up the license, and tossed it to Leo. "Not to my knowledge, but I'll find out," he replied as Leo left the room.

With Leo gone, I felt a little more comfortable. "How long are you going to be here?" I asked him.

"As long as it takes."

Even though I thought I knew the answer, I asked him anyway, "You weren't just going the see the kids, were you?"

His silence spoke volumes.

"Why did you bring me in on this?" I asked him.

He heaved a sigh. "Like I said, Jake. You're like a son to me."

Here we go again.

"We've been through this before. I can't use my own people. Nobody knows I'm here. Very few people know you and I are acquainted, and you just happened to be here. Also, in your blundering way, you seem to get results." I took that as a compliment until he said, "And you're expendable."

So much for being a son.

I had a lot more questions, but none that I wanted the answers to. I got up to leave. Hoping to reassure him, I said, "I'll be touch tomorrow. Don't worry, Tony. I'll get to the bottom of this. You can bet your life on it."

"You already have," he replied, turning the sound back up on the TV.

10

I took the River Walk from Harrah's back to my room at the Riverside, passing Tres Palms along the way. It gave me time to think and digest everything that had happened in the last six hours. It was like being in another shitstorm. Things were happening fast—too fast. It was hard to get my head around it.

One, Dudley was probably murdered. Two, he didn't have the cards on him or in the car. Somewhere before I caught up to him, he'd gotten rid of them. Three, since he'd spent most of that time in a bar with his two pals, the logical assumption would be that one of *them* had the plastic.

It was too late to go back to the Tiki Lounge to talk to Ruby. Besides, I was worn out. Ruby always got in bright and early to clean the place, so I'd catch her then. In the meantime, I was going to need more boots on the ground here.

I pulled out my cell phone and called Arliss.

Arliss was my associate and my best friend. Hell, he was my only friend. He was on the big side, looks Black, but he's also Hispanic, French, and mongrel. He's a free spirit, loves guns, living on the edge, and drama. Fortunately or unfortunately, I provided a lot of that for him.

He answered on the second ring. "Yeah, what do you want?"

If you didn't know better, you'd think he was being rude, which he was.

"Some help, you rude fuck. I'm in trouble," I replied, which I knew would please him immensely.

"Already? It's only been two weeks. I think that's a record."

"Where are you?"

"Momma Rose's," he said through a mouthful of donut. Momma Rose's was his mother's donut shop that she'd just opened in Flagstaff. She had the best donuts in town, and everybody knew it.

Flagstaff was only three hours away. I told him what I needed, and he hung up before I could say thanks.

The warm breeze and the moonlight reflecting off the river had its usual calming effect upon me. I watched an excursion boat with a raucous wedding party in full swing pass by, headed upriver. The locals called it the party boat. A few salt and peppers walked by me, even though it was past their bedtime.

By the time I got to the Riverside, I was feeling much better. As I wandered through the casino, a number of slot machines whispered to me as I passed by. *I'm the lucky one. Come play me.*

I resisted until I got to the three Sizzling Seven's dollar machines at the T that goes to the North and South Towers. By far the most popular dollar slots in the house, you usually had to wait to get a machine. Sometimes these three machines thought they were ATMs, seemly giving the money away and spitting out actual coins, not paper receipts. I love them. To see all three of them empty was more temptation than I could take. Even though you're only supposed to play one at a time, I stuck a hundred-dollar bill in all three of them and started pushing buttons.

One hour later, and fifteen hundred bucks to the good, I cashed out. There's something about loading fifteen trays of one hundred gold coins each and then walking them to the cashier's window that's right up there with sex.

Speaking of which, I hadn't had any in a week and I could use some.

Looking around, I saw a field of blue hairs. Nothing under seventy, so I retreated to the bar. Tom was still working. I sat down where he was cutting limes.

"Working overtime?" I asked him when he looked up.

He was pulling a Coors out of the cooler. "My relief didn't show up. Kids nowadays, they don't wanna work, and the immigration people are running off the Mexicans. That's okay. I need the overtime. Gotta pay the bills." He went back to cutting limes. "By the way, a couple guys came in earlier, looking for you. Showed me a photo. You're still wearing the same clothes."

Uh oh.

"Really," I said, trying not to let my surprise show. "How long ago?"

"A couple hours."

About the time Dudley got to meet Sister Mary Katherine in hell.

"What did they look like?" I asked him, sliding a hundred across the bar.

"Two steroid addicts in dark shirts. Fire plugs. Five-ten. Thirty years old. Dark hair. Beady eyes. Pretty much your basic pair of thugs." He made change at the register and placed it in front of me. "They were just fishing. I acted like I didn't know shit. Which I don't," he said with a smile before going back to cutting limes.

I left the ninety-five bucks next to my empty Coors bottle when I got up. Service was everything.

11

I couldn't go back to my room, because I had to assume that if they were sniffing around, they were still here. Who *they* were didn't matter. How they found out didn't matter either. Whoever snuffed Dudley probably wanted to do the same to me.

Time to get along, little doggie.

Not knowing where else to go, I left through the South Tower and struck out across the parking lot and Casino Road to the RV park across the street. That's where Don's high rollers in their big RVs got to stay for free. I sat down on a picnic table in strip of grass among the six-figure modern-day behemoth campers, like the ones Willie Nelson used on tour.

I caught my breath while I watched to see if anybody had followed me. It didn't appear so. I looked around. Most of the lights in the Greyhound-sized RVs were out, but not all. Some of the owners were probably across the street, still raising hell and blowing their children's inheritance. More power to them. It's their money.

A door opened to my right, and a woman in her fifties stepped out holding a little dog before setting it on the ground. She looked a little older than me but was petite, auburn-haired, and built like a brick shithouse in three-inch heels. I'm kinda partial to older women. Not only are they more experienced, but they were so much more appreciative, as well as forgiving.

The dog shook, she shook, and they both moved off into the darkness. Sure, it was dark, but not that dark, and I wasn't that drunk. She looked pretty damned good, strutting along the land yachts toward a piece of desert where Poopsie could poop. I noticed she wasn't carrying a plastic poop bag. Maybe the rich didn't have to pick up their dog's shit. Maybe I was just cynical.

I looked at the stars for ten minutes until she returned, with Poopsie leading the way. When she got to her million-dollar bus, she picked the dog up and disappeared into the door, which closed with a hydraulic hiss.

After two minutes, it hissed again, and she appeared with a bottle and two glasses, headed my way. You could tell when two people were sexually attracted. They did too.

12

The next morning, I woke up on a queen-sized bed with a beautiful white comforter over me. Buck naked. The smell of frying sausage, eggs, and coffee assaulted me. I was so hungry I could have eaten roadkill.

As I pulled myself to a sitting position, a woman in shorts, sandals, and a pink polo shirt in the kitchen said, "Ah. You're alive. Would you like some coffee?"

"Please," I said, trying to orient myself. Poopsie came over to hump my leg.

"Just knock him away," she said, laughing. I did, but that didn't stop him. I was forced to get up and join her, where she handed me a cup. Poopsie, now renamed Ratso, disappeared into the bedroom in back.

"Hi, I'm Lucille." She held out her hand and I took it. It was warm and dry.

"I'm Jake," I replied, chagrined that she'd put me to bed and I didn't even know her name.

"I know," she said, handing me my wallet. Seeing my surprise, she continued, "What? Did you think I'd take a man in and not know who he was?"

I didn't know what to think. "I'm sorry if I did anything inappropriate."

She laughed. "Don't worry, it was consensual."

I guess that was a compliment. Now I felt even worse. "I don't know what to say," I said, uncertain whether she'd enjoyed it.

She led me to a breakfast nook and handed me a plate of sausage and eggs with toast. She gave me a bright smile. "Don't worry. You promised me a repeat performance tonight."

She looked as good as my breakfast. This might turn out to be a good day after all.

While I ate, Lucille put Ratso on a leash and headed out the door. I promised her I'd see her tonight. I washed my dish, fork, and coffee cup and locked up and left.

Slipping across the street to the Riverside, I gave the valet my claim check, and he dashed off to collect my twenty-year-old Corvette. In the meantime, I kept my eyes open for twin dark-shirted thugs.

They must have slept in. Five minutes later, I was crossing the bridge to Arizona, and I didn't appear to have a tail. I turned right and headed for Bullhead City.

Along the way, I spied the skeleton of a half-completed high-rise across the river on my right. A well-known casino developer who later became a politician had started it and tried to persuade the city council that they needed one more. He was unsuccessful and, lacking the necessary permits, was forced to abandon the project. It reminded me of a bombed-out building. Twenty floors of concrete floors held up by steel beams. It looked forlorn, ghostly.

The Tiki Lounge was showing every day of its fifty years as I pulled into the potholed parking lot. If I ever decided to move here, I was going to give Ruby a hell of a deal on a paint job. I could fix her asphalt parking lot too.

The door was open to let some of the stale beer and cigarette stink out. Cigarettes had been banned indoors for five years, but the smell was still in the walls and was never going to dissipate. I heard Ruby rattling around in the women's bathroom, so I helped myself to a breakfast beer and took a seat at the bar.

When she finally emerged with her mop and yellow bucket on wheels, she looked as withered and stringy as a creosote bush. She'd been doing everything here, day in, day out except Christmas day, for a half century. Tough old bird.

She spied me at the bar and smiled. "Well, howdy, Jake. You're up early today." She pushed the bucket toward the other bathroom. "You want to do the men's room?"

I started to get up, but she waved me back down. "Just kidding. You'd probably do a shitty job anyways." She straightened up with her hands massaging the small of her back and then walked over to join me at the bar.

"Big doing's last night," she said as she sat on the stool next to me. "Did you hear about it?"

I gave her my best innocent look and shook my head.

She searched my face for a moment, and her eyes twinkled. "Right. Seems Dudley, that weasel you were inquiring about, got his butt blown to hell and back last night at his house. The fire chief came in for a snort after it happened. Said it might have been a gas leak."

Gas leak my ass.

"Damn. I guess that means I won't get to talk to him," I replied, trying to look disappointed. I sucked down some more of my Coors so she wouldn't inspect my face again.

She got up and glided over to the coffee maker. "No big loss. I'm just thankful he paid his bar tab before he went to meet Satan," she said, pouring herself a cup, "If he thought it was hot here…"

"Didn't you say he had a couple buddies that he hung out with?" I asked as she putzed around behind the bar.

"Yeah, two lazy redneck no-goods. Cousins. I don't know what they're gonna do now that Dudley's gone." She took a sip of her coffee. "He was their meal ticket. They rent a trailer down the road apiece, at the Water View Trailer Park. It's on the left as you head back toward the casinos. You can't miss it. It's older than this place. An old Nazi owns it. Don't tell him I said hi. He and I don't exactly get along."

I polished off my beer and slapped a c-note on the bar. "You're a jewel, Ruby," I told her as I walked out the door.

SIZZLIN' 7S

It didn't take long to find the place. Beat-up trailers dating from the sixties, pit bulls chained to the rundown porches, and rusted-out pickups parked in the dirt driveways gave it away. With upscale high-rise waterfront condo complexes on either side, I was surprised that the city hadn't condemned the property or a developer hadn't snatched it up. I drove by slowly to get a feel for the place, then headed for the IHOP to meet Arliss.

13

Arliss's forty-year-old VW van was parked in a handicap spot by the front door. He had a valid handicap sticker hanging from the rearview mirror. I think it's his mom's. I walked in and scanned the interior.

He was hard to miss. Big, dark, and with dreadlocks. He was really a gentle giant, but you wouldn't know it to look at him. He was a weapons freak and lived with his mom. I wasn't sure, but I thought he was gay. Not that I gave a shit.

I sat on the vacant stool next to him.

"I see you made it through the night," he said in way of greeting.

"Yeah, and I don't know how. Did you have any problems getting here?" The van was old, smoked like a chimney, and used a *lot* of oil.

He shook his head. "She did real good." Even though he could have used an SUV I had in Flagstaff, he had an attachment to the VW and preferred to drive it. I think he had hidey-holes built into it for his toys.

I explained to him what had happened to me since yesterday, when everything was just fine, until now, when everything was *not* fine.

"Wow" was all he had to say when I finished.

"No shit," I replied.

"So what's the plan?"

Good question.

"Don't have a clue." And I meant it. "I thought I had a plan last night, but that got blown sky high, literally. His two redneck cousins are my only lead. I think we should go visit them."

We took the VW van and left my 'vette in the parking lot. The trailer park wasn't far away, and it only took a few minutes to get there. Arliss pulled the van up to the first trailer on the right. The trailer was a lot nicer than the others, with a sign on the side that read Office.

I got out and knocked on the door. I heard a dog, a big dog, barking until it was shushed.

The guy that opened the door looked like he was in his nineties—high nineties. *What's the deal with all the old people here? Must be the heat.* A hundred-pound German shepherd was at his side. The dog eyed me like I was a steak.

"How can I help you?" the old man asked with a pronounced German accent. The dog continued growling.

"I'm new in town and I was wondering if you had any vacancies?" I said to him, ignoring the wolf. They took eye-to-eye contact as threatening.

He looked at me suspiciously, then at the ancient van. Then he appeared to relax. "Yes. I have one unit available."

Unit? Is that like shithole?

"Great! Can we look at it?" I replied, trying to act like I'd rent an outhouse to sleep in for the next month. First and last, with a damage and utility deposit, no problem.

As soon as I said *we*, he took another look at Arliss filling up the driver's side of the van. He seemed to decide that we weren't much of a threat, just transients like the rest of his renters.

I didn't care what he thought we were, just as long as I could get a look around without raising any suspicion.

"Let me put the dog on a leash and I'll show you the unit," he said before closing the door. I went back to talk to Arliss.

"Follow us," I said, when I got to his door. "We're looking for a white Ford pickup with lots of dings and rust." Then I walked away to join the old man and his attack dog. I let them lead the way.

There appeared to be fifteen *units* on each side of the gravel road that led to the river. Thirty small trailers of different makes and years lined the gravel drive. They all shared one thing, however. They needed to be in the landfill.

About halfway down on the left side, I saw the pickup. I made a motion with my hand to Arliss behind me. He'd scope it out. One thing I did notice, however, was that the front door of the adjacent trailer was open. I heard Arliss slow as I followed the old man and the dog to the end of the road and a trailer that was straight out of *Grapes of Wrath*. Only eight hundred a month. First and last, plus a damage deposit, the old Nazi informed me. Two thousand and I could move in immediately.

I suspected he used to be a concentration camp guard for the Third Reich. I went through the motions of inspecting the dump while Arliss did his thing. The old man was more concerned with me stealing something than why Arliss had stopped. He didn't see Arliss get out and walk to the other trailer.

I should have pulled out my cell and called the Center of Disease Control in Atlanta. That's how bad the rental was. Instead, I told the old man that this wasn't quite what I was looking for, but thank you very much. I could tell he was disappointed.

When we headed back up the road, Arliss was standing beside the van. As we walked up to him, he stepped in front of the old man. For some reason, the dog didn't try to take a chunk out of Arliss's ass.

"You got a problem," he said to the startled old boy. Then to me, he pointed to the trailer and its open door. "You need to call 911."

I did.

Then I walked to the dilapidated trailer and looked in the front door. The place was torn to pieces. A dog lay on the kitchen floor in a pool of blood. A man was sprawled on the couch, and I went in to check on him. He was still breathing. Two shots to the chest. The blood on the shirt was black. He had been shot some time ago. He looked like he was on his last legs.

His eyes tracked me as I approached him. He tried to lift his right arm, but only got it up about six inches before it fell back. He had something in his hand. I opened his hand and found a matchbook. The dying man tried to say something, but he didn't have the strength to get it out. His eyes closed, and I thought that was it. There was a throw pillow next to him with two blackened holes in it. Whoever shot him used it to muffle the sound.

I looked at the pack of matches. It was from a casino in Las Vegas. The Bellagio.

Before I could wrap my head around *that,* the dead guy groaned and opened his eyes again. He appeared lucid this time.

I held the matches up so he could see them. "What the fuck does this mean?"

He coughed up some blood but didn't seem to care. "That cocksucker Nicky lied to us." Then his eyes rolled up into his head and he slid to the side. Dead for sure, this time.

I turned to see the old man making his way through the door. He took one look at the mess, the dog, and the dead guy. Instead of appearing shocked, he looked pissed.

We exited the trailer before the cop car and ambulance pulled up. The old man and I were standing in the road when the car stopped and two officers hopped out. Arliss had backed the van up to the office, out of the lane.

The first thing the cops did was talk deferentially to the old man, ignoring me. He told them the door was open, he looked in, saw a crime scene, and had me call 911. That wasn't exactly how it happened, but I kept my mouth shut. He didn't mention either one of us going in. The cops acted like they were talking to the mayor.

I knew right away why the city hadn't condemned the property. The old Nazi had too much juice. He'd probably hid out here after the war, thinking this was the middle of nowhere, never expecting a gambling Mecca to grow up around him. He most likely got in on the ground floor and owned large tracts of land, and this was his own little concentration camp until he died.

Now there had been a murder on his property. It would invite scrutiny. I don't think he wanted that.

After going in and looking around, the cops came out and asked me a few questions. I told them that me and the old man were looking at a rental *unit*, and I didn't know anything. They took my name, told me I could leave, and turned their attention to the old man.

Time to go.

As I hustled back to Arliss and the van, I took a quick look back. The old man was watching me intently. He was spooky. I could see him seventy years ago in a black uniform, riding boots, a riding crop, and a death's head emblem on his peaked cap, standing on the platform as the trains arrived.

I barely got my door closed before Arliss pulled out onto the street, and off we went in a cloud of smoke.

14

"**What do you think?**" Arliss asked me.

"I think we're behind the eight ball and somebody's a couple steps ahead," I replied, retrieving the matchbook from my pocket. It was glossy, red, and had *Bellagio Hotel and Casino* imprinted on the cover. I opened it up and noticed a phone number scribbled on the back of the cover. From the prefix, it looked local. I spied a Circle K with a pay phone out front.

I pointed to the phone. "Pull in there." I didn't want to use my cell.

Pay phones were practically extinct, but not yet, thank God. They had their uses, anonymity being one of them. For that reason, I always carried a roll of quarters with me. Plus, if you have a roll in your fist when you hit somebody, they're going night-night. I extracted two quarters from my roll, fed them into the phone, and dialed the number on the matchbook cover.

A machine answered. "Thank you for calling Nicky's Italian Restaurant. We are open from eleven a.m. to eleven p.m. Tuesday through Sunday. Please call back then. Thank you."

I hung up the phone, went into the Circle K for directions, and then returned to the van.

Arliss looked at me expectantly.

"How about Italian for lunch?" I asked him.

We headed south back through town, past the Walmart and Albertsons. Nicky's Italian Restaurant was on the left, by itself. It was a nice stucco building with trees and flowers in front. Green canopy over the front door. Big parking lot. Looked expensive.

It was little after eleven, so I figured they were open. Arliss parked close to the front door. We got out of the van and entered the restaurant. The place didn't smell like spilled beer and stale cigarette smoke. It smelled like Mama Rose's kitchen, only with oregano.

We waited at the hostess stand to be seated. A brass plaque attached the stand read "No checks. Cash and Credit Cards Only."

I wondered if some of those credit cards were Tony's.

An attractive thirty-year-old woman approached. "Two for lunch?" she asked in a soft, breathy voice. If the food was as good as the hostess, I didn't care if it was expensive.

"Something by a window please," I replied. We looked like the first customers, so I didn't think it would be a problem. It wasn't.

Grabbing two menus, she escorted us to window seat that faced the front with a good view of the bar and kitchen door as well as the main dining room. After she took our drink orders, I watched her fluid movements all the way to the bar.

"Earth to Jake," Arliss said to get my attention. "What's the plan here?"

I opened my menu. "I don't know. Let's eat some good Italian food and keep our eyes open. See what happens."

Ms. America returned with my Coors and Arliss's Bud Lite. "Have you decided what you would like to have?" she asked in her honey voice.

I almost told her. Instead, I asked, "Do you have Chicken Jerusalem?"

"Why, yes. It's not on the menu, but it's the owner's favorite, so the chef makes it." Her words were like a lover's touch. Woody was starting to wake up, so I dropped my napkin on my lap. That just made it look like a pup tent.

Arliss would eat anything, so I ordered for both of us. "Well, then, make it two. What's good for Nicky is good for us. Oh, is Nicky here, by any chance?" I asked like I was an old pal.

She didn't miss a beat. "No. He was delayed this morning."

SIZZLIN' 7S

I'll bet. He had a busy night last night, blowing up and shooting people.

"But I expect him shortly. Now if you'll excuse me, I'll get the chef right on it," she said, smiled, and did her model walk back to the kitchen.

I thought about my rain check from Kim. I was primed and ready to go for tonight. Assuming I made it through today.

15

The chef was fast, and our food was out in no time. The place was starting to fill up. Most of the clientele were well-dressed retirees, with the rest being businesspeople. Two attractive women took over the waitressing, and a brawny bouncer type kept bar. The food was delicious, the service excellent. This was starting to look like a bust. No shady-looking characters, no gangsters or murderers in sight.

We were finished and nothing was happening, so I decided our time could be better spent somewhere else. I was about to ask for the tab when all that changed.

Ms. America escorted two no-neck twins in dark shirts to the bar, then went into the kitchen. Two minutes later, your stereotypical gangster walked out and joined them. Some people you just can't dress up, and you can't shine a turd. I assumed that it was Little Nicky.

Nicky did all the talking. They did all the listening. After about five minutes of instruction, the minions nodded in unison and left. They didn't even order drinks. I guess it wasn't a social occasion.

We didn't have time to wait for a check, so I dropped a hundred on the table and we followed the twins outside. As Arliss and I passed the bar, Nicky was still sitting there, talking into a cell phone. He didn't sound happy.

The twins piled into brown Crown Vic and pulled out of the parking lot and headed south toward Needles.

Halfway there, we passed the remains of Dudley's trailer, though you couldn't see the wreckage from the road. We stayed quite a ways back from the Crown Vic because we were throwing up smoke like there was a house on fire driving down the road. I didn't know how they couldn't see us behind them. Maybe they had other things on their mind.

I was glad for the drive because it gave me time to think. I instinctively went for following the followers in this case, not their boss. Nicky wasn't going anywhere, and if I hung around there all day, I'd put on a hundred pounds, and it would cost me a fortune.

Nope. The only lead we had was hauling ass down the road to Needles, California. And we were right behind them.

The dead cousin in the Nazi's trailer was only one of a pair. For some reason, the other one got away. He had the plastic. Had to be.

And Dumb and Dumber in front of us knew where he was.

Before I knew it, we were there. We crossed a bridge over the Colorado River and were magically back in California. Needles straddled the border with Arizona. It hosted Interstate 40 and major rail depot. Not to mention a major drug conduit.

The Crown Vic slowed as it passed the train station. Across the street was a Victorian cottage. They braked for a moment and then continued down the street before turning right again.

"Pull over and park at the depot," I told Arliss, pointing out a vacant space directly across the street from the cottage. An Amtrak train was pulling in as I jumped out of the van and dashed into the station. Maybe the surviving cousin was attempting to leave town using the train. The pickup was still back at the trailer, so maybe the Amtrak was his only way out of town.

A quick scan of the waiting customers told me the cousin wasn't there. I walked back to the van and was almost to the door when the Crown Vic turned the corner across from us and cruised by again. I turned slightly and saw they were both looking at the cottage across the street as they went by.

The Crown Vic continued on down the street and turned right again. They were going to go down the alley behind the house.

They'd seen it on their first pass and had rightly figured that was their best approach.

We sat in the van to see what transpired. We didn't have long to wait. A man flew out the front door, headed for the train depot. It was the other cousin. He must have heard Nicky's boys breaking down the back door and decided the Amtrak, preparing to depart, was his best shot at getting away.

He ran across the street and was flying by the van when Arliss suddenly opened his door, catching the man in the chest and face. He went down like he'd been poleaxed. I jumped out, ran around to Arliss's side, and helped drag the unconscious man around to the side door, where we unceremoniously heaved him in. I jumped in and slid the door shut. Arliss got in, started the van, and pulled out of the parking lot just as the two thugs burst out the front door of the Victorian, looking around frantically.

I ducked down, and all they saw was a big black guy in dreadlocks driving by in a smoking VW van.

16

On the way out of town, I used the roll of duct tape that Arliss always kept under his seat to truss our package hand and foot. I slapped a piece across his mouth. Once I was satisfied he was secure, I gave him a couple of not-so gentle slaps to bring him around.

Upon regaining consciousness, he realized two things: he was tied up, and he was in big trouble. I could see the terror in his eyes. He started to gag, so I ripped the tape off so he wouldn't drown on his own vomit. I rolled him on his side, but all he did was dry heave. Pushing him on his back, I asked, "What's your name?"

He seemed resigned to his fate. "Earl. Earl Nickerson."

Even though I thought I knew, I had to ask, "Why were those guys chasing you?"

Confusion ran across Earl's face. "You mean…you're not with them?"

He was probably thinking, *Then why did you knock me out and kidnap me?*

Just to freak him out, I said, "We're competitors. They wanted to kill you." Then I gave him the hook. "We don't. We just want some information, then you're free to go."

I wouldn't have believed that hogwash if my mother had said it, but Earl was desperate enough to go for it.

"Fucking Dudley. He got us into this. Sold us the plastic for a grand. Said we wouldn't have any problem with the cards. They were fresh. Do the limit on all of them until they quit, he said. Three to five grand each. Piece of cake. Only problem was, the fuckers didn't work. Got a bunch of bullshit questions from the machine." He started to cry. "Then that asshole Dudley hooks us up with some dude with money. Next thing I know, shit rains down from the sky, and Charlie gets killed. Fucking Dudley. I'm gonna kill that rat, fuck."

Obviously, Earl didn't know anybody in the fire department.

"Somebody already did," I said to freak him out some more. "Who's Charlie?"

"My cousin," he replied as he pulled himself together, and once he started talking, he wouldn't stop.

I was curious. "How come they didn't kill you too?"

"I was banging the woman that lives next door. Her bedroom window is next to our living room. I saw the whole thing." He paused to catch his breath. "And I couldn't do anything." His shoulder sagged.

"How'd you get to Needles?" I asked. He didn't take the pickup, and I needed to know how many more players there were.

"I knew I was next. Susan, the woman I was with, saw the whole thing too. We both knew I had to split. She said she'd help. I went out her back door, over the fence, and took off down the road. She got in her car picked me up at the Circle K, then drove me to Needles. I told her to go stay with her sister until I called."

It made sense. The only reason Nicky's boys didn't finish Charlie off was because Susan came out of her trailer and got into her car. She wasn't one of their targets, so they left quickly before she pulled out.

"Why were you in that house across from the depot?" I asked next.

"It's my aunt's. Charlie's mom. She's in Phoenix and won't be back for another month. She always keeps a key under the flowerpot. I figured I'd wait there until the last minute and hop the train to LA. I already bought my ticket so I could just get on and go."

I could tell Earl was worried about how he was going to explain to Aunt Molly that her son was dead, and why.

SIZZLIN' 7S

Earl held the key to this clusterfuck. "Tell me how it went down, from the time you met up with Dudley at the Tiki yesterday until now."

I've heard that eyes were a window to the soul. I believed it. The surprise in his eyes confirmed to me that that was where the three of them had hooked up. I also saw that he realized that if I knew *that*, there was no sense in lying to me if he wanted to survive.

He told me that Dudley had called, all excited, and wanted to hook up with them. They met at the Tiki where Dudley bought them all drinks, showed them the credit cards, and said he'd sell them for a grand. He also said they could pay him with the first thousand they pulled from the ATMs. After four or five drinks each, they left and started with the Bank of America ATM down the street and then Chase Bank a few blocks away, with the same results. The machines didn't ask for a pin number but started asking a bunch of questions.

In ten years of working stolen credit cards, they had never run into this before, he told me. Spooked, and knowing that Charlie had been photo'd at each ATM, they knew not to push their luck at Wells Fargo. They decided Pussy Willows was a good place to retreat and formulate plan B. He also said that they were behind him the whole way and Dudley hadn't stopped anywhere else.

That's where I found them. I thought back to it. While I was watching them, Dudley had only left the bar one time, apparently trying to make a call, and then walked out because the noise was too loud. He had returned within minutes, joining Charlie and Earl. That was the only time he was out of my sight. That must have been when he called Nicky.

Or Nicky was calling *him.*

Nicky had no reason to buy stolen cards—that was small time— unless he knew who had lost them. But how could he know that? The only way he could know that was if somebody told him. It damn sure wasn't Tony. Only two other people knew—me and Shane.

Well, shit.

I could see it. Shane lied to me about not knowing Dudley. Hell, he was head of security at the casino, so he *had* to know all the cheaters, scammers, and pickpockets, especially the locals. But it took Shane a while to place Tony. I knew he would eventually. When he did, two and two equaled a chance to score some real money, and that was when he could have made the call to Little Nicky, who my best guess was a front for the Vegas syndicate.

The Vegas bunch had been salivating over Laughlin for years. Las Vegas was way over the top now, too well regulated. Corporations and government watchdogs had slashed the mob's profit line.

The antiquated casinos of Laughlin were scoring record profits from the old farts that didn't want to screw with Vegas anymore. Unlike Vegas, the average age of gamblers on the floor was over sixty. It would be good pickings, but so far their efforts to elbow and buy into any of Laughlin's casinos had been frustrated. Nicky was their straw man here to watch and wait for an opportunity. Any opportunity.

And Shane dropped it right in their lap. He dropped a dime on Tony to Nicky and got the ball rolling. Nicky didn't know what Tony had lost, but whatever it was, Nicky wanted it. Once he got it, he'd figure out what to do with it.

Then he may or may not tell his bosses about it, depending.

I hated to think that I was in the middle of some kind of guerilla action by Nicky against Tony. There was no other explanation, though. Sherlock Holmes would have figured it out long ago.

At least I was getting an idea of who all the players were. Ruby had said that Dudley floated from Vegas to Laughlin and back. Dudley was connected to Nicky. Nicky was connected to the Vegas mob, Tony's main competitor. It was all starting to fall into place.

Whatever Tony lost, they wanted it and had killed two people to obtain it. The question was, did they get it? Apparently not, because they had tried to run Earl down and lost him.

Now I had him.

Earl was starting to babble, glad to unload everything. This whole episode had been more than he had bargained for.

"This dude, Nicky, was supposed to meet me and Charlie at our place. Charlie thought we might need insurance. He kept one card to show and gave me the others to hold until they showed the money. He told me to go next door and hang out. Me and Susan climbed into the sack. Two dudes showed up, killed my dog, and stuck a gun in Charlie's face. I watched the whole thing. He gave up the one card, then they shot him." Earl started crying again. I cut his hands loose. It took a couple of minutes before he could continue.

So they got one card.

"Which one did they get?" I asked him.

"The Chase Bank Visa."

"Where are the other five cards?" I was hoping like hell he still had them on him. That would be the jackpot.

He looked up at me like he hoped I wouldn't just throw him out of the van at sixty miles an hour. "I gave them to Susan."

Fuck. Was this never going to end?

17

I retied his hands, stuck some more tape over his mouth, and rolled him over so I could check his pockets. Twenty bucks, a train ticket, a driver's license and a pack of rubbers was all he had on him.

I left him there on the floor and climbed into the front passenger seat so I could think.

Arliss had heard pretty much everything. "What are we going to do with him?"

I winked at Arliss, knowing that Earl couldn't see me. "Aw, let's just take him in the desert and kill him."

That brought some muffled protests from the back.

Arliss caught on to what I was doing and took up the good cop part. "I don't know, man. That don't seem right to me. I think the guy was up front with you. Maybe you ought to give him a break," he said, loud enough for Earl to hear.

I heard noises of affirmation from behind me. "Mmhhmm. Mmhhmm. Mmhhmm."

"What did you have in mind?" I made sure Earl could hear me.

"Maybe we could put him in a safe house so Nicky doesn't kill him," Arliss replied, smiling hugely. He was having a good time at Earl's expense. More affirmations came from the back.

I acted like I was mulling it over.

"Okay. But *you* gotta watch him."

That brought an exhalation of relief from the back.

SIZZLIN' 7S

Arliss and I tried to keep from laughing as we made our way back over Don's bridge and headed for the casinos. When we got to the Edgewater, I motioned for him to pull in.

While Arliss found a parking place, I slipped into the back of the van and cut Earl's restraints, then ripped the duct tape from his mouth. He yelped.

"Don't fuck with me, Earl, or I'll feed you to Nicky. Arliss has talked me into giving you another chance, so don't fuck it up. Do everything he tells you to, or I swear to God I'll kill you myself. Are we clear?" I meant to terrify him, as if he wasn't already.

He nodded. "Can I call Susan? I told her I would when I got away."

He wasn't away by any stretch of the imagination. "Sure." I powered up the phone, put it on speaker, and handed him my cell. I knew that I'd capture her number when he called. "But here's how we're gonna do it. You tell her I'm your friend and that I'll be contacting her. Tell her you're on the train to LA, everything is cool. Your friend's name is Jake. I'll be listening. You got it?"

He didn't have much choice. The conversation was brief. I could tell he wanted to talk to her some more. Apparently, she was more than a one-night stand to him. Somebody cared for him, and he for her. He ended with "Bye, baby" and handed the phone back to me.

I saved the number to my phone SIM card. I'd call her later.

Opening up the side door, I told him, "Go with Arliss. There's a lot of people out there that want to see you dead. If you do what he says, you just may survive. He tells you when to breathe. Got it?"

Earl nodded.

I got out in front of him and brushed him off. Arliss came around and loomed over him. "We're going in here. I'll register and you will stand off to the side and be invisible. When I head to the room, you will follow. Are you with me here?"

Earl looked up at him and nodded again, glad to be alive. Not only that, he was apparently going to spend the night in a nice hotel instead of a rathole. At this point, he'd follow Arliss anywhere. Maybe he could even hit the buffet, he was thinking. Earl loved buffets. He didn't need much prodding.

I climbed into the driver's seat as they headed into the Edgewater Hotel and Casino. That was one thing less on my mind. I pulled out onto Casino Road and drove to the IHOP, where I swapped the VW for my Corvette.

I drove the 'vette to Lucille's mansion on wheels across the street from the Riverside, parking next to her front door to make an impression. My car was old, but like me, it cleaned up well, and all the important parts worked.

She met me at the door wearing a short yellow sundress. I was standing three feet below her. I guess I hadn't noticed her legs last night, but I did today. Well-toned, well-tanned, and, well…fucking gorgeous. Woody stood right up and saluted.

Lucille looked down and smiled.

I wasn't ready to hit the sack yet, so I said as I walked up to her, "How about I take you out for a cocktail?"

She looked over at the 'vette and said, "Vintage and looks good. Like you. Let me get my scarf and I'll be right with you." She disappeared back into her million-dollar bus.

When she came back out, she looked like a million bucks herself.

Instead of opening the door of the Chevy, I said, "Let's walk across the street."

If she was surprised, she didn't show it. I held her hand as we negotiated the hill down to Casino Road, across it and the Riverside casino parking lot without getting run over. Once inside the casino, I guided her up the escalator to the Gourmet Room, a fancy French restaurant that overlooked the Colorado River. Real cozy.

It was an excellent restaurant. The only reason I could afford it was because Don—God bless his soul—kicked me back 10 percent of all my losses on food services. I couldn't eat enough lobster to use up all my comps.

I didn't have a reservation, but Victor, the maître d', was used to that with me. He seated us at a table next to a floor-to-ceiling window in the bar.

"I guess you've been here before," she said after taking in the view. "Victor seems to know you well."

SIZZLIN' 7S

"I try to eat here often. The buffet downstairs is excellent but gets a little old, and they don't have lobster," I told her with a smile. "Now tell me everything I missed last night."

18

We watched the sun play off the Colorado River. I had a couple of drinks, and she ordered something I couldn't pronounce for an appetizer. We spent a leisurely two hours getting to know each other. She did most of the talking. She was a retired lawyer. Go figure. She'd been a widow for five years and decided it was time for a change, so she bought a land yacht and took to the road. She was thinking about moving to Laughlin, at least temporarily.

When she asked me what I did, I told her I was a contractor. If she had any idea what I was involved in, she would undoubtedly get up and leave, so I kept my answers brief, steering the conversation back to her.

The part about her having been a lawyer, though, opened up interesting possibilities. I mentally ticked off the felonies I had committed in the last twenty-four hours: conspiracy, assault, kidnapping, unlawful detention, obstruction of justice, and maybe racketeering too, seeing as Tony was involved. I was probably going to *need* a lawyer before this finished playing out.

After leaving the restaurant, I managed to get past a bank of Sizzling Sevens slots without acting like I had a gambling problem, which I did. My problem was that I couldn't do it all the time.

We made it across the boulevard without getting run over by pickups pulling boats and headed back to her RV. Lucille let Ratso out for a walk, and I went along. It was nice to do mundane things every now and then. I was actually starting to relax.

That's when my phone rang.

I didn't recognize the number, but when I answered, I recognized the voice right away. It was Leo, Tony's butler.

"He wants a report" was all he said and hung up.

I knew it. It was too good to last.

I put my phone back in my pocket and looked at Lucille. She smiled and said, "You don't have to tell me. You have to go, right?"

I nodded. "Business. I don't know how long it will take. I'm sorry." I genuinely was. "Can I call you later?"

Instead of being hurt, she hugged me and whispered in my ear, "I'll be here all night, Jake. Go do what you have to do." She gave me a quick kiss and pushed me away.

She was scoring points left and right.

19

As I got back onto Casino Road, I called Arliss on his cell.

"Triple A Storage. How can I help you?" he answered.

"How's our package doing?"

"Happy as a clam," Arliss responded. "He's watching pay-per-view porno, and I had room service bring up a six-pack. He's not going anywhere. He *is* concerned about his girlfriend, though."

"Tell him I'll take care of it."

He gave me his room number, and I disconnected. My next call went to Earl's girlfriend, Susan. She was probably worried and expecting my call. I wasn't disappointed. She answered on the first ring.

"Susan, this is Earl's friend, Jake. Can you talk alone?" I didn't want anybody else around her when I talked to her.

"No. I'm at my mother's. She's in the kitchen, but she'll be right back. Is Earl okay? Please tell me," she said in a rush.

"He's fine, but we need to talk. Can you get away so we can meet?"

She didn't hesitate. Obviously, Earl meant a lot to her. "Yes. Where?"

"Do you know where the Tiki Lounge is?"

"Sure. I've never been in there, but I know Earl likes the place. He was going to take me there when he got paid. He was going to take me out to dinner too, he said. I guess that isn't going to happen now." I could hear her sadness over the phone.

SIZZLIN' 7S

"Maybe I can help with that. Meet me there in an hour," I said and hung up before she asked any questions.

I gave my keys to the valet at Harrah's and went straight to the twenty-fifth floor. I didn't know how many Sizzling Seven slot machines I passed along the way. They were all whispering, *Yoohoo.* I ignored them. At this rate, I was going to be cured before I knew it. Some people might say that the threat of imminent violent death may be rough gambling addiction therapy, but hey, whatever works, right?

As usual, I was met at the elevator door by one Tony's heavies, frisked and escorted to his suite. Leo took over from there.

Leo had been with Tony since they moved from New York to Phoenix in the sixties. Leo was butler, bodyguard, and confidante. On top of that, he was a pretty nice guy. Up front, most of the time. But he could kill you without blinking an eye.

Tony was in the living room watching a football game. He turned the sound down when he saw me but didn't try to get up. He didn't ask me if I wanted anything to drink. I sat down in a chair next to him. Leo was standing behind me again.

"Give me some good news, Jake," Tony said, still watching the game.

I took a calming breath and said, "I got good news and I got bad news. But before I tell you the good news, I need to ask you something."

Tony turned his attention to me but didn't say a word. I took that as a yes.

"Do you know a guy named Nicky Mosconi?" I asked and waited for the tell, and the lie. To my surprise, it manifested itself as a blink of surprise and then silence. He turned his gaze back to the game, but I could tell he wasn't watching it. He recognized the name, and now he was running the scenarios through his head.

I kept my mouth shut until he figured it out. Leo still didn't ask me if I wanted anything to drink. After a minute or two, Tony apparently came to a decision and turned his gaze back to me.

Rather than answer my question, he said, "What does this Nicky Mosconi have to do with my cards?"

"I have reason to believe he has one of the five cards."

Tony's eyes hooded slightly. "Do you know which one?" he asked quietly.

I felt like I was downstairs on the roulette table betting the farm. "Chase Bank Visa," I told him, hoping that was the right answer.

Apparently, it was. Tony had been holding his breath, and I heard him release it. Leo asked me if I would care for a beer.

I wasn't going to learn anything if I didn't ask, and now seemed to be the best time to do it. "So you know this Nicky? Is he Vegas?" All the dots seemed to point that way. "Look, Tony. I need some guidance here."

He didn't smile, but he nodded. "I know. You're right. Little Nicky is the point man for Vegas."

He continued, "Little Nicky. That's what everyone calls him behind his back. His father is Big Nickolas Mosconi. Big Nicky. He has what's left of the Vegas organization. Since the corporations moved into Vegas, they can't skim like they used to. Their cash cow dried up. He'd like to move in here and take over that uncompleted casino and use it as a base, but he's having a rough time. But that don't stop him from trying. He's stepping out of bounds." Tony frowned. "I'm told they're heavy into drugs and *other things*. I-40 and the train are right down the road. No transportation problems. The commission is not happy."

That little bombshell told me that this was a turf fight. That moved everything up to a new level. Leo brought me an ice-cold Coors. I downed it in three swallows, handed it back to Leo, and asked for another.

"Okay, and what's the good news?" Tony asked.

Even though I was starting to feel sick to my stomach, it was my time to shine, so I smiled. "I think I know where the other cards are."

20

4:00/5:00 p.m.

Five minutes later, I'd given Tony an extremely abbreviated version of how Nicky got the Chase card. Actually, I left out just about everything except Dudley and Charlie getting killed. Tony didn't want to know the details anyway. All he wanted to know was when I going to get his plastic back. Hopefully soon, I told him, and got up to leave, but Tony wasn't finished.

"Jake, one other thing. Do you know if Little Nicky accessed that card with his computer?"

I wondered if it was a trick question. I didn't know if you could do that shit, and I was even more surprised that Tony did. It must have shown in my face.

"He'd need a card reader hooked to his computer, but I'm sure his restaurant is wired for that. I don't want that to happen. Am I clear?" Tony said.

"Perfectly," I lied. I'd figure out what that meant later. I didn't waste any time getting out the door.

On the way back out of the casino, I gave into temptation and surrendered to the first Sizzling Seven dollar slot that called out my name. Two minutes later and a hundred bucks lighter, I walked out the door to claim my car.

The parking lot at the Tiki Lounge was almost empty when I pulled in. I parked around back out of habit. The back door was unlocked, so I went in that way.

There was a young couple in the corner, two old geezers playing pool, and a fortyish woman sitting at the bar. She wasn't what I expected. She looked like a librarian. Her hair was up in a bun, and she had clunky black glasses. She wasn't fat, and her dress looked a size too large. She definitely wasn't fashion conscious. And she looked nervous.

Had to be Susan.

I sat down on the stool next to her but didn't say anything right away. Ruby was behind the bar. She smiled and said, "Howdy, Jake. Coors?"

That got Susan's attention. Some of her nervousness melted away. When Ruby put the beer in front of me and said, "On the house," Susan relaxed and turned to me. She didn't beat around the bush.

"I'm Susan, Earl's friend. How is he?"

Ruby had moved away, so I was able to get right to it. "He's fine, but he's got a problem. You saw what happened this morning, didn't you?"

I could see the fear in her eyes. Her hands went to her mouth. She couldn't speak, so I did it for her. "Charlie and Earl were trying to sell stolen credit cards, and some really people bad people want those cards. The only way he's going to walk away from this is if I recover those cards." I saw the tears start to flow. God, I hate it when women cry. "He said he gave them to you. Do you still have them?"

I watched her nod and dig into her purse. She pulled out an envelope and handed it to me. I couldn't believe it was that easy.

"If you give them back, will he be okay?" She wasn't wearing much makeup, thank God, so her mascara wasn't running. I smiled and told her yes, everything was going to be just fine now. She smiled back and reached over to hug me. I hugged her back. I noticed the librarian wasn't wearing a bra. Ruby gave me the hairy eyeball.

When we disengaged, I handed her a bar napkin so she could dry her eyes. "Would you like to see him?" Her eyes got real big, and she nodded.

"I'm with the government, and Earl is helping us with a big case, so this is all a secret, okay? We've got him in a safe place so the bad guys don't find him. If I take you to him, you've got to promise me you'll do what I say and keep Earl under control. This has to be strictly voluntary. It might take a day or two. Can you do that?"

She was laughing, crying, and nodding at the same time. I didn't feel guilty about feeding her that load of bullshit because it would probably keep her alive. More importantly, away from the cops. She was a witness to a murder. A mob murder. Those kinds of witnesses generally didn't last long in the real world. Especially in *protective custody*.

"What are you drinking?" I asked her after she'd composed herself.

She told me iced tea. It figured. I ordered her a Long Island iced tea and told her I had to use the bathroom. Rudy was still giving me the hairy eyeball.

When I got into the bathroom, I called Arliss and told him to switch to a two-bedroom suite. Then I opened the envelope and inspected the contents. Five credit cards. Wells Fargo, AMX, Chase, and one I'd never seen. APEX. White letters on a black background.

I noticed something else. It was slightly thicker than a normal credit card. I sealed everything in the envelope, put my room number on the outside, wrote *Hold* on it, and left the bathroom.

Susan was still at the bar. When I sat down next to her, I saw that her drink was already half gone.

"This is really the best iced tea I think I've ever had," she said with a little slur.

Oh boy.

"You don't drink much, do you?" I asked, although I thought I knew the answer.

"Hardly ever." She giggled. "I'm a grade-school teacher, so I can't do that. Besides, I can't afford it."

Yeah, Earl was going to have a great time tonight.

I motioned to Ruby for my bill.

21

I got Susan's keys and stashed her car across the street in the K-Mart parking lot. Then I drove us to the Edgewater Hotel and Casino across the river. She giggled the whole trip.

I called Arliss on the way, and he was there to take her off my hands when I drove up to the front door of the casino. I told her he was my partner and to do what he said. I pulled off before she could ask any questions and found a spot in the parking lot so I could take another look at Tony's credit cards.

Four of them looked like credit cards. The name on all the cards was William Smith, except for the APEX card, whatever the hell that was. It was just a black card with white letters. The name on it was Carousel Industries. It was slightly thicker than the other four, but other than that, unremarkable. But it got my antennae twitching.

When that happened, I've learned to do something about it and save myself a lot of grief.

After sticking the other four cards in my shoe, I put the APEX card back in the envelope, took a stamp out of my console, attached it, addressed the envelope to myself, and stuck it in my shoe.

I needed a change of clothes, so I decided to take a chance and make a run at my room in the Riverside. It didn't appear that anybody had followed me. I parked down the street between two eighteen-wheelers in a dirt lot and entered the casino through the north doors. Essentially the back door.

SIZZLIN' 7S

I made it as far as the elevators before I spotted an older guy in a rumpled suit sitting in a chair about fifty feet away. He looked like he should have been retired, but his outfit and demeanor screamed cop.

I wasn't wrong.

Columbo practically sat up and barked. He slid into the elevator just before it closed. It was just the two of us, and he didn't push a button. I watched his reflection in the polished stainless-steel doors. He appeared bored.

Unless you're in New York, when somebody doesn't even give you a passing glance in such a confined space, you know something's up.

As soon as the doors opened and I stepped out, he did too. I immediately did an about-face and said, "Oops, wrong floor."

He held up his badge with his finger over the bottom. "No, Mr. Leggs, this is the right floor. I have a few questions for you."

"Here?" I asked.

"In your room, or downtown. Your choice." Colombo said with a smile that didn't reach his eyes.

"How about my room. It's just down the hall," I said, trying to be helpful.

"I know," he replied, opening his coat and showing his weapon.

He followed me to my room, and as soon as I opened the door, he said, "Assume the position."

I did, leaning against the nearest wall, my hands over my head and my legs spread. He frisked me like he'd done it a million times. I noticed the cops never checked your nuts. Must be a guy thing. I could have had a .22 nestled there in my jockey strap.

"Am I under arrest?" The badge he flashed me was from Bullhead City, across the river—a different town and another state. He had no jurisdiction here, but I let it play out.

"Not yet, but I'm working on it," he said when he finally quit manhandling me. He pointed to the table and chairs. "Turn your pockets out, lay the contents on the table, and have a seat."

I did as he said.

He was clearly disappointed with the five hundred-dollar bills plus change, a stick of gum, and a package of Trojans that lay on the table. He went through my wallet with a vengeance. Finding nothing there other than my driver's license, some business cards, and some dirty pictures, he threw it on table in disgust. "What are you, some kind of pervert?"

I saw my chance and counterattacked. He was out of his jurisdiction and couldn't arrest me, but he obviously had information. Information that I needed.

"Why are you hassling me? I have no idea what this is about, and I'd like an explanation." I was trying to fend off a strip search. If he made me take off my shoes, I was fucked.

He studied me for a moment then seemed to come to a decision.

"Look, Mr. Leggs, I've been a detective for a long time. This is my second career job. I put in thirty at the LAPD, pulled the pin, then moved here. It took me about two weeks of retirement to drive me and my wife crazy. I took a job here as the chief of detectives, and now we're both a lot happier." Columbo didn't mention that it was in another state, across the river.

"The reason I'm questioning you is your presence at a murder scene yesterday."

I've found that when you're talking to cops, saying nothing is the best option.

When I didn't respond, he nodded as if he expected that. "We hardly ever have violent deaths here. Most of the old folks just keel over from the heat or old age. Never had one from shoveling snow, though." He wanted to show me he had a sense of humor. "Now I've had two suspicious deaths in one day. That's bad. So I figure something's going on." He waited for me to respond.

When I was with the old Nazi, at Charlie's murder scene, the young cop made me show my driver's license, so that's probably how he knew who I was. There was no point in asking how he had tracked me from there.

Unfortunately, I was registered under my own name at the Riverside, so all he had to do was wait for me at the elevator. He'd probably already been in my room.

I wanted to sidetrack him from what I knew was coming next. "I'm sorry, but I didn't catch your name."

"I didn't throw it. It's Sabbatini, but let's not get distracted," he replied with smile. "I did a routine NCIC search on your name, and the computer practically imploded. You've got quite a history, Mr. Leggs. Mind if I call you Jake? I made a call to a buddy of mine in Flagstaff. He informed me that they were still sorting through the last of your misadventures. He also told me to tell you to don't come back for a while."

Must have been Sarge. He could have at least sent me an e-mail. I tried to look like I didn't know what he was talking about, but it wasn't working.

"So my question to you is, what were you doing at that shithole trailer park?" He made a show of looking around my suite. "You weren't there to rent one of Heinrich's hovels. I gotta tell you, I've my eye on that old bastard since I started here. He's got some juice, but I'd love nothing better than taking him down for something. Now I've got him, a murder, and known troublemaker in one place. I know it isn't coincidence."

He was damn sure about that, and I could see he was going to be a problem. He proceeded to tell me how *much* of a problem.

"You're like that Lil Abner character, the one with a rain cloud over his head. It follows you everywhere. So I'm going to follow *you* to see where all this leads." He tossed my wallet back at me, took out a Sharpie, wrote a number on the table, and got up.

"Get used to seeing me 'cause I'm going to be watching your every move."

Having read me the riot act, Sabbatini walked to the door. Sure as shit, he did the Columbo thing and turned around as he opened it.

"That includes your buddy and his van. Damn thing needs a ring job."

With that, he was gone.

Well, fuck. I pulled out Mohammed's card and gave him a call.

22

Mo answered on the first ring. I think he was bored, coming down from our last adventure.

"Mr. Jake! How good to hear from you! What can I do for you?"

"You can meet me outside the Riverside in five minutes."

He didn't hesitate. "I will be waiting for you," and he hung up. I suspected he was out in front of Pussy Willows at the moment, across the street but across the river. One minute as the crow flies, but five minutes by way of the bridge was about right.

I grabbed a pair of socks, jeans, and a T-shirt as I blasted out of the room, down to hall to the stairs—screw the elevators—and came out fifty feet away from the VIP office.

My hostess, Deborah, was at her desk and on the phone. I threw the envelope in front of her along with a c-note and headed out the glass doors before she could say anything. She was used to my antics.

I thought I was going to need some legal representation soon, and since Lucille was waiting for me to call, I decided there was no time like the present. I pulled out my cell as I headed for the west entrance doors and called her.

"Hello?" she answered, tentative.

"Lucille, its Jake. You're probably not hungry, but would you like to join me for dinner?"

"Of course," she replied. "Are you going to pick me up?"

"No. I'd love to, but I can't. Can you meet me?"

SIZZLIN' 7S

She agreed to, and I told her where. She said she had to get dressed but would try to hurry.

My next call went to Tony. Leo answered.

"Talk to me," he said.

"Tell Tony four of his cards are secure." I hung up. I didn't want to hear any shit from Leo.

Mo was waiting by the back door—the north exit—for me. We were out of the parking lot within fifteen seconds and across the river in two minutes. I didn't have to tell Mo anything. He seemed to know. I took those minutes to regroup.

Now the cops were on to me, and it wouldn't be long before Nicky was too. The way I figured it, the best defense was a good offense. I felt bad about involving my lover in what was obviously a dangerous situation, but then again, I figured she was my lawyer, sort of, and I didn't think anything was going to happen. Yet.

"Take me to Nicky's Italian Restaurant," I told Mo. He smiled like he knew something I didn't and simply nodded.

We were there in five minutes. Bullhead City was not that big. Highway 95 was pretty much the main drag. Mo pulled up in front of Nicky's, and I got out after telling him he was on retainer.

"Don't get lost," I think my exact words were.

As I went through the front door, I was hoping nobody was still working that had seen me there this morning. No such luck. Luscious Lips was still working the hostess stand and smiled when she saw me. The change from my hundred at lunch probably made her day. Twenty years ago, I would have made a run at her. I was tempted, but my date would be unhappy.

"Well, hello again," she said, searching her memory for a name that I'd never given her. I was considering donating to her college fund.

Instead, I gave her my best "I'm old enough to be your father" look and said, "I'm sorry I missed Nicky at lunch."

I laid a hundred in her palm. "If he's still here, would you ask him to join me? Tell him it would be to his benefit to do so."

Other than a slight widening of her eyes, you wouldn't know she thought this was unusual. She simply smiled and walked away. And what a walk it was. I should chase her down later, if only for the principle of the thing. At my age, you don't get that many opportunities.

Nobody offered me a menu or brought me water. The word was apparently out there that I was not here to eat. I was fish food.

Ten minutes later, Nicky sat down across from me. He didn't look pissed off, just curious. And that was just the way I wanted it.

23

"**So what's up?**" Nicky asked.

"I'm a contractor," I stated, which could mean anything. "I have a client. That client…he lost some property, and he wants it back."

Nicky's expression never changed. "And why would you think I have your client's property?"

I gave him a shark's smile. "Let's just say somebody dropped a dime on you."

His calm veneer cracked ever so slightly. "Not that I know what the fuck you're talking about, but what did you have in mind?"

"You've got some plastic of his. He wants it back."

Nicky was trying to think of a way to kill me before I could leave his place. I could see it in his eyes.

"I'll be right back," he said, getting up. I figured he was going back to the kitchen to tell the twins to whack me. Make it happen anywhere but in the parking lot.

Luscious Lips saved the day by escorting my date to the table, and then leaving.

Lucille looked great. I stood up and hugged her. She didn't know she was my lawyer yet, but she would soon. "I'm sorry for the short notice. You look beautiful," I said. "Something has come up, and I may need your professional opinion." I slid a dollar bill across the table to her. "Please accept this as a retainer. I think that makes it official."

Lucille smiled, nodded, and took the dollar.

"Just before I met you, I ran into a *situation*." I paused to let that sink in. "Why don't we have dinner and I'll try to explain it to you? In the event we get interrupted by gangsters, just follow my lead, okay?"

She laughed again. She had a beautiful laugh. "Somehow that wouldn't surprise me, Jake."

Before she could ask any questions, a waiter appeared and took our orders. I guess we were allowed a last meal. As usual, she ordered something I couldn't pronounce, and I got the spaghetti with meatballs. Couldn't screw that up. I also ordered the most expensive thing on the menu as a takeout, just in case.

After the waiter left, I tried to make frivolous conversation, but she wasn't having any of it. She kept staring at me until I broke down and told her everything. Well, almost everything.

Her expression ran the gamete of incredulity, skepticism, humor, and concern. My tale went from Tony's wallet being lifted to my recent visit from Bullhead City's finest, leaving a few things out. By the time I was finished, she was looking at me with different eyes.

"Jake," she said, "you're a criminal."

I didn't need to pay her a dollar to know that. I was about to thank her for that observation when our food appeared, followed by Nicky.

Lucille's presence obviously threw Nicky off. He had nowhere to sit down, and I let him stew on that before I said, "Nicky, this is my lawyer, Lucille Dombrowski. Ms. Dombrowski, this is Mr. Nickolas Mosconi Jr., recently of Las Vegas."

The twitch in Nicky's right eye told me that I'd hit a nerve. He didn't like being called Junior.

Lucille went with the flow and shook hands with Nicky while giving him a smile that didn't reach her eyelashes. She was still assimilating the information I'd given her and doing it well. Her demeanor prompted another eye twitch from him.

For once, Nicky was at a loss for words. He probably expected to sit down across from me and cancel my food order because I wouldn't be getting a last meal. My lawyer—a woman, for God's sake—had screwed that up. My execution was going to be postponed, temporarily.

Before he had a chance to bail, I read him the riot act.

"Look, Nicky. I don't want this to go south. You can't kill me *and* my lawyer." That got me a look from my lawyer.

"Call your boys off and let's talk."

He wasn't happy, but he didn't have a choice, so he got up and went back into the kitchen to tell the boys they couldn't kill me. Yet.

As he was doing that, I had Lucille move across the booth and sit next to me so that when Nicky got back, he would have a place to sit while I eviscerated him. I also liked the skin contact that I got with my date. I think she liked it too.

"What are you planning to do with this guy?" she asked.

"Rattle his cage. Throw him off-balance."

"I'd say you've already done that." Lucille dug into her dinner. No shrinking violet. I liked that. I joined her, and we ate in companionable silence until Nicky emerged from the kitchen and joined us, sitting down without an invitation.

We ignored him for a couple of minutes until he could no longer stand it and spoke up. "So talk."

"I'm going to assume you *found* the lost property in question and was about to return it to the owner." That brought a slight smile from Nicky. "I'm here to offer you a reward for its return. A substantial reward."

"Since you're *assuming* I have it, and I'm not *saying* I do, how much reward are we talking about?" Nicky asked after glancing at my female lawyer.

I lowballed him. "Ten thousand dollars."

He looked suitably indignant and couldn't keep the sneer off his face. He suspected it wasn't an ordinary credit card, and he knew that if I offered ten grand, it was worth a hell of a lot more. He had no intention of letting the card go now. What he *didn't* like was me fucking with him. He got up to leave.

"I don't have the property you are trying to recover, so I guess we have nothing to talk about."

"Sit back down, Nicky," I told him. "You blew up Dudley last night, then you had your two boys shoot and kill Charlie shortly afterward. I have a witness. You return my client's property and I'll make the witness go away. Otherwise, your shooters are going down. I doubt they'll want to take the ride by themselves. We're talking murder one here. Two counts."

Nicky sat back down, his interest renewed.

"Fifty...assuming I can find the lost property," he said after looking first at Lucille and then me.

"Might take a while, but I can do fifty. But you have to give half of that to Charlie's mother," I told him just to be shitty. I wasn't going to give him a penny, but I wanted to taunt him before I set the hook.

He didn't bother to ask who Charlie was, and he had no intention of giving me anything but a couple of .22s to the old noggin.

"Can I talk to you privately?" Nicky asked.

Lucille used her napkin to wipe her lips. "If you gentlemen don't mind, I think I need powder my nose." Pretty funny, because she obviously didn't use any makeup and didn't need it.

I got up and let her out of the booth.

Nicky was talking before I could sit back down. "Who the fuck *are* you?"

"I told you. A contractor. A fixer. I'm here to fix this situation to everybody's satisfaction. That's all you need to know. Tell you what, I'll up my offer twenty percent. Sixty thousand."

The greed showed through his eyes. He would get me to show the money, then give me a couple of bullets instead of the card. Your classic rip-off.

"*Assuming* I can locate the property in question, I think we got a deal," Nicky said. "How do you want to make the exchange?"

I must look really stupid. "I'll call you in an hour and let you know. I have to go get the money." I almost added, "Moron."

Nicky nodded, as if he should have thought of that himself.

"Oh, by the way, if you interfaced the card with your computer, the deal is off. I'll know if you did when we make the exchange."

I saw the wheels turning. This was good information. Maybe he should be doing that as soon as I left. Before he could pry out why that was important, I got up and intercepted Lucille as she came back from the john, gently steering her to the door. She asked no questions, and I didn't bother to wait for the takeout or pay the tab.

When we got out the door, I said, "Let's take your car. Let me pay my cab and I'll be right back." Much to my delight, she didn't ask why I had a cabbie hanging around and headed for her Jeep.

I hustled over to Mo, who was parked in handicapped slot next to the front door. He rolled down the window as I approached.

Mo was jazzed, I could tell. He was practically salivating.

"I'll be leaving with the lady in the Jeep. We might be followed. If we are, try to keep them off us until I get her home. Then meet me at the Riverside casino, north entrance."

Mo grinned. He had a mission. His life was getting a lot more exciting. He was a happy camper. The money helped too.

I ran off to Lucille's Jeep and hopped in.

"I have to tell you, Jake, you sure know how to show a lady a good time," Lucille said as she pulled out of her parking place. "I didn't even get to finish my dinner. Not to mention involving me in a criminal conspiracy for which I could be disbarred, convicted of a felony, and incarcerated. What's for dessert?"

"You're my lawyer, and I gave you a retainer. You left before any conspiracy was hatched. You are now advising me on the consequences of any of my actions, which I will tell you forthwith as privileged information. You're covered. I'm sorry about dinner." I gave her a peck on the cheek. "By the way, step on it. We're probably being followed, and if they find out where you live, they'll kill us both."

She burned rubber pulling out onto Highway 95. I put my seatbelt on.

24

If you didn't count in the roar of the wind in the topless Jeep, the ride across the bridge was fast and in silence. I got the impression my date was unhappy with me.

I had to admit, she would make a superb wheelman. Wheel*person*. She hauled ass, did some shake maneuvers, and went through a couple of casino parking lots before coming into her RV park the back way. I was impressed. With Mo bringing up the rear, I don't think the twins had a chance.

When we pulled up in front of her RV and she turned off the engine, the silence was deafening. My tinnitus was killing me. That happens when you forget to take your high blood pressure meds.

She kept her hands on the wheel and stared straight ahead. Didn't say a word.

"What would you like for dessert?" I asked just for the hell of it.

That earned me a laugh.

She turned to look at me. "I can't decide if I'm more angry or more excited than I've ever been in my life. I'm leaning toward angry."

"I vote for excited," I ventured, and then I told her of my conversation with Nicky while she was in the lady's room.

By the time I was finished, she was rubbing her eyes. "Do you have any idea how many felonies you've committed in the last twenty-four hours?"

"I've lost count. Ran out of fingers and toes."

"You're hopeless."

We sat there in not-so companionable silence for a while.

"What do plan to do now?"

"I'm shooting from the hip here, so basically I'm clueless."

She laid her hand on my arm. "Since you're paying me big bucks to be your lawyer, how about some legal advice?"

I put my hand over hers but didn't reply.

"Turn this over to the police. I'm sure I can negotiate a short prison term, say ten to twenty years with the possibility of early release with good behavior. I promise I'll come visit you every month."

Until she smiled, I wasn't sure if she was serious or not.

"That advice is worth about what I'm paying you." I smiled back. "No thanks. I think I can manage to wiggle out of this on my own. I may bring the cops in later, but I've got some things I have to accomplish first."

I started to get out of the Jeep, but she kept her hand on my arm. "Where do you think you're going?"

"To visit some people."

"Not without me, you aren't."

I shook my head. "No way, sweetheart. I think you're safe here. There's no telling where this is headed now that I've poked the bear in the ass. These guys have already killed two people, and they won't hesitate to kill more. I don't want you hurt."

She hopped out, walked around the Jeep, and got right in my face. "You should have thought of that before you invited me to dinner. Until this is done, consider us attached at the hip. Besides, you owe me dessert."

I was liking her more and more every minute.

"Your choice, baby," I said and started walking. She dogged my footsteps as we reached Casino Road and dodged the traffic getting across it to the Riverside Casino parking lot.

We skirted the main entrance, passed by Don Laughlin's classic car showroom, and made our way to the north entrance, the one used by the locals. If anybody was watching, they'd probably be at the south or west entrance where the majority of people entered the casino.

Mo was waiting in a handicapped slot near the back door, the cab running and pointed toward Casino Road.

"Where to, boss?" he asked as we climbed in.

"The Edgewater, and quit calling me boss. Did you have any problems on the way over here?"

"Nothing I could not handle." Mo grinned, looking at me in the rearview mirror. "You were correct about being followed. They kept trying to get around me, but I acted like a woman driver, switching lanes every time they did. I finally drove them up on the sidewalk and into a newspaper box in front of the Panda Express. I do not think they are very happy with me."

"Did anybody else see you do it?" I was concerned that his exuberance would get his cabbie license revoked.

"No, that is why I waited until there was no other traffic around. Except for the newspaper dispenser and a broken headlight, I do not think much damage was done. They will not call the authorities." He was obviously pleased with himself.

I reached forward and patted him on the shoulder. "I believe a bonus is in order."

"Thank you very much, boss." He returned his attention to the road.

"By the way, keep an eye out for the cops. They may be watching." If that alarmed him, he didn't show it. He nodded like I was commenting on how nice the weather was.

So far, Lucille had said nothing about the cab waiting for us or Mo's recital of his recent exploits, but she then took the opportunity to poke me in the ribs with her elbow. When I turned to her, she gave me the same expression Sister Mary Katherine, my fifth-grade teacher, would give me every time I tried to look up her habit.

25

Mo let us out in front of the Edgewater Hotel and Casino and then drove off to the cab area. I didn't have to tell him to wait.

Lucille and I made our way through the casino to the bank of elevators servicing the hotel. Thankfully, we weren't alone on the ride up or in the hallway, so she didn't get a chance to grill me.

Arliss opened the door on my first knock. If he was surprised to see a woman with me, he didn't show it. He stepped aside as we entered, then closed and locked the door behind us.

"Arliss, this is Lucille. She's my lawyer, so you can talk freely. Lucille, this is Arliss, my associate." They shook hands, giving each other the once-over.

"How are Earl and Susan doing?" I asked.

"I think they're probably watching Roller Derby or wrestling. After I cut them off from the porno, they settled down a bit. How are things going on the war front?" Arliss asked over his shoulder as he headed for the living room.

The suite was impressive. I wondered how much it was costing me. Lucille joined me on the couch, still quiet and taking everything in.

I told Arliss about the cop showing up and my encounter with Nicky. He listened without questions. When I was finished, he just nodded.

My lawyer finally decided to put her two cents worth in. "Arliss, you have to give me a dollar."

He raised his eyebrows but did as she asked, digging into his pocket for a buck. He could only find a twenty but handed it to her anyway.

"Hot damn, a tip. I'm now officially your lawyer, so you can say whatever you want in front of me from this point on and it's privileged information," she said, putting the twenty in her purse. "Shucks, two new clients in one day. Maybe I should go shopping."

She was smiling at me, but it wasn't a real warm smile, if you know what I mean.

Lucille turned back to Arliss. "As your lawyer, I have to advise you that your activities have left you open to prosecution for numerous felonies and too many misdemeanors to list at the moment, as well as civil actions—lawsuits and the such. Do you understand that?"

I saw that Arliss was trying to keep from laughing, but he managed to control it and merely nodded again. He shot me a sideways glace and saw I was having the same problem but with limited success.

Lucille turned to me and gave me that Sister Mary Katherine look again. "Look, Jake, you may think this is funny, but it's not. You're up to your eyeballs in trouble. I can't even count the number of criminal acts you've engaged in in the last day. Let's start with the feds. We've got kidnapping, transportation across state lines, engaging in organized crime, extortion across state lines, interstate fraud, civil rights violations, and conspiracy. Forgive me if I've missed something. That's good for a century, running concurrently. If they run consecutively...a millennium.

"Then there's the state charges. Pretty much the same thing—assault, kidnapping, unlawful detention, extortion, fraud, conspiracy, obstruction of justice, harboring a witness, impeding an investigation. I could go on and on, but that's good for *another* hundred years. I won't even bother with the misdemeanors. Neither one of you will live long enough to worry about it, because you'll probably have to do the state time first. No cushy federal country club camps for you guys."

Arliss tore his gaze from her and looked at me. "I like her," he said. "She's got balls."

I returned his grin. "I do too. I think I'm in love."

Lucille rolled her eyes but plowed ahead. "Fine. Just so you know. But here's my only rule: if you expect to get out of this relatively unscathed, I have to be with you the whole way, *and* we have to resolve it in twenty-four hours. We don't have time to screw around, and I can't cover you for more than a day. Otherwise, as an officer of the court, I have to pull the plug. Is it a deal?" she said, turning to me.

If she kept this up, I was going to have to propose to her. Trying to keep it professional, I took her hand. "You have a deal, counselor."

I don't think she noticed that I didn't say *we*.

26

Arliss broke the sexual tension. "So what's the plan?"

I thought about it for a moment.

"I'm not quite sure. I'm supposed to be calling Nicky about now to tell him I've got his money so he can kill me. Screw him. He can wait. I've got Tony on hold, but he won't hold long. I think I need to see him. I've got a few questions for him."

I looked at Arliss. "You keep an eye on things here. By the way, give me the keys to the VW. The cops don't know where we're at yet, but they know about the van. It's only a matter of time until they find it. I'll move it to the Aquarius to throw them off. Then I'm gonna go see Tony. After that, I'll be in the wind. If you need me, call," I said, getting up. Arliss and I didn't do chitchat.

He tossed me the keys, and I headed for the door. It took Lucille a couple of seconds to realize that I was leaving. I was almost out the door before she could grab her purse and get off the couch. I knew I'd pay for it later, but she was learning.

I didn't have long to wait. Ten feet down the hall, she pushed me against the wall.

"Don't jack with me, Jake. Are you going to play fair or not? No bullshit." She was surprisingly strong for such a little thing.

"We'll do it your way," I said, taking her face in my hands and kissing her. She didn't resist.

It was heavenly. Time stood still and bells rang. I think she felt the same way. After that, I had no trouble dragging her back down the hallway to the elevator. Fortunately, there were other people in it on the ride down.

I took her hand as we left the elevator. I wanted to alleviate any second-guessing on her part. I was beginning to *really* like her, so I was eager to please. We made our way past the slot machines and out the front door.

Mo was vigilant and spotted us right away. He started moving before we hit the curb. I was thinking about promoting him to salary status. I put Lucille in the back seat and told him to meet me at the Aquarius. I hoofed it over to the parking lot.

It took me about ten minutes to locate the VW van. A quick look around didn't turn up any suspicious cars watching it. I got in and drove it next door to the Aquarius Hotel, parking it in the back lot. Mo was waiting, and he must have figured I'd be parking somewhere way in the back, so he was behind me as I pulled in.

I was back in the cab in a minute, and Mo was moving before I could shut the door.

Expecting to get another ration of shit from my lawyer now that she had a few minutes to think, I was pleasantly surprised when she reached over and gave me a lip-lock. How many people can say they've kissed their lawyer? I can understand *fucking* your lawyer, but a French kiss?

Mo broke the moment. "Where to, boss?"

It took me a moment to focus. "Find me a pay phone."

Pay phones were practically extinct, so it wasn't that easy. We found one in front of the convenience store next to the In-N-Out burger joint.

I got out of the cab, pulled out my roll of quarters, and called Tony's room at Harrah's.

Leo answered on the first ring. He didn't even say hello, just "What."

"I need a meet with Tony."

Leo knew my voice, so he didn't ask who I was. "He's eating dinner at the moment. How soon are we talking about?"

"Yesterday."

He hesitated for a moment and said, "I'll see what I can do," and left me on hold. I hated being put on hold, so I hung up.

I was going to see Tony whether Leo liked it or not.

I climbed back into the cab. "Harrah's," I told Mo.

27

My date seemed unconcerned about the turn of events. Apparently, going from the Edgewater, where I was keeping two murder witnesses sequestered, to the Aquarius to stash a car, to Harrah's to meet with a mob boss was like going to Walmart after Walgreens and Safeway. I may be wrong, but I think she was enjoying it.

Mo pulled up in front of Harrah's doors. "Don't get lost. This shouldn't take long," I told him as we got out. He was gone before we got to the doors.

Several Sizzling Sevens slot machines called out to me on the walk to the elevators, but I didn't have time. I walked fast, and Lucille kept up. An open elevator was waiting. I punched the button for the twenty-fifth floor.

Cube, one of Tony's bodyguards, was waiting when the elevator doors opened. He hadn't been here on my previous visits. Cube and I went back a ways, so he apologized before he gave me a cursory pat down. He took one look at Lucille—with her scowl, arms crossed, and tapping her foot—and decided to forgo that with her.

Leo opened the door when we got to the suite. He led Lucille and I into the living room, where Tony and Francine were sitting on the couch watching *Dancing with the Stars* on the ninety-inch plasma screen mounted on the wall. Looked like you were two feet away from the dancers.

Tony looked relieved to see me. I suspected he needed a reason to bail and watch football on the bedroom TV. Two feet from the quarterback was better. He pointed that way and turned to Francine.

"Sweetheart, Jake and I need to talk some business. Let me know how everybody dances," he said like he cared and gave her a kiss on the cheek. Francine gave me a little wave, noticed Lucille, and got up to greet her. Francine was a really loving woman and probably the only woman that could have put up with Tony for sixty years.

Francine insisted that Lucille join her in watching DWTS, leading her to the seat her husband had just vacated. After all, the men were going to talk, so what else was she going to do? She told Leo to fetch Lucille a glass of white wine. My lawyer shot a me look of venom but was helpless against Francine's insistence.

I followed Tony into his bedroom. I grew up in houses smaller than it. I shut both of the double doors while Tony eased himself into a chair by the window. I sat down across the table from him in the other chair. He reached over, grabbed the remote, and turned on the TV to *Monday Night Football.* He adjusted the sound up, but not too much. Any bug would have a tough time weeding out our conversation.

He turned to me. "So."

Translated: *report.*

I gave myself a couple of moments to gather my thoughts. When you talk to a guy like Tony, you have to watch your every word. So I lied.

I had all these parts in my head, but they weren't fitting together conveniently. I hated those hundred-piece puzzles when I was a kid. I could do the corners, but the rest never jelled. That's what this reminded me of.

"I will have access to the four remaining cards in the morning. I expect to recover the Chase card shortly, but that's a work in progress. Tonight, tomorrow at the latest."

Tony nodded, apparently somewhat satisfied. I figured I was outta there. "Who's the woman?" he said, throwing me off momentarily.

I should have thought a moment before saying, "My lawyer," which was probably the last thing you wanted to say to a mob boss. I should have said, "My new girlfriend."

But it was too late. Another classic case of putting mouth in motion before putting brain in gear. So much for watching my words.

I held my breath until Tony chuckled. "So you're porking your lawyer? Jake, I'm proud of you. I wish I could fuck *my* lawyer, but he's my brother-in-law. Francine wouldn't approve."

I let my breath out.

"It's strictly professional." I lied like it was going out of style. "She knows next to nothing, but what she does is protected by attorney-client privilege. I'm doing a lot of damage out there, and I'm probably going to need one sooner or later. I figure sooner is better."

He watched me for moment and seemed to come to a decision. "Maybe I'm wrong. She's not your type anyways. She's not a blond with big tits." He thought that was funny.

I laughed along with him. When the king laughs…

I figured now was as good a time as any to get some answers out of him, so I plunged in. "What is the significance of Nicky accessing the card with his computer? Is there something about these cards I should know?"

His eyes tightened slightly. He took his time answering. "The Chase card has, shall we say, *sensitive* information encoded in it. It was meant to be used at a meeting with some association in Los Angeles the day after tomorrow. If the card has been compromised, it is of no further use to me."

That's when I saw a glimmer of light from the end of the tunnel. I *had* the Chase card. Earl must have been mistaken about which card Charlie had. Depending on how important the other cards were, I could complete this contract in a matter of hours.

"How important are the other cards, Tony?"

"Some of them are regular credit cards. Fictitious name, but good. They're not important. Two cards have different capabilities. The Chase card is the priority. The APEX card is second and almost as important. The others are peripheral."

Bullshit bells were clanging in my head. Tony lied more than I did. He'd manipulated me more times than Sister Mary Katherine had whacked me with her ruler.

The APEX card held the cardinal spot. The Chase card was the red herring. Either way, I was covered. Then something occurred to me.

"How many Chase cards were there?" I asked him, dreading the answer.

He smiled as if surprised by my question but quickly suppressed it. "Two. One regular, one enhanced."

That should have explained something, but damned if I knew what.

I nodded, letting Tony think I was going for his bullshit. "My problem right now, Tony, is how can I determine whether or not Nicky has compromised the card. You have any suggestions?"

"As a matter of fact, I do." He pulled himself out of his chair with some effort and made his way to a table next to his bed. Opening the drawer, he got something out and brought it to me. When he laid it on the table, it looked like nothing more than a hardpack of Marlboros.

"I don't smoke."

He ignored my riposte, seating himself with obvious effort. His new knees were killing him. The black bags under his eyes had gotten more pronounced in the last two months.

"This is a reader. You can't see the flasher 'cause it's tiny, but that little baby will let you know the moment the card gets close to it. It'll flash green or red from an LED in the lid. Just hold the card close to it, within a foot or so, and a light will flash for two seconds. Green is good, red is bad."

I picked up the Marlboros. It was surprisingly heavy. I had no idea Tony was so plugged in, technology-wise. Tony was always surprising me. That's why I am so wary of him.

"If it's red, then the card has been compromised and I don't care if it's recovered. Turn your attention to the APEX card. Do whatever you have to do. I'm leaving in the morning. I need this situation resolved by then."

I was pretty confident I could do that, so I didn't let the unspoken consequences of failure bother me. Usually it would have scared the shit out of me, but there was something else going on here that I was missing.

Tony had done this to me before, and I was lucky to get out of it alive and free the last time. He was always sucking me into shitstorms and I was tired of it. My last "Get Out Jail Free" card got used up two weeks ago. I had to assume that everything that came out of his mouth was a lie and go from there. Where *there* was, I had no idea.

The second understated reference to APEX got my antennae twitching again, and I tried a new tactic. "So the APEX card will read too?" I asked, pointing to the Marlboros.

Tony usually had no tells, but he let one slip. His right forefinger started to point, then stopped. "Yes." He looked at me to see if I had noticed.

I had, and I figured it was time to get the hell out of there.

"Okay, Tony. I'll have the plastic back to you by check-out time tomorrow. I've got some things I need to take care of before then," I said, grabbing the Marlboros and getting up. "I'll be in touch."

Tony turned up the sound on the football game as I left the bedroom and went to collect my lawyer.

I could tell when I turned the corner to the living room that she was not a happy camper. My personal best time for watching DWTS was just shy of fifteen minutes. It had been about that long, and Lucille looked like she was ready to scream, another point in her favor. Francine was oblivious.

Lucille shot off the couch as I approached and headed for the door. I said goodnight to Francine. She smiled, waved, and went back to watching DWTS. She didn't bother to ask me where Tony was. Marital bliss at the half-century mark.

Cube was waiting outside the suite door, then escorted us out the door, down the hallway, and to the elevator before shaking my hand. I think he wanted to give me a hug, but guys didn't do that. At least some guys. "Say hi to Arliss for me, will you, Jake?" he said as the elevator doors closed. I didn't know he and Arliss were that close.

Then again, you could have knocked me over with a feather when my favorite weatherman announced one morning that he was gay.

Lucille, livid, was on me a second later. "How dare you push me off like that? I should have been in there with you. I thought our deal was that I know everything that goes on now. That was total bullshit!"

Luckily, a blue hair and her doddering husband got on two floors down, giving me a chance to make up something. I was ready by the time we hit the casino floor.

"I'm sorry," I told her as we negotiated our way through the casino to the front door. It wasn't easy because one of the Sizzling Seven dollar slots whispered to me that if I would just stick a hundred bucks in her, she would reward me with a progressive jackpot, currently $1,869, after three pulls.

I tried to focus on my immediate problems.

"Tony's old-school. He doesn't do women and business. I'll tell you everything when we get outside." I grabbed her hand and she followed me. I took that as a good sign.

Mo must have seen us coming through the doors because he was there in a heartbeat. As soon as we got into the back seat, I started talking. "Take us to the Tiki, Mo."

Turning to Lucille, I told her everything, verbatim, that Tony and I discussed. She listened and didn't say anything.

Then I told her what was bothering me, besides maybe Tony sticking it to me without kissing me. "Something is going on about these cards that I can't figure out. Half the time I think Tony wants them back, and the other half, I'm not so sure. I've got all the cards but one, and as far as I can determine, it's not that important. Or so he claims. Tony can say one thing and mean something else."

I took a moment to catch my breath. "He does this to me all the time. Don't get me wrong. So far the rewards have exceeded the blowback, but I always gotta watch this guy," I told her. "I've got a gut feeling he's setting me up for something. He's playing me."

She looked at me for about ten seconds and then relaxed, taking my hand.

I felt like I'd passed her test. We had crossed the bridge by now and were back in Arizona. Back on Sabbatini's turf.

Lucille was mulling over what I'd told her, so I leaned forward to talk to Mo. "Do you know where the Rivers View trailer park is?"

"Of course. That is where the old man that owns half of the town lives."

Something about his tone got my antenna going again.

"When we get there, take a cruise through. I want to take a look at something."

We were there in five minutes. Mo turned right off 95 and slowed as he passed the office. The whole park didn't take three minutes to traverse. I had Mo slow down as we passed Charlie's trailer. The crime scene tape was still up.

Standing in the shadows across the street was a figure. There was a dog heeled to his side. A really *big* dog.

28

When we pulled back onto 95, I knew I had another player in motion, and I was still trying to figure how many guys were on the other side.

I didn't think the old Nazi was connected, more like sniffing around. He sensed something was going down, but he just hadn't figured out what it was yet. I put him off on the side, mentally.

Lucille spoke up, breaking me out of my thoughts. "I think you may be on to something with the APEX card. Didn't you tell me it was thicker, not like a regular card?"

I gave her another point.

"My thoughts exactly." I pulled the Marlboros out and showed her the device. When she took it, I could see she was surprised by its weight.

"Do you know anything about this stuff?" I asked. I didn't want to tell her I was a Luddite. Dr. Ludd organized the first antitechnology group back in the 1800s. I was probably one of his last advocates.

"Quite a bit, actually," she replied. "My kids dragged me kicking and screaming into twenty-first century. I've had clients that were accused of stealing millions over the Internet. I got them off. They paid part of their bill tutoring my daughters, and then me. I can call on them at any time, for anything, but I'd prefer not to."

I was seriously considering running down to the mall and grabbing a big diamond ring from Zale's. I figured her for a six-and-a-half ring size. Three carats. It would set me back for a while, but what the hell, I was making a killing on my lawyer's fees.

She was still studying the reader when Mo pulled into the Tiki's parking lot. He just naturally pulled around to the back door and put the cab into park, not saying a word.

Lucille put the device in her purse and got out first. I followed her. Mo glided the cab off to a dark corner.

The bar was packed with old farts, and we were lucky to find two seats together at the bar. Lucille intimidated an eighty-year-old guy into moving over, and she did it so well, he thought she was doing him a favor.

Ruby materialized out of nowhere, chipper as can be. She took one look at Lucille and gave me a shit-eating grin. She'd seen me last week with the blond that was gone and earlier with Susan. "Hey, Jake, you sure get around. What's *up*?"

"Cute," I told her. "Bring us a couple of shots of Cuervo with Coors chasers." She scooted off like she was on skates. Kind of reminded me of *Star War*'s Obi-Wan Kenobi on roller skates, except skinnier and with tits down to her knees.

I turned my attention back to Lucille. "So what do you think?"

"What do I *think*? I think you're a friggin' idiot, and I don't know why I'm wasting my time on you."

Oops. On hindsight, I probably should have asked that question after she'd had a couple of drinks. Women could be so unpredictable at her age. A Valium, applied judiciously, did wonders. I was fresh out of Valiums.

I decided to keep my mouth shut until she'd downed her tequila. I nudged my shot glass closer to her when she wasn't looking.

She slammed her shot then reached over and did mine too, without asking. She wasn't screaming at me, so I took that as a good sign.

I waited for the tequila to take effect, which wasn't long. When she pulled a cigarette out of her purse and fired it up, I was tempted to remind her that, as a lawyer, she should know that that was a violation of the law in Arizona.

What I said instead was "No. I meant the card reader. What do you think?"

Lucille sent me a sideways glance that told me she was still pissed off about me sidelining her at Tony's. She went back to looking anywhere except at me. She punished me for another minute before answering.

"Pretty sophisticated. RFIDs. Radio frequency identification devices. They're in everything now, from tires to sneakers. Manufacturers use them to collect data on their product, but it's become something of a Frankenstein. Wafer-thin, enough to fit into the hem of a dress. What you have here is a RFID reader, able to access the card wirelessly, no physical contact, just proximity, a foot at most. The newest readers that I've heard about that can do it remotely at that distance are the size of a suitcase. Not exactly inconspicuous next to a cash register. You've got one the size of a cigarette pack. Very impressive. I'm somewhat surprised that that old man is plugged into this kind of technology." She took another drag and blew it in my face.

I hated cigarette smoke. I think she knew that.

Ruby didn't come over and tell Lucille to kill the cigarette, seeming to sense the tension.

"I'm not kidding about pulling the plug tomorrow if this isn't taken care of. The witnesses have to turn themselves in. I'll arrange it. Give me two more bucks," she said, putting out her cigarette in my empty shot glass.

"So what's your plan?"

I reached into my pocket and fished out her retainer for two more clients, which I laid on the table.

"Get the card back or find out if it's compromised, what I've contracted to do. I'd rather not have you around, but since you insist, you're in." I was glad we were back in a professional mode. "I'm going to call Nicky and set up a meeting. He's probably waiting on my call now."

I got up, went into the bathroom, pulled out my cell, and called Nicky's restaurant. Luscious Lips answered.

SIZZLIN' 7S

"Put Nicky on the line," I said, not bothering to identify myself. He picked immediately, like he'd been waiting.

"Yeah."

"Nicky, this is your contractor buddy. I've got the payroll checks, and I'll need to meet with you to drop them off." I had to talk like that because you just couldn't trust the airways anymore. Everybody seemed to be listening. Nicky was apparently like-minded and didn't express any confusion over my code.

"Where and when?"

"Riverside Casino. The dollar Sizzling Seven slots across from the cigarette concession and next to the high roller lounge. There's a bank of three machines. I'll be at one of them. One hour. Be there," I said and terminated the call. An hour gave me plenty of time to put everything in motion.

29

When I walked out of the bathroom, I found Detective Sabbatini sitting on my stool. He was talking to Lucille, and she didn't seem to be bothered at all. I walked up to them.

Sabbatini saw me coming and greeted me with a wolf's smile. "Well, well, isn't this a coincidence. I stop in for a beer, take the only seat at the bar, and it happens to be yours, Mr. Leggs. I thought my boys had you under surveillance. I'll have to have a talk with them when I get back to the station." He motioned to Lucille. "I presume this lovely lady here is your date."

"Actually, I'm his lawyer," she butted in with a smile. "And I *presume* you are a law enforcement official. Can I see your credentials, please?"

Taken aback by her professionalism, it took him a moment to pull out his badge and present them to her. Continuing to screw with him, she actually took the creds from his hand and inspected them. Nobody had ever taken his badge from his hand when he'd presented it. You could see it.

After writing down his name, badge, and ID number on a bar napkin and placing it in her purse, she returned it to him. The look on his face was priceless.

Invading his space, she went on the offensive. "I don't believe in coincidences. Since you've stated that you have my client under surveillance, I must conclude that you are here to question him. Is that correct?"

I think he was telling the truth about just being here for a beer and running into me, but I wasn't about to throw him a lifeline. I kept my mouth shut and enjoyed the show.

"No, counselor. I really am here for a beer, but now you've got my curiosity up."

Before he could start in on me, I had a couple of questions for him.

"What's the deal with the old Nazi that owns the trailer park? I could tell from our earlier conversation that was no love lost there," I said.

Sabbatini thought about it while he took a slug of his beer. "The old man was dirty when he got here sixty years ago. Bought in cheap, a lot of property that is now worth tens of millions. He uses his clout to do as he pleases. He's a slumlord with a little sick sex thrown in. He's got his finger in everything around here. I haven't been able to pin anything on him, but I'd love to. He's just plain evil."

He turned to me with a touch of wishful thinking. "Why? Are you here for him? A relative of somebody he killed back in the war maybe?"

Sabbatini was probably right. That's why the old man was so paranoid. One day somebody was going to show up and do justice for crimes the old boy had committed when he was a very young man.

But it wasn't me.

"No, Detective. Like you, I am merely curious. However, if I learn anything that can help you in that respect, I'll call you." I motioned to Ruby for my bill. She glided right over.

Laying a couple of twenties on the counter, I touched Lucille's elbow to let her know it was time to go. I don't think she was quite finished with the detective, but she slammed her beer like a pro and got up.

Taking his hand, she said, "It was a pleasure meeting you, Detective Sabbatini. I'm sure we'll be talking in the future."

"No doubt," he replied, giving me a hard look.

As we walked out the door, Mo pulled up like he came out of a starting gate. Lucille and I dived into the back seat, and he shot out of the parking lot like his ass was on fire, throwing us around the back seat. I don't think Sabbatini had time to pay his bill and get to the door before we were long gone.

"Edgewater," I said to Mo as we pulled out onto 95 headed north. Lucille and I were trying to pull ourselves into semi-dignified positions. I think she was giggling when we got ourselves upright. It might have been the two shots of tequila with a beer chaser.

"I'm sorry, boss. I saw him pull up in his police car and go in, but I had no way to warn you. I could only be ready for you when you came out," Mo told me, looking in the rearview mirror.

"You did great, Mo," I reassured him. "Drop us off at the Edgewater, then go to the Riverside and wait." The casino was a quarter mile from the Riverside, close by if I should need him.

Lucille was still trying to suppress her giggles as I put my arm over her shoulder. "I haven't had this much excitement since a bunch of us snuck into the drive-in movie in the trunk," she confessed. I was glad she was enjoying herself.

I was impressed with her steely attitude with the cop at the bar, the whole lawyer thing.

"I have to tell you, I'm considering giving you a raise. You did an excellent job acting as my counselor back there. You blew him away," I told her, our lips close together.

She allowed me to kiss her. The usual sparks and stars went off. Way too soon, Mo had us parked in front of the Edgewater's front entrance.

That broke the moment, and we disengaged. She jumped out of the cab like "that was nice but let's take care of business." Mo looked at me expectantly in the rearview mirror. I shrugged.

"I'll call you," I told him as we got out. He drove off as soon as I shut the door.

The cops might to be on him, so I figured he needed to be someplace that had nothing to do with Arliss and the two stashed witnesses. The Riverside was perfect. Mo could hang out there and draw off any heat, if there was any. He'd let me know if there was.

I had a fondness for the Edgewater Casino. After my father died, unbeknownst to me, my mom took up gambling, traveling with five of her bridge-playing buds to Laughlin from New Mexico on a monthly basis. It was a twelve-hour drive for six old ladies. I can't imagine how many pit stops they'd have had to make.

She played the nickel shots at the Edgewater. That was when they actually spit out coins. When she died, I found fifty thousand dollars in nickels in her garage, in five-gallon pails. It took the bank three days to count them. Every time I see a blue hair playing the nickel machines, I think of Mom. She was real card.

It didn't take us long to pass through the old casino and exit through the back door to the River Walk and then back to Casino Road. When we got there, I asked if we could cross the street to her RV and regroup. She held my hand as we dodged the traffic. She didn't let go, and we didn't get killed. I took that as a good sign.

The fifty yards to her luxury coach was calming. I was going to do a swap within the hour, but I had yet to nail down the details. It was all in the details. Guys like Little Nicky, you missed a detail, it was the deep sleep. Adios, amigo.

When we got there, Ratso was shaking so hard when Lucille opened the door, I was afraid I'd have to give him doggie CPR. Personally, I'd come to the realization that pets were like kids. Someone once told me that children sharpen their teeth on their parents. I believe it. The last time I moved, I gave my dog away to a Korean family, my cats to widow lady, and the fish to some Native Americans. The girlfriend left on her own.

Downsizing.

As much as I liked little Ratso, I liked his master more. I was thinking I might have to modify my behavior concerning pets. Maybe Ratso could get lost sometime in the future when I took him out for a walk. Coyote Kibbles. It was a possibility.

30

While Lucille took Coyote Kibbles out for a walk so he'd quit peeing on the floor, I spent the time going over my options.

I had the local cops on my ass. I had a Vegas mobster front man on my ass. The head of the Phoenix mob had paid me big money up front to recover his property. His cards. I was 80 percent there. I held four of the five cards.

I played Texas hold 'em all the time, and I knew four was not enough. That was when you bluff.

Added to that, there was something bothering me about Tony's rendition of the cards and what I'd seen. He had a history of playing me, and it was probable that he was doing it again.

Two of the cards were players—important to Tony. One of the Chase cards, and the other was the APEX. I was putting my money on APEX. The other three were dummies. Something didn't quite click, and as much as I liked Tony, I was gun-shy.

All I had to do was go across the street, get the cards from Deborah, come back, and scan them with the pack of Marlboros in my lawyer's purse. That would tell me everything I needed to know. But I held off.

I wasn't quite sure, but I thought my lawyer would tell me when she got back from walking Kibbles.

When she climbed back into her luxury bus, I figured I had my ducks more or less in a row. I sensed that her mood had changed.

She'd obviously had a chance to think about events while walking her dog. I kept my mouth shut and let her get it out.

"Okay, Jake. What aren't you telling me?"

I gave it my best shot. I looked her straight in the eye and said, "There is more going on here than you can imagine. I think there's some kind of turf war going on between two factions of the mob, and I'm smack in the middle of it. And as my attorney, I think you should give me some advice."

I think that was one of the smoothest lines I've ever delivered.

She wasn't having any of it. In fact, it made her laugh.

"That's rich," she said when she caught her breath. "I don't think I'm your attorney anymore. I'm pretty sure I'm your coconspirator at this point. I think we should turn ourselves in. Maybe we can get into one of those federal co-ed minimum security facilities. That way, we can see each other every day, and the ten to twenty years will go by a lot faster. The upside is, I can still act as our attorney until I get convicted along with you. Then I'll be disbarred."

I like a woman that doesn't beat around the bush.

"Don't be negative," I told her. "If we play our cards right, we could come out of this smelling like a rose. I've got most of cards, and I've negotiated the return of the last one. What's my liability for buying it back?"

She looked skeptical, but I could almost see the wheels turning in her head. "The DA might consider it buying stolen property. On the other hand, it could be called paying a reward, authorized by your client for recovering and returning lost property, assuming you don't commit any felonious acts to make the exchange," she speculated. "It might fly."

Usually when I hear legal mumbo jumbo like that, I want to barf, but coming from her, it sounded erotic.

"Okay, it's settled," I said, deciding not to appraise her of the aforesaid felonious acts I'll probably commit during the swap. As an officer of the court, she couldn't be privy to them, and I didn't want to discourage her. "I'm going across the street and get the cards. I want to use that gizmo to check them out before I meet with Nicky."

I got up to leave, but she grabbed my arm and pulled me to her, kissing me long and hard. It was the kind of kissing that led to sex. If I didn't have a date with a gangster killer in an hour, I would have stayed and done it some more.

"Go get the cards and come back, Jake," she said, letting me go. I almost stepped on Ratso before making it out the door. I had to take a couple of breaths to clear my head when I got outside.

I took off at a brisk pace, got across the Casino Road without getting hit by an RV, and entered the Riverside by the west side, near the host offices.

Deborah was sitting at her desk as I entered the glass-enclosed office. She was on the phone, and as soon as she saw me, she held up one finger, reached into a rack next to her desk, and pulled out my envelope, handing it across her desk to me. I smiled, took my envelope, and waved. She went on with her conversation, and I went out the door.

I had one more thing to do here, so I headed to the three most popular slot machines in the casino, the one-dollar Sizzling Sevens that sat in a row halfway between the north and south towers, right next to the high roller slots. That was where the meet was going to happen.

The problem with that was that the machines were busy all the time. Usually you had to wait in line to get one. Sometimes it was hours before somebody gave up and went back to their room. The kicker was that the machines paid off in dollar coins, not paper receipts. There was something profoundly satisfying about loading up racks of dollar coins and lugging them to the cashier's window.

Believe it or not, the machines did seem to pay out more frequently than any others. I know because I was a skeptic and now I'm a believer.

I was in luck. Two of the three machines were flashing jackpot lights. One for $1,288 and the other for $1,545. Two little old ladies were dancing in the aisle, literally. That meant that for the next hour or so, people would shy away from those machines, erroneously thinking that neither machine would pay out again anytime soon.

SIZZLIN' 7S

I've seen the machines hit two jackpots in a row several times, but then I've played them a lot.

A young guy playing the machine in the middle looked on in dismay as the old girls did their thing. By the number of butts in his ashtray, it looked like he'd been there for a while. I didn't see any coins in his tray, and the counter on the machine indicated he was down to less than a hundred credits. A hundred bucks.

The flip side of the Sizzling Sevens is that sometimes a particular machine would seem to get a wild hair up its ass and break you before it paid out. It looked like it was his turn. I hoped he could hang on until I got back.

I didn't see any thugs or detectives hanging around, so my next stop was the front desk, where I asked to see the manager. When he showed up, I explained that I needed to get my briefcase. He took me back to his office and retrieved it from his safe. I thanked him with a hundred. On the way out, I stopped at the gift shop to buy a canvas shopping bag.

I exited the casino by the portico on the west side, dodging cabs and valets until I got to the street, then dodging tourist cars and trucks as I crossed. If anybody was following me, they had a good chance of being run over before they could catch up with me. I jogged a block south, then a block west, and came into the RV park from the side. I rested against what looked like a rock band tour bus and watched for a tail.

At my age, jogging was not all it was cracked up to be.

Satisfied that I hadn't been followed, and having caught my breath, I made my way to Lucille's rig.

She opened her door at my first knock, obviously relieved. Ratso was beside himself as well, but I think he was that way with everyone. At least he didn't hump my leg. I made sure I didn't step on him as I came in and locked the door.

I followed Lucille over to her kitchen table, and we sat down across from each other. I saw that she had the Marlboro gizmo on the table between us. I pulled out the envelope and handed it to her. She hesitated a moment before taking it. So far, she hadn't said a word.

Opening the envelope, she pulled out the self-addressed stamped envelope and gave me a questioning look.

"I didn't know if I'd have to dump it on the run. Better safe than sorry," I said by way of explanation. Shaking her head, she tore the end off and dumped the cards into her hand. There was a Wells Fargo, a Chase, an AmrExp, and an APEX card.

"All right," I said. "Place one of the cards next to the gizmo and let's see what happens."

She laid the Wells Fargo credit card next to it. A tiny LED in the Marlboro pack lid flashed green three times.

So far so good.

"Okay, now do the rest one at a time," I told her.

That's what she did. The cards came up green every time.

I didn't expect any surprises, but at least the gizmo seemed to work like Tony said. Now I had to try it on the other card the first chance I got.

Opening the briefcase, I pulled out the five one-pound bricks of hundreds out and stuffed them in the canvas bag. Her eyes widened. Not too many people got to see that many hundreds at one time, vacuum-packed like steaks.

I was impressed the first time I saw one. My first thought was, *Where the hell is my box cutter when I need it?*

"How much *is* that?" she asked.

"Two hundred fifty thousand," I replied. "More or less."

"You're actually going to give it to Nicky?"

"I have to at least show it, otherwise it's not going to work. He's expecting sixty, but it won't get that far. It's a case of 'you show me yours and I'll show you mine.' I think I was five, and my neighbor, she was six the first time it happened to me."

That got a smile out of her. I'm sure she had her own fond memory of that. Practically everybody did.

"So what's your plan, Jake?" She was running her hand over the bundles. All lawyers were alike.

"The exchange is going to take place at a bank of slot machines in the middle of the Riverside casino. They're called the Sizzling Sevens. I'll be sitting at one of the machines so that he can't shoot me right there. Too many people. These bundles here," I said, pointing at the bricks of bills, "are easier to deal with in a shopping bag than a briefcase. He's planning on ripping me off, so the extra cash will throw him. I'll put the Marlboros in my shirt pocket so I can pass the card over it without Nicky knowing what I'm doing. All I have to do is look down to see if it's a go or not."

She nodded as if seeing it. I palmed the cards and put the them back in the envelope and acted like I was putting them in my back pocket when I was actually sticking them in the crack between the seat cushions.

"The deal is, I need two seats. Two machines next to each other. I think we can swing it if you help."

Lucille's guard went up again.

"What's your favorite charity?" I asked.

"Women's shelters," she responded without hesitation. "I sponsor one in Phoenix."

"How about if you go with me on this, and if we pull it off, I add a hundred grand bonus on top of the eight bucks you made today?"

She thought about it for a minute or two.

"The downside is, we could both go down in flames," I said to nudge her along.

"This would make a good book," she said. "I might have a lot of time on my hands to write it if you fuck this up."

"I won't, sweetheart," I told her. "If I'm right, we'll each have a hundred grand to make things better. I run into this stuff pretty regularly lately, and I like to take the money and give it away. Good for my karma. God knows I did enough terrible things when I was younger."

"How much younger?" she asked.

"A couple years?" I ventured.

31

So I need you to take a seat at one of the three machines. I'll sit next to you in the other. When Nicky gets there, you get up, give him your machine, and leave immediately by the west door. I'll point it out to you. Mo will be waiting for you outside. Get in the cab and leave."

"What about you?"

"Don't worry about me. As my lawyer, you really shouldn't be there when the transaction takes place. Not to mention, I might need you to bail me out if things go all to hell."

What I really wanted to say was that I didn't want her in any more danger than she was already just being around me. Mo would take care of her until I could clear the Riverside.

She looked dubious but said, "I'm ready when you are."

Lucille put out some dry food and water for Ratso, and we left. The night was warm, and the moon was full. It was a gorgeous night, and I wished we were just out for a stroll. Maybe tomorrow night, if I wasn't dead or in jail.

Traffic was still heavy, and I almost dropped the bag holding the bricks of hundreds as we dodged a dozen Harleys. Having safely made it to the Riverside parking lot, I got on my cell and called Mo.

He answered on the first ring. "Yes?"

"It's Jake. I want you to come over to the Riverside and wait outside the west entrance. My lady friend will be coming out in about twenty to thirty minutes. When she does, take her to the

Aquarius, then come back and wait for me. Okay? Make sure you're not followed."

"You got it, boss." And he hung up.

I picked the Riverside Sizzling Sevens slots precisely because they were in the nexus of the two wings of the casino, and even in the dead of night, foot traffic was heavy. That and the eye-in-the-sky would discourage Nicky and his entourage from whacking me there. But once I was outside the door, it was another story. Depending on his resources, he could have a man waiting at each of the four main entrances.

As we approached the west entrance, I pulled five one-hundred-dollar bills out of my pocket and handed them to her.

"When we get inside, I'll get us a machine. Act like you don't even know me. You use this money to play it until Nicky shows up. Then you leave, regardless of how much is still in the machine. When you're gone, I'll do the thing with Nicky. In the meantime, I want you to go with Mo to the Aquarius and hook up with Arliss. He's in room 1520. He'll be waiting for you. I'll call you when I'm finished with Nicky."

I stopped short of the door and sent Arliss a text message. Once inside the door, most cell phone didn't work for shit.

While I was texting, I could see Lucille looking at me like I was a zoo specimen. I think she was having second thoughts.

I hit send, slapped my phone shut, and hustled her through the doors before she could change her mind.

32

When we got through the door, it was like entering a fifties nightclub. The smoke was so bad it almost knocked me over. My clothes were going to have to go to the cleaners. The building had been around for a half century, occupied by a thousand smokers twenty-four seven the whole time and smelled like it.

A lot of gamblers smoked, and in an age where you couldn't even smoke outside in some places, that was part of the draw. I put up with it because I loved this casino. Reminded me of Las Vegas before it turned into a cross between Disneyland and Gomorrah.

The bank of Sizzling Seven slots was only twenty steps away. The one on the left was open, and I nudged Lucille to that machine. Queenie, a regular local, was on the machine to the far left. I'd played beside her before. She had to be ninety, played with a cup of coffee in one hand and a cigarette in the other. She only had one eye and couldn't see well out of that one, so her face was plastered against the machine so she could see what came up on the reel.

She had a tendency to play a machine for as long as it took to pay out.

Didn't matter that it might take three thousand to win fifteen hundred. She wouldn't be getting off that machine anytime soon.

The middle machine was occupied by the same young guy I saw earlier. He was still plugging away but not doing well, if the empty tray below his machine was any indication.

SIZZLIN' 7S

Lucille sat down next to him and fed a hundred into the machine. The LED above the machine read the progressive jackpot to currently be $1,296 and climbing. I leaned against the wall across from the machines and looked at the payout on the middle one. Fifteen hundred bucks and change. It was due for a pop. Hopefully not while he was still sitting there. I couldn't take the chance. I needed that seat.

He looked like he'd run out of money because he was feeding it tens instead of hundreds. I stepped across to him and tapped him on the shoulder.

When he turned to look at me, I held out five c-notes. "I'll buy this machine from you for five hundred bucks."

He glanced up at the payout number and then back to me. "Serious?"

"Does the pope shit in the woods?"

He must not have been Catholic or a hunter, and he didn't get the joke, because he snagged the money, put it in his shirt pocket, got up, and said, "Good luck."

I sat down as he walked away, and as I stuffed a hundred into the dragon's mouth, I heard her whisper, *Good boy. Now I'm going to reward you, big time.*

And she did. I hit three red sevens on the first pull. Three hundred one-dollar coins started spilling into my tray. Lucille's machine hit the same thing thirty seconds later. The clatter of the coins started to attract a crowd. It was a voyeur kind of thing, like car accidents. It was just what I was looking for; my sweet little machines didn't let me down.

We didn't have time to stack the coins in racks of a hundred, so I grabbed some quart-sized plastic cups from between our machines, handed a half dozen to her, and told her under my breath to start shoveling the dollar coins into them. Within minutes, we filled up five of them.

One elderly woman tapped me on the shoulder as I went back to playing my machine.

"How much did you have to put into it before you won?" she inquired.

In all honesty, I told her three bucks. She looked at me like I was jerking her around. "Right, asshole." She snorted and walked off.

She probably never won. Negative energy. You gotta talk to the machines like they were women. Talk nice. Stroke them enough and they'll give it up.

I continued to play my machine and ignored Lucille. She was doing the same. I hit another three red sevens. The coins banged into my tray, and the crowd got larger.

Under cover of the noise, I said to Lucille, "As soon as Nicky shows up, you grab as many of those buckets as can and leave. Don't bother to stop at the cashier's window. Just go out the door we came in and get into Mo's cab."

"I *got* it. You don't have to tell me again," she replied somewhat testily.

"Excuse *me*," I whispered and went back to punching the max play button.

At three bucks a pull if you use the arm—figuring three seconds between pulls—works out to be $3,600 per hour if you don't hit anything. More if you hit the max button. Not exactly your penny slots and not for the faint-hearted.

Even if you win half of it back, you're screwed. I'd watched Queenie do it for days at a time. She had to have money or she wouldn't still be doing it. Her three dead husbands must have left her a bunch.

One minute later, Lucille hit another three red sevens. By this time, the crowd had gotten so large, Jimmy, one of the floor managers, came over for a look-see.

Seeing all the buckets of coins at Lucille's feet, as well her shapely legs, he called for a handcart and asked her if she wanted him to buy them, saving her a trip to the cashier. She agreed and batted her eyes. He loaded them up and said he'd be right back.

He didn't bother to ask me if I needed help too. Maybe I should have batted my eyes at him.

But at least it took care of one problem. Nine hundred one-dollar coins were too heavy for a woman to carry off, especially if she was running.

SIZZLIN' 7S

Jimmy showed up five minutes later with nine crisp one-hundred-dollar bills and gave them to Lucille. He also gave her legs one last look. Only then did he notice me.

"Hey, Jake. Good to see you." He looked down at the tubs of coins under my less shapely legs. "Looks like you're doing okay," he said but didn't offer to buy them to save *me* a trip to the cashier.

He got a call over his radio, patted me on the shoulder, and left. Lucille was snickering beside me but not acknowledging me in any way. She probably never got any speeding tickets either. Nicky showed up a minute later. He only had one thug in tow, one of the guys from the train station. One of Charlie's killers. He was leaning on a wall by the cigarette concession, trying to look inconspicuous. He might as well have been a nine-hundred-pound rhino. The old people took a wide berth around him.

I nudged Lucille, and she immediately got up and left without looking back. Nicky sat down in her seat. He looked pissed, but I couldn't figure out why. Ignoring the machine, he turned to me. "You got the money?" he asked without so much as a "How ya doin'?"

Not wanting to appear unprepared, I pointed to the cloth shopping bag between me and Queenie. She was eyeball-to-reel with her machine, oblivious to me or the bag.

"Right here. You got the card?"

He nodded, reaching into his jacket pocket. I noticed he was carrying a no-no in a casino—a gun. He pulled out the Chase card and showed it to me.

For the eye-in-the-sky, I continued hitting the max button on my machine, acting as if this was a chance exchange between two players.

"Start playing your machine," I said as I took the card from him. "You're drawing attention."

Looking around, it finally dawned on him he had an audience. His machine had been so hot, everybody wanted it and would ask him to move his ass out of the way if he wasn't going to play.

"I need a hands-on inspection," I told him.

"Me too." Nicky was eyeing the bag. He didn't know there was four times his money in there.

"Me first, then you." I wasn't about to front the money and he knew it. He tried to stare me down, but it didn't work. Shrugging, he handed it over. Then he reached over and hit the play button on his machine, but he kept his eyes on me. Lucille had left almost sixty credits on it, so he didn't have to feed it first.

He wasn't paying attention to what came up, but I did. Triple bars all the way across. Sixty bucks. Not bad for a three-dollar investment. The machine was hot.

I played my machine with my right hand and used my left to inspect the card, which I held close to my shirt pocket. The pack of Marlboros in there gave off three quick red flashes from the LED in the lid. Nicky couldn't see it, but I could.

The card was compromised. It was of no value to my client. And I had no intention of turning over sixty grand for a worthless piece of plastic. I started to hand the card back to him.

"This card is fucked up. It's no good. I don't know what you did to it, but I'm not paying for it." I hit my max button again for the cameras, as if I'd told him, "Nice business card."

Nicky was pissed off to begin with, and I think that took him over the edge. His mouth dropped open, his eyes bulged out, and his hand went for his gun.

That was when the love of my life, machine 6504-06, saved my bacon.

I watched the three Sizzling Sevens come up one at a time as if in slow motion. Before Nicky could clear his gun from his jacket, strobe lights went off, bells started ringing, and the tune "You're in the money" began blaring out of speakers over the slot machine. His hand froze inside his jacket, unsure what was going on.

But by then, he was screwed. Two dozen spectators crowded around, asking how much I won. Nicky was almost pushed out of his seat by all the attention and was clearly frustrated by why he couldn't just kill everybody. Jimmy pushed his way through the crowd, congratulating me on my win. I got up so he could secure the machine. Nicky saw the armed casino guard standing on the periphery of the crowd.

SIZZLIN' 7S

"Hey, Jimmy," I said, drawing him close to me. "I gotta piss like a racehorse. Can you watch my machine while I go? And my buckets too? I'll take care of you later. In case I don't come back, hold on to my cash."

He laughed like that was the funniest thing he'd heard all day. Who wasn't going to come back for the payout on a jackpot? Plus all those buckets?

"Not a problem, Jake. I gotta lock the machine down and go get your payoff anyways, so you got plenty of time. I'll have Ralph watch your stuff while I take care of that," he said, beckoning to the armed guard.

I didn't look at Nicky as I picked up my bag, dropped the card in it, and traded places with Ralph—who was about six-four—then slipped through the high roller's lounge, finding the closest escape. Nicky's thug had his view blocked by a dozen people and never saw me leave. I'm sure Nicky was fighting his way through the crowd to get to his pal, but I would be out the door before they could give chase.

I knew I couldn't hang around in the parking lot waiting for Mo to get back, so I headed for the east door where most of the employees came and went. Once outside, I walked the twenty yards to the water taxi that ferried customers and employees across the Colorado River to a large parking lot on the Arizona side. The boats ran every few minutes, and I was lucky to catch one leaving as I stepped on it.

The ride across was brief and uneventful, giving me a chance to take a breath and think. I needed a plan because up until now, I'd pretty much played it by ear up till now. That wasn't going to work much longer.

I called Mo as I stepped off the boat. He answered on the second ring. "Pick me up next to the Home Depot," I said, sure he would know what I really meant since Home Depot had closed hours ago.

I hung up and pulled the battery out as I walked across the parking lot to Highway 95. The six-lane highway was busy but negotiable. After another hundred-yard walk, I stepped into Pussy Willows. By then, I was pretty sure nobody had followed me.

It was close to one in the morning, but the place was packed and rocking. There were two girls on the stage and another three doing lap dances. I found a dark corner near the door and parked my ass on a stool.

33

Willow must have seen me come in because she appeared out of the gloom, handing me a Coors as she sat down beside me.

"Well, Jake, this *is* a surprise. I don't see you for a month or two, and now it's twice in two days." She had a beautiful smile.

I smiled back. "I just couldn't stay away from you."

She punched me in the arm. "Hah! Now I know you're up to something."

I took a long pull on my Coors. It tasted great, and all that walking had made me thirsty. "Actually, I'm hiding out from some Mafia killers, and I'm just waiting for my getaway car to show up," I told her in all honesty.

She gave me a concerned look. "Now *that* I can believe." Willow glanced at the bouncer by the door. "Am I going to have a problem?"

"No," I assured her. "I don't think they know where I am, and my ride should be pulling up any minute now."

Willow looked relieved.

While I slammed the rest of the beer, Willow hesitated a couple of times then said, "Some old guy came in when we opened. He acted like a customer, but he was asking about you. Think it might be connected?"

I put the empty bottle down. "What did he look like?"

"*Really* old. That's why I don't think he came in for the show. Thick accent. German, I think. He really creeped the girls out."

The old Nazi.

Why the hell was he interested in me enough to come sniffing around?

How'd he know to come asking here? I thought about that for second but came up with zilch. I'd worry about it later. My plate was already full.

I tried to put her at ease. "Nah, I don't think it has anything to do with my immediate problem, but thanks for letting me know."

"Good. Beer's on me," she said, grabbing the empty bottle and getting up.

"Is there anything I can do to help?"

I picked up my canvas bag, which she noticed for the first time, and said, "Thank you for asking. Yes, there is. You think I can get your bouncer to escort me across the parking lot to my ride?"

She gave me a mischievous grin. "Only if you let me look in your bag."

I held it up and opened it so she could take a peek. Gamblers appreciated sights like that. She laughed, slapped me on the shoulder, and then gave me a peck on the cheek.

"Don't get yourself killed, Jake. Then I won't have the pleasure of kicking your ass at Texas hold 'em every time we play. Now that I see you've got some *real* money, I'm going to really enjoy taking it from you. I've got all your tells down," she whispered to me, batted her eyes, and walked over to the bouncer. He nodded after she said something, and he glanced uneasily at me.

I took a moment to put the battery back in my cell and called Mo. He told me he was waiting outside. I pulled the battery out, put it back in my pocket, and headed for the door.

The bouncer preceded me outside without a word, staying two steps ahead of me. He looked like an NFL guard but with a military bearing. I could see the bulge of a weapon in his waistband at the small of his back. His head swiveled from side to side until he picked out Mo's cab on the edge of the packed parking lot.

When we got there, I palmed him a c-note when I shook his hand. He nodded, closed the door for me, and stood there until Mo pulled away. Willow was smart, using good people. Maybe I could subcontract the guy from her. It was looking like I might need him.

"Where to, boss?" Mo asked as we pulled out of the parking lot.

There was a fast-food franchise at the end of the Home Depot parking lot and next to the highway. "Pull into there and park. I need to think for a minute. And quit calling me boss."

Mo parked in the far corner, where we could watch everything coming and going. I was sitting in the front seat with him.

"Have you eaten?" I asked.

He shook his head no. I pointed to the Chinese place. "Why don't you run in there and grab something while I make a few phone calls?"

"Very good, boss. I *am* hungry, but I was afraid to take the time."

"Go. I'll be fine. And quit with the boss shit."

"Yes, boss," he said as he got out.

I could see I wasn't going to win this one.

While he was gone, I popped the trunk and tucked the money bag behind the carpet in the corner of the quarter panel behind the taillight, then shut the trunk. I stood outside the car stared at the stars as I thought about everything that had happened so far.

Tony had gotten his credit cards stolen.

I found the guy who stole them, but he got blown up. Then I found the guy he gave one to, but he got shot to death. I found the guy who had it now, and he wants to kill me.

I think I'm seeing a pattern here.

I pulled out my cell, put the battery back in, and called Arliss at the Aquarius.

"National Association for the Advancement of Colored People, how may I direct your call?" he answered.

"Cute, Arliss," I said. "How's everything?"

"Fine, I guess, if you count me being relegated to the living room and kitchenette area as acceptable. Your lawyer took over *my* bedroom, and the fuck bunnies haven't come out of the other one. How big is this party going to get?" He was on a roll. "Should I get another room just in case?"

I knew he was just joking around, but he had a point. We had all our eggs in one basket, and that wasn't a good strategy.

"No. I'm coming over to brief you, but I've got a stop to make first. Shouldn't take long, then I'll take the lawyer off your hands. In the meantime, keep an eye on the door."

"You got it," Arliss replied and hung up. As I pulled my battery out of the cell, I thought about Nicky trying to pass off the compromised card for sixty grand. It looked like that after I'd told him *not* to do something, he did it anyway. He must not have cared whether I knew because he planned to kill me anyway and take the money and card back. But it didn't explain his being pissed. He should have been smiling.

The only thing I could come up with was that something happened when he swiped the card into his computer, and whatever it was, it wasn't good.

That's why I needed to talk to Tony. Now.

I had a sneaking suspicion he was playing me again. Actually, it felt more like a certainty. What he was up to, I didn't have a clue.

I intended to find out though, because at the moment, I had all the cards, literally.

34

I had Mo drive me to Harrah's Hotel and Casino when he got back with his Chinese takeout. The aroma coming out of the bag on the seat between us reminded me that all this running around was making me hungry. Really hungry. Maybe I should have had him get *me* some too.

Then again, I was probably better off confronting Tony on an empty stomach.

"What do you know about the old German that owns the trailer park by the river?" I asked him as we approached Harrah's.

Mo obviously knew who I was talking about because he made a face. "He is an evil man. I myself rented from him when I first came here. His trailers are cesspools. He takes advantage of the fact that some people have no other choice. When some of the young women cannot pay, I have heard that he makes them do things instead of rent. Things that I find hard to believe because he is so old, but I do not think the women are lying. I moved after one month. I did not want my family around him."

It was clear he didn't relish talking about it. I wanted to know more about the old guy, but I let it go. I couldn't be distracted right now. My biggest problem at the moment was to get Tony to answer some questions before I gave up the cards.

I don't know why I was bothering because he would probably lie to me anyways. Just maybe, though, I could figure out what was going on by what Tony was *not* telling me.

I decided I would have to settle for that as we pulled into Harrah's portico. I stepped out, and Mo drove off. I didn't have say a word to him.

As I made my way to the elevators, none of the machines called out to me. Good thing, it wouldn't take much for me to just forget all of this and spend some time lost in a slot machine's one-armed embrace.

I didn't think Tony knew I was coming, so I was surprised when the doors opened, I found Cube and Knuckles waiting for me. I knew Knuckles too. One big happy family. Knuckles put me up against the wall and patted me down. He made sure I wasn't hiding a .22 taped to my nut sack.

Cube apologized, I shrugged, and the two of them marched me down the hallway to Tony's suite.

Leo, the gatekeeper, opened the door and took it from there. "What's up?" he asked. I noticed his jacket was open, and his right hand was free.

I brushed by him. "I need to talk to Tony." As I headed down the hall, I was sure he had his gun out by now and had it pointed right at my head. I didn't think he'd shoot me though, and I needed to make a statement here.

Tony was sitting on the couch by himself. Francine had probably gone to bed hours ago. He was dressed in his trademark Polo shirt and gray slacks, with a nice pair of Allen Edmonds on his feet that rested on the leather ottoman. The Weather Channel was on the big plasma screen mounted on the facing wall. The weather lady was young and hot. I guess that was all the T&A he could find.

He turned the sound down when I sat down, uninvited, in a chair next to the couch.

Not saying a word, he just looked at me, waiting for me to begin.

I took the cue, and before he could start with "You know I think of you as the son I never had" shit, I said, "You know I think of you as a father, so I've come here for some guidance. I need some information."

I was doing an end run on him, and I could see that he was amused by it.

"So what do you need to know?" Tony tried to appear concerned.

"I think I'm going to have a problem with this Little Nicky." I had to talk to Tony in terms that he could understand yet remain respectful. I've learned the hard way that Tony was the stereotypical old-time mob boss.

"I had a *meet* with him tonight to reclaim your lost property. It didn't go well. I think he's going to come after me."

That was when Tony started to show *real* concern, not feigned. Not concern about me but his plastic. He was anxious to know what happened.

"What is it you need to know?" Meaning: *What happened?*

"Tell me everything you know about Little Nicky. If I got to take him down first, I need to know everything about him." Meaning: *I'll tell you when you give me what I want.*

He accepted that with a nod, as if it was just a cost of doing business. Tony pulled his wingtip brogues off the ottoman and leaned forward to me. Meaning: *Pay attention to my words.*

"Big Nicky and I grew up together in New York." He paused for a moment. "We used to be friends."

I let that alone. TMI.

"Little Nicky caused some problems…so he was sent here until those problems went away. That's all I know." Meaning: *That's all you need to know. Deal with it.*

Right.

He hesitated. "I think Big Nicky's trying to make a move on Laughlin."

That was all he was going to give up, but what he didn't tell me said volumes. I was fucked.

He took control of the conversation. "What happened at the meet?"

I felt I had no choice but to tell him. "It was at the Riverside. We had slots next to each other. I made him show first. The card was compromised, I refused to pay, and if it hadn't been for a diversion, I wouldn't have made it past the parking lot alive."

I'm pretty sure he didn't give a shit about whether I lived or died, but I thought the news that his card was accessed would trouble him.

I was wrong. For a millisecond there, I even thought I saw a flash of triumph in his half-hooded eyes.

"I'll return the other four cards in the morning, when I can get access to them." I don't know why I said four. I'd worry about it later. "I'll have them here before you check out. I'm sorry I couldn't retrieve the last one. You told me you didn't want it if it was compromised. I'll return the money too, since I was unable to complete the recovery of your property." Meaning: *Asshole. Take your money and your problems back and leave me alone.*

He played the benevolent role to the hilt. "Keep the money, Jake. You did a great job, and I knew I could count on you. You're like the son I never had. Francine wants to move on to LA at the crack of dawn, so don't bother. Keep them safe and meet me there as soon as you can. Can I trust you to do that?"

I didn't think Tony could even spell the word *trust*, let alone believe in it. My antennae started twitching again.

Tony tried to get up. He made it look painful. Leo rushed over to give him a hand. "Go and enjoy the rest of your vacation, Jake. I'm going to bed now. My bionic knees are killing me. It's hell getting old." He paused for a moment to give his last words of wisdom. "And say hello to your new girlfriend for me. She's pretty. You should think about settling down." Meaning: *Meeting's over. I'll call you when I need you. Fuck off and good luck.*

I couldn't push it anymore, so I got up and left.

Cube and Knuckles made sure I got on the elevator, safe and sound—and gone.

35

I was so focused on remembering every word Tony had said that I didn't hear the beckoning siren song of the slots as I exited Harrah's. I was in a daze.

Mo had apparently seen me headed out the doors because he was there in a heartbeat. He pulled up as I got to the curb. We were out of the portico and booking down the road before I could shut the door.

"I think somebody is onto you, boss," he said, looking into his rearview mirror. "Two men in an Escalade have been watching the entrance since shortly after we got here, and they are following us now."

I should have put my seat belt on before saying, "Lose them."

He didn't answer, just blew through the red light at the entrance to Harrah's and rocketed down the boulevard to Tres Palms where he executed a tire-squealing right turn into their parking garage that slammed me against the console and then the dash. I thought I was going to throw up as he negotiated the three levels up and then down like it was a carnival ride, spitting us out on the other side of the building.

We were back on the main drag before I could roll my window down and hurl. I can't get on a swing without getting nauseous. I washed out of flight school when I was younger because I kept barfing on my instructor. I still knew how to fly, but if it didn't have two jet engines and a liquor-dispensing attendant, preferably female, I was not getting on it.

"I think we lost them. Where to now, boss?" he asked me with one eye on the rearview mirror.

"Aquarius." I finally got the window down and stuck my face into the wind. I was glad I passed on the Chinese takeout.

I had Mo pull into a dimly lit corner, and I got out of the cab. "Park where you can see the front. This shouldn't take too long," I told him before working my way through the parking lot to the main entrance. I didn't pick up any bad vibes on the way.

When I got into the casino, my bladder was killing me, so I made to beeline to the restroom, avoiding the Sizzling Seven machines. An old associate of mine once told me the only thing better than a good fuck was a good fight. I think a long-delayed piss, once released, was right up there.

The restroom was empty when I unzipped at the urinal, but as I was rolling my eyes to the ceiling in ecstasy at letting go, two men came in and occupied the pissers on either side of me.

My eyes were still closed in bliss when one of them stuck a syringe into the side of my neck.

I don't remember zipping up.

36

I woke up in a closet. I could tell it was a closet because I was a contractor and I built a boatload of them. Two feet deep, six feet wide, eight feet high. Ninety-six cubic feet. The quarter-inch gap halfway across told me the two doors were bypass, probably mirrored on the other side to make the room look bigger. I was in a hotel room.

Better to rent a crime scene. Funny what goes through your head when you're naked, zip-tied hand and foot, and hanging by a belt around your chest to a hopefully well-secured hook on the back wall. I felt like side of beef out of *Rocky*. I hoped it wouldn't morph into the something out of Pacino's *Scarface*. My mouth was duct taped, and I had to pee. Again. That was what probably woke me up. I guess I wasn't allowed to finish last time.

I immediately thought about Mo. I wondered if he got away. If he didn't, I was toast.

I was right about the doors being sliders, because one of them opened. I couldn't see who it was because he was backlit. When he got close enough to rip the tape off my mouth, I saw that it was Little Nicky.

"Well, well, well, you're awake. Good," he said, grinning like he was about to dig into a good meal.

I think I lost most of my mustache and the top of my goatee to the duct tape when he did it. It made my eyes water. He must have thought I was crying, because he laughed.

"You ought to be scared." And he meant it. "You have caused me some serious problems, and I want some answers."

Other than him missing out on robbing me of sixty grand, I couldn't imagine what *serious* problems he was talking about, so that's why I replied, "I don't know what the fuck you're talking about, shitwad."

My mother always said that my mouth would be the ruin of me. She was right. Nicky punched me in the nose, and while I watched the stars exploding in my eyes, he slapped another piece of duct tape across my mouth.

When I could see better, I noticed one of the no-neck twins, the one that reminded me of Porky Pig, was approaching me with a hair dryer. All the bathrooms in the upscale hotels featured them. Some had cords that were longer than others. His one was *real* long.

Porky flipped the hair dryer onto *hot* turned it on and stuck it against my nut sack. At first it felt pretty good, actually.

I thought, *Thank God these guys are too cheap to buy an electric chainsaw across the street at the Home Depot. What kind of pussy-ass torture is this anyway?*

Boy, was I wrong.

I was starting to get an erection with all that hot air on my balls when Nicky stepped up, ripped off the tape again, and said, "What the fuck did you do to my computer?"

"Bite me, Nicky. I don't know what you're talking about."

Porky flipped the blow dryer to *fry*, and the fun began. Ten minutes later, I'd given up the name, address, and combination to the safe of a rich sister that I didn't have, along with next week's winning Powerball numbers. I was even willing to share with him the results of next month's Belmont Stakes Triple Crown horserace. The trifecta was gonna pay huge.

But nothing about computers. I couldn't even bring up my e-mail without help. That was the problem with torture. You can't rely upon the information you get. Nicky saw this was getting him nowhere, so he finally pulled the plug, literally. I think that was when I passed out again.

When I woke up, I was still hanging around in the closet. I didn't know if it was because I still had to pee or whether it was the bang of a door being kicked in that brought me to. Then what sounded like a brief struggle was followed by the sliding closet door being flung open.

It was Arliss.

37

I'd already lost most of my facial hair by the time Arliss removed the tape from my mouth, but I was losing a substantial amount of skin now as well, and it made my eyes water again. Arliss mistook the tears running down my cheeks for gratitude.

"Aww, don't cry, Jake. Everything's going to be okay."

"Get me off the goddamn wall, Arliss," I said when I quit crying.

He cut the ankle and wrist restraints so I wouldn't fall like a sack of potatoes when he undid the belt around my chest. I wasn't sure my legs would hold up, even untied. Fortunately, he held on to me when my feet hit the ground.

When he was sure I could stand by myself, I ducked into the bathroom to relieve myself and grab a towel to wrap around my waist. My nuts felt like soft boiled eggs, and even the towel brushing against them was excruciating. I didn't even want to look at them.

As I stumbled out of the closet and into the bedroom, I saw it was an Aquarius room, but smaller than Arliss's room. On the floor by the king-sized bed was the prone figure of Porky Pig. His pants were down around his knees, and he was tied up with strips of the shower curtain. Earl was standing guard over him.

When I looked at him, Earl said, "Can I kill him? This cocksucker shot my cousin."

I just shook my head as I grabbed my clothes off the bed and got dressed. I was too exhausted to explain to him why an individual citizen couldn't murder a murderer. That was the state's prerogative.

It only took me a minute to put my clothes on. My cell phone was still attached to my belt. Arliss was already holding the door open, obviously ready to leave. I pushed Earl toward the door and turned to give Porky a parting shot in the groin with my shoe. Hard.

As I stumbled down the corridor to the elevators, Arliss told me he had stashed Porky's gun under the mattress, minus the magazine. I fished Detective Sabbatini's business card out of my shirt pocket and gave him a call on my cell.

"I don't recognize this number," he grumbled by way of greeting. "Who is this?"

"Doesn't matter, but what does is that the trailer park killer is in room 563 at the Aquarius Hotel. If you hurry, you just might catch him. Oh, and he might have the murder weapon with him." Then I hung up.

I already had enough hostages, so there was no way I could drag Porky along, but I didn't want him to get away either. I knew that Sabbatini would eventually track the call to my cell, but I figured this business would be over before that happened. I still had a little time. I pulled the battery out of my phone. I knew there was a residual signature on some phones, but short of destroying the phone, that was all I could do.

I looked at Arliss as we piled into the elevator. "How did you find me?"

"Mo did. You left your keys on the seat. He ran into the casino to catch you and saw two guys taking you out of the bathroom, acting like they were helping an intoxicated buddy to his room. He followed them to the room and called me. By the time we got there, one of them had left, leaving the other one to watch you. The dumb shit was watching porno movies instead, and we caught him with his pants down, literally," Arliss replied, hitting the button for the tenth floor where our room was. Earl snorted out a laugh.

I figured Nicky had left, probably to find something nastier to use on me. Hopefully he'd be dumb enough to come back while the detective was there.

"I sent Mo back outside to be ready if we needed him, then took Earl with me for backup. I kicked the door in, and we gang-tackled the dumb ass. The rest you know. Your lawyer is with the other half of the newlyweds."

We got out of the elevator then walked down the hallway to our room. Earl kept his council. Arliss used a key card to let us in. Lucille and Susan were sitting on the living room couch with the TV on, but muted. They were obviously relieved to see us, but I could tell by their expression that I probably looked like the leftovers of a mugging.

Lucille's nurturing instincts must have kicked in because she immediately dragged me into one of the bathrooms, sat me on the commode, and started cleaning me up.

"Do you think you could get me a plastic bag with some ice in it?" I asked as she wiped my face with a hot washcloth.

She looked at me curiously then did a quick inspection of my scalp. "I don't see any bumps or lacerations. Did they injure your head?"

"No, but they were only inches away."

Confused, she looked down at my chest.

"Lower," I told her.

She blushed and said, "Oh," then hurried off to get an ice pack.

I got up, turned on the shower, stripped off my clothes, and stepped in. It had nozzles on both sides and felt like a massage. I cranked the water up as hot as it went and kept the spray above my waist.

The shower door opened, and a slender arm holding a ziplock plastic bag of ice cubes materialized out of the steam.

I pressed the ice pack against my tender loins and stood in the steaming, pulsating cascade of water for a half an hour. It was bliss.

Lucille was waiting with a terry cloth bathroom as I stepped out of the shower. "Feel better?" she asked.

"Much."

"How about the other parts?" She smiled, checking out my equipment. My cock was swollen now from all the abuse it had taken and may have given her a false impression of its potential size.

"They could probably use some hands-on physical therapy," I told her. Maybe the beating could be a good thing.

She grabbed the hand lotion, gently took my hand, and led me to the bedroom.

38

8:00 a.m.

When I came out of the bedroom in the morning, I wasn't all that rested. Arliss was awake but on the couch. I could tell from his expression that he wasn't all that thrilled with me at the moment. Earl and Susan had the other bedroom, so he'd been stuck with guard duty. I don't think the couch was long enough for him to lie on, let alone sleep.

"What time is it?" I asked him as I fired up the coffee maker.

He looked at his watch. "Almost eight."

I figure I got to bed around three, which should have given me almost five hours of sleep. I *might* have gotten three, thanks to my lawyer. Not that I'm complaining.

"Hey, thanks for rescuing my ass last night—this morning—and watching the door. I wasn't in much shape to do anything."

"Bullshit. The walls here aren't that thick, but you're welcome." He got up and stretched. "What do you want to do with those two?" He pointed with his thumb to Earl's bedroom door.

I handed him a cup of black coffee then fixed mine the way I liked it. Sweet and tan.

"I'm sure Detective Sabbatini has Nicky's hitter on lockdown by now. I suspect when I turn my phone back on, there'll be a message from him." I paused. "I think we need to hang on to them for another day. Call down and tell the front desk that you're staying another day. That way, we don't have to move them before check-out time. Might throw off anybody that's paying attention as well.

"I'll find a place to stash them tonight. After that, one way or another, I'm gonna have to give them up to Sabbatini. Get them ready to move on a phone call. What's Mo doing?" I was hoping he hadn't been sitting in the parking lot all night.

"I sent him home after Lucille shut the bedroom door. I gave him a big bonus for using his head. He's a happy camper. I think he likes this stuff and can't wait for your next call." Arliss knew because he was the same way.

If it hadn't been for Mo's quick-headed thinking, I might have disappeared into a shallow grave in the desert. I was racking up a lot of IOUs.

I pushed away from the counter I was leaning on and headed back into Lucille's bedroom. I had a lot to do today, and I was burning daylight.

When I walked back into the room, the sight of her sprawled on her belly with only a tendril of white sheet covering her shapely and well-tanned ass was enough for me to reevaluate that plan.

A higher power drove me back into the bathroom, though, for yet another shower—only colder this time.

Much to my surprise, Lucille was dressed and sitting on the bed, looking fresh as a daisy when I finished. I was impressed. I figured any woman that could be ready before me was a keeper.

I barely had time to tell Arliss that I'd call him before she was out the door. I hurried to catch up with her.

"Are we in a rush to get somewhere?" I asked her half-jokingly as she stabbed the down button on the elevator with more vigor than was necessary.

She didn't answer me until we were in and the doors shut. "Jake. You're a dinosaur. I'll bet you don't even have a computer. This is a classic example of future shock. Fifty years ago, a writer predicted that by 2010, guys like you wouldn't be able to operate a Coke machine. And that was before the Internet."

I was trying to take this in a positive way, but I was having a hard time. I was pretty sure she was calling me a dummy, and I didn't like her attitude. "Just exactly what are trying to say?"

"I'm not calling you a dummy or anything," she said, confirming my suspicions. "But you're in over your head."

I couldn't fault her on that.

She was suddenly sweet. "I have a friend that is into this kind of stuff. She's got more computers in her rig than the NSA." She actually batted her eyes at me.

Déjà vu all over again. I'd seen this behavior before with some of my previous girlfriends. A one-hundred-and-eighty-degree flip from one minute to the next. I was pretty sure I was getting a glimpse of a possible hormonal imbalance here that she couldn't help, so I forgave her for calling me stupid. I didn't say a word.

"We run into each other from time to time because she has a rig like mine and travels like I do. We've gotten to be good friends, and we keep in touch. She's in Las Vegas now, but that's only an hour and a half away."

I figured a ride to Vegas in my Corvette was just what I needed right now, and I had the valet claim check in my wallet. I got on the house phone and told Arliss to hunker down until I called him.

When we got back to Lucille's, I retrieved the four cards from under the dining room seat cushion while she was packing like we were going to go far, far away. I had one change of clothes and a toothbrush.

39

10:00 a.m.

We were in Vegas by ten that morning. The temperature was already in the high nineties. Compared to Laughlin, it was downright cool. I called ahead and got us a suite at the MGM Grand. Thirty years ago, I used to stay at the original MGM before its fire and eventual demolition. Every time I come here now, I marvel at how over the top Las Vegas has become, and yet the sidewalks are always so crowded with tourists even in the early morning that it reminds me of downtown Manhattan.

I let the valet park the 'vette and the porter carry off our two small overnighters to our room. I led Lucille straight to the bar so I could have the breakfast of champions. She had a cup of coffee from the Starbucks that was next to the bar.

Yoo-hoo, I'm over here, I heard.

I looked around to see where it was coming from and saw a bank of Sizzling Seven slots about fifty feet away, with a good line of sight to Lucille. The line at Starbucks was a lot longer than the bar, so when I got my Coors, I sucked half of it down in two pulls. Then I just naturally wandered over and stuffed a hundred into the pie hole of the seductress, machine SS-1111. Three pulls later, I hit three red sevens, paying me three hundred bucks plus the ninety-one I still had in credits. I cashed out with one of those paper receipts that I hate and was back on my stool before Lucille returned with her overpriced latte. I congratulated myself for being up two hundred and ninety-one dollars, as well as another beer the roving waitress had given me. It wasn't even noon yet. I figured I was on a roll.

She hadn't even noticed I was missing and started right in on the plan. She had her lawyer hat on and got right to it. "My friend's name is Kim. She's going to meet us here any minute now." She took a ladylike sip of her seven-dollar triple mocha no-fat frappe latte while I took another healthy pull on my free Coors, finishing it.

That got me a mildly disapproving look, but she continued nevertheless. "Try to be on your best behavior," she scolded me, as if two beers were all I needed to be an obnoxious asshole. She didn't know it yet, but sometimes I don't even need that.

I gave her my best innocent look. "I'll do my best."

"Good. Kim used to work for NSA and DARPA. She won't talk about it, but she's got to be the most computer-wise person I know. Her RV is stuffed with electronics, few of which I can even identify, and I think I'm pretty savvy technologically. When she gets here, let me do the talking, okay?"

That was just fine with me, so I gave her my "Aw, shucks. Thanks" look, but before I could formulate a sarcastic reply, an Asian woman sat down next to Lucille. It was obvious that this was Kim because they went through the whole woman thing of squealing, laughing, hugging, and trying to talk at the same time. I took the opportunity to snag another beer from a passing waitress.

I hadn't quite finished it and was eyeing my new best friend, machine SS-1111, when Lucille finally got around to introducing me to her pal.

"Nice to meet you," Kim said, sticking her hand out. It was petite like her, and dry. That was the extent of the formalities, and she didn't waste any time. "Lucille says you have a problem. It's delicate, highly technical, and possibly dangerous."

And here I thought they were talking girl stuff all this time. I looked at my lawyer. She smiled and shrugged.

I smiled back and turned to Kim. "I think that pretty much sums it up."

"Goody. Whatcha got?" She was actually rubbing her hands together in anticipation. Her eyes twinkled. She was obviously not a stay-at-home granny.

I laid the cards out on the bar and pushed them to her. I told her the story about them being stolen and then recovered, leaving out any mention of casinos, gangsters, mayhem, and death—pretty much everything except the part about the card reader.

She looked disappointed. I hadn't given her anything dangerous.

"Plus, there's this guy that wants to kill me because he thinks I did something really bad to his computers with these cards. I have no idea what he's talking about," I said, laying Tony's card reader on top of the cards. Its LED immediately started flashing green.

She brightened considerably and gave the cards a cursory inspection, devoting more attention to the card reader. When the bartender passed by, she ordered a round of Patrón Silver tequila then turned to me. "Are you willing to spring for a computer?"

That perplexed me. "Sure, but I thought you had a bunch of them."

"I do, but if I what I suspect is true here, I don't want to toast any of my stuff. What I need is a couple disposable laptops, some monitors, a bunch of cable, and a printer. These cards are probably so toxic that any computer interacting with them would be radioactive afterward."

I must have had a look of horror on my face because she hastened to add, "Not literally, but they might become so contaminated that they'd be worthless for anything other than word processing. We're going to need some diagnostic stuff too. You going to pay for it?"

At this point, I didn't care what it cost. I needed information, and I needed it now. "Go whole hog," I told her.

The bartender had put a shot of Patrón in front of each of us. Kim reached for hers and slammed it. "Then let's get hell out of here," she said. I took a quick look at my lawyer. She shrugged and slammed hers too. I was not fond of tequila; it reminded me of my college days down in the Mexican border town of Juarez. Not wanting to look like a pussy, I followed suit, and to my surprise, I found it was nothing like the rotgut I remembered, but still had the same bite.

When my eyes quit watering, I discovered Lucille and Kim were already headed for the door. The cards and the reader were gone too. I threw a fifty on the bar and hustled after them. I didn't have time to cash out my paper voucher, dammit. I had thirty days to redeem it. I wondered if I could do that from jail.

A cab was just dropping off a couple of salt and peppers when Kim commandeered it. I barely managed to get in before the cab pulled away.

40

11:00 a.m.

Thirty minutes later, my wallet was five grand lighter after we left the nearby Office Max and took another cab to Kim's tour bus parked behind the old Circus-Circus RV Park. The cabbie helped me with the packages while the girls unlocked the door and went in. Two minutes later, I was another hundred bucks lighter and the cab was gone.

Other than painted stealth black, her home on wheels was indistinguishable from a couple dozen others parked cheek to jowl like ultrachic tour buses lined up for a decadent race.

Walking into it was like dropping into a miniature space station. Computers, plasma screens, and electronic equipment covered every square inch of the walls except the dining table, the ceiling, but presumably not airliner-sized bathroom.

We took seats at a table. Kim scooted to one side while Lucille and I took over the other. "What I think what you've got here is some sophisticated RFID stealth-ware," she began without preamble as she laid the cards and the reader on the table.

I nodded and tried to look like I knew what the fuck she was talking about. Lucille laid her hand on my leg under the table.

Kim took pity on me and explained, "Radio-frequency identification devices. Ultrathin computer chips capable of transmitting over short distances. Most people don't know it, but they're in everything from passports to tires. Credit and ID cards are a given. It won't be long before they're even in clothes. No big deal normally." She picked up the reader and held it up in front of her face, inspecting it again. "This baby *here* is the problem."

Lucille was kneading the inside of one my thighs. I think all the technical talk was getting her off. I could see me getting her all hot and bothered while I read to her tonight from my monthly issue of *Scientific American* before I turned out the lights.

Kim noticed the smile on my face and misinterpreted it as having an inkling of where she was headed with this, so she continued.

"Last I heard, unless you swiped the card on a reader hardwired to a register, gas pump, or anything computerized, you'd need something the size of a suitcase laying within inches of the card to steal or analyze the data on it. The data is on the magnetic strip on the back. It would have to be a lot bigger than this," she said as she placed the reader a foot and a half away from the black and white APEX card. It immediately flashed its green LEDs.

Coming from the NSA, she probably knew stuff I couldn't wrap my head around. This was the first I'd heard of RFIDs. George Orwell strikes again.

Trying to not sound as stupid as I am, I said, "So whoever made this succeeded in miniaturizing an existing technology. For what purpose? Identity theft? Fraud? What?"

"Well, think about it. Some poor shmuck lays his wallet down on the counter, waiting for the clerk to finish swiping his card and giving him the receipt. You lay your peanuts and this pack of cigarettes down near his wallet, like it's a purchase, and voila! You've captured all his credit card information on the remaining cards in his wallet on your reader. You pay for your peanuts, go to your car, turn on the air conditioner, pull out your laptop, upload the captured data on the reader, and max all the victim's cards out before he even gets home. Five, ten, twenty grand a pop."

Whoa.

I knew Tony was into making money through illegal activities, but this seemed way above and beyond the call of duty even for him.

I didn't think he could program his cell phone, let alone be masterminding something of this scope.

I must have been shaking my head because she said, "Why don't you let me work on this with all the stuff you just bought? There're a hundred restaurants within walking distance. You two go have a nice romantic lunch and stay gone for a while. I'll have something for you when you get back."

It wasn't a suggestion, more like a command. That was fine with me. By now I was more horny than hungry, and the nearest hotel was a minute away, walking distance.

41

2:00 p.m.

While Lucille showered, I grabbed a ten-dollar beer out of the suite's mini fridge and stared out the window overlooking the strip. In the four decades I'd been coming here, it had remade itself so often I couldn't even recognize where the original hotels had stood. The mob was gone, pushed out by corporate. Vegas was a chameleon, changing its covering every year of so. The Strip was getting closer to a science fiction amusement park than a place for guys to get away, take their mistresses, and gamble. Nobody brought their kids to Vegas back then.

Thirty years ago, all that changed.

It was only a matter of time until corporate realized that they were forgetting about three quarters of every nuclear family. There was no reason for the two kids and the little lady not to have fun at the water park while Dad wagered their college money at the blackjack table. Enough of them won to keep the myth alive and Vegas exploded. Half Disneyland, half *Star Wars*.

That's why I liked Laughlin; it was closer to the way Vegas used to be.

Lucille roused me from my reminiscing by hugging me from behind. She was out of the shower, but I could tell she had forsaken the towel. The warmth of her body against my backside caused my little redheaded friend to stand at attention. Again.

The next thing I remember, we were back in the bed, and it was almost three in afternoon. The TV was on, and I could smell coffee brewing. Lucille was singing in the bathroom.

I stumbled in and turned on the shower. She was combing her hair. She was dressed and looked great. I, on the other hand, looked like shit.

She was gracious enough to say nothing. After a minute or so, she moved back into the bedroom, but I could still hear the singing over the shower. I jacked the hot water up as far as it would go.

It occurred to me while I held my head under the shower that I'd opened myself up to two women that I barely knew, and the rest of my life was pretty much in their hands. One of them was happy as a lark. The other one wanted her to be happy too. That almost never happened. I had the feeling that events were moving out my control.

I think I looked much better when I emerged from the bathroom. Lucille was talking on her cell phone but smiled and terminated it when she saw me.

She got up and poured me a cup of coffee while I got dressed. "I just talked to Kim. I don't know what she found, but she seems pretty excited. We need to get back there." She handed me the coffee.

I was pretty much screwed every way you could imagine, so I agreed and followed her out the door. We didn't have any luggage, and it only took us about three minutes to take the elevator down and walk out the hotel door to Kim's RV a block away in companionable silence, with the exception of Lucille's singing. It was so unnerving that I was about to mention it when Kim opened her door, obviously expecting us.

"You still singing 'Hotel California,' girl?" Kim asked, ignoring me.

"Yeah, I can't get it out of my head," Lucille replied with a laugh.

"I could hear you a block away. Get your ass in here."

I was absent the leash, but I figured this was how Ratso probably felt following his mistress. Kim must have picked up on my vibes and paid some attention to me. "Jake, I think I have some good news for you. Or bad, depending."

"Depending on what?" I sat down next to Lucille at the table. Even that was taken over by reams of paper. I was worn out and in no mood for sparring.

"On what you want to do with what I have to tell you," she replied without smiling.

That got my attention.

She waited a couple of beats before beginning. She was looking at me, not at her friend, my lawyer and lover.

"Do you remember what I told you about RFIDs and credit cards?"

I nodded, unsure that I should reveal my lack of knowledge as to its importance.

"We've moved to a higher plane," she said as she started stacking all the paper in front of her. I said nothing because I knew nothing.

"I don't know what you're into, but I've got to tell you this: we need to consider bringing the feds in on it."

Not. My response was simple and understandable. "Why?"

She sighed and looked up at the ceiling as if seeking an answer.

"Because what you have here is a fundamental breakthrough in wireless technology." She paused for a moment, formulating her words. "Whoever made this device has tapped into quantum physics. Harnessed chaos theory and given it practical application." I could tell she was passionate about what she was talking about. I could barely spell quantum mechanics, but I was happy for her all the same.

I couldn't help myself. "And that means…what?" Lucille gave me an elbow in the ribs.

"It *means* that whoever made this thing, if he revealed it today, would be an instant billionaire. So what's the deal?" She turned to look at me. "What the hell have you gotten us into?"

As a thirty-year veteran of the NSA, I was sure she had a gun under the table and would console her friend after the fact.

A couple of decades ago, after numerous bouts with enforcement agencies and outrageous fees to lawyers, I started taking law classes at night. What the hell, if you can't beat 'em, join 'em. After civil law, I moved on to criminal law because that was the only course the local college offered.

The first thing my teacher, the municipal judge, said to us when he walked up to the lectern was "Never plead guilty to anything. That's rule two. Rule one is contact your lawyer before you say a word." After that statement, I adopted that philosophy.

My lawyer was sitting next to me, so I moved on to rule two. "I don't have a clue. Why don't you tell me?"

What she said next surprised me more than if she'd pulled out a sleek pearl-handled Glock nine-millimeter with a foot-long silencer.

She held up the APEX card and placed it a foot away from my new laptop, which was up and running. A stream of data was zipping across the screen. "The computer is running off its internal battery pack, but the card has no apparent power source. There is no cable or direct physical connection. Yet the card responds to queries and the computer replies. These two are talking to each other…and they're not swapping recipes. They're discussing chaos theory."

42

Lucille was the first to speak. "How can that be? It's so small."

"Good question," Kim replied, never taking her eyes off me.

I felt my bowels loosen and in immediate need of the bathroom facilities. Without a word, I got up and hit the head, barely in time to avoid doing something I haven't done since I was a toddler.

I was right. The bathroom was free of unrecognizable electronic devices. But I couldn't believe how wrong I was about Tony. Whatever he was up to went far beyond what I thought he was capable of. Both technically and ethically. What was I thinking? He was a gangster—the head gangster. Despite all that crap about my being the son he never had, it looked like he'd strapped a suicide vest on me and sent me on my way.

I needed more information. I washed my hands, threw some cold water on my face, and went back to face the ladies.

They were both watching me when I sat down.

Lucille jumped in first. "I think you need to tell her everything."

I looked at her then at Kim. The thought that she might not have entirely severed her ties to the ultra-secret government agency she had worked several decades for crossed my mind. I wondered how deep her friendship was to my lawyer and lover. I guess I was about to find out.

I started at the beginning.

I had already told her about the unnamed client losing his cards, so I left out the part about the pickpocket being blown up, his fence getting murdered, my kidnapping of the fence's cousin, his illegal detention, but I tossed in my aborted exchange in the Riverside with Nicky and escape, my own kidnapping, torture, and subsequent rescue. I didn't bother with all the misdemeanors, just stuck to the felonies. I left Tony out of it entirely. Even so, the abbreviated version took almost a half hour.

The whole time Kim said nothing nor showed any surprise or, for that matter, any emotion at all. I suspected that after all that time with the NSA, nothing surprised her.

I was wrong again.

When it was obvious I was finished, she looked me for a full minute before leaning back in her seat and saying, "Holy shit."

That would have been my response, too, if I hadn't already lived it.

She looked at Lucille for verification and got another shrug.

Kim looked out the window next to her, seemingly lost in thought. Lucille put her hand back on my leg. Nobody said anything for a couple of minutes. Kim turned her attention back to the APEX card, studying its thickness against the other cards.

Finally, she turned her focus on the Marlboro pack. Leaning forward again, she moved it another foot away from the computer. Lines of data continued to scroll on the screen. She moved it another six inches, and the connection was broken. She sat back, still looking at the reader. Then she looked around at all her high-tech equipment.

"Call a cab, Lucille," she said after only a few seconds. She got up and went into her bedroom while Lucille got on her cell. Thirty seconds later, Kim came back out with what looked like a wallet. Grabbing the APEX card off the table, she inserted it into the wallet. She held the wallet out to me.

Not knowing what she was trying to tell me, I said, "Thanks, but I've got my own wallet."

"Not like this one. It was developed by DARPA."

I was not totally ignorant, so I knew that DARPA stood for the super-secret government science agency that brought us the Internet. I had mixed feelings about that.

"With the introduction of RFIDs and eventual use of devices like this," she said, holding up the cigarette pack, "for ID and data theft, one of our eggheads cooked up a card shield that looked like a wallet. The problem was that it only worked when the card was in the wallet, so when you took it out to pay the cashier, the card was now vulnerable. Hence the idea was flawed and shitcanned. A few prototypes were produced. You can find knockoffs on the Internet now, but not like this one. It's not perfect, but for our purposes now, it's the best thing going. I have no idea if the card can be tracked or what it can do to any computer you pass within a couple feet of, but I don't want to find out."

I took the sleek-looking calfskin wallet and put it in my shirt pocket, glad I didn't have a pacemaker. I didn't want to get it close to my nuts either, so it damned sure wasn't going into my pants pocket.

It didn't slip my attention that she had said *our eggheads*.

I would have bet a grand that even in retirement, she was still dialed in, and not with just the NSA. In which case she should have tried to keep the card, but she hadn't. She gave it back without my asking.

While I was trying to figure that out, Lucille ended her call. Kim went to a closet and pulled out three large black duffle bags. Walking to boxes of electronic we'd purchased earlier, she started stuffing them in. I got up and began to help.

"Put in all the stuff we bought today. We'll need some more specialized items, but I'll sacrifice some of my own. You can pay me later," she said, moving off with a bag and disappearing into the bedroom. I hoped it wasn't to make a phone call. Or maybe, like most women, she just kept the best stuff close to her bed. Lucille was back on the phone, hopefully chartering a plane leaving McCarren Airport in fifteen minutes—destination Area 51.

The only thing I recognized while I was packing the duffel was a printer. The rest of the boxes had a picture and a number. There were a ton of cords. I was working on the second bag when Kim emerged from her bedroom with half duffel full. I was hoping it wasn't clothes.

She stopped at what used to be a seating area that was now shelves of esoteric electronic hardware and started cannibalizing it until her duffel was full. Seeing that mine was only half full, she filled it with a few more items.

Three bags, three people. It finally dawned on me. She had the logistics down. I wondered then if she had been a field agent.

I heard a car pull up and then a honk. Our cab, but I looked out the door just to make sure. I lifted all three bags to see which one was the heaviest. It was my first bag, so I grabbed it and headed out the door.

The cabbie had the trunk open, and while I threw mine in, he helped the ladies. I knew what the cabbie was thinking: three big black duffel bags? White, middle-aged. No problem. Three Chinese, bags full of money, no problem. Three Pakistanis? Big problem.

The land yacht and the fact that we spoke English, along with my hundred-dollar bill, made him feel a lot more comfortable.

"MGM," I told him as we all piled in. If we were going to Area 51, I wanted to pick up my change of clothes. We might be there for a while. Like forever.

Kim didn't object, so I took that as a good sign.

The cabbie did his thing and had us at the MGM in record time. I doubt anybody could have followed him. The three of us and our bags were in front of the golden doors before you knew it. Good tips, good service. But you've got to tip up front.

The black duffels had extendable handles and rollers, undoubtedly also developed by DARPA. I think they should have used a light blue color. Nevertheless, we quickly traversed the casino before working our way to the elevators. I ignored the beckoning calls of the Sevens. They could come later.

The elevator was empty; another good sign. The ride up was quiet. No one said anything until we got into the room.

"Whew," Kim said, dropping her bag. Lucille did the same when she found some room to put hers down. I carried mine in all the way to the far end of the room to show I was manly. I tried to remember if I'd taken my high blood pressure medicine this morning.

I immediately started on my bag. The sooner I could get out of that room, the better. I stacked the boxes against the wall and waited for Kim to explain why we couldn't do this at her place.

She must have picked up on it. "I think all that data you saw was picked up by the reader when you passed the compromised card over it. It looks like captured financial data, but I'm not sure. I don't know what that thing is capable of. It could even be a transmitter," she said, pointing at my shirt pocket. "Until I know otherwise, I'm not going to jeopardize a million dollars of my own equipment for your little project."

My little project? How about my death here?

"I appreciate your help, Kim," I replied. After a half century, I've learned not to aggravate women who had you by the balls.

There was a shitload of things I had to do, and I couldn't have my lawyer around while I was doing them, so I decided to dump Lucille on Kim and get on with it.

I'd finished with my duffel bag and started helping Lucille with hers.

"How about you work with Kim while I go out and take care of my immediate problems?" I said, hoping I could slip away.

Much to my surprise, she agreed.

I gave Lucille a peck on the cheek, and I was out the door before it could hit me in the ass.

43

4:00/5:00 p.m.

When I got to the casino floor, I wasted no time hitting the front door. I ignored the insistent whispers of the Sevens as I passed by. *I'm over here. Come get the jackpot!*

I pulled my cell out and called Arliss. He assured me that he had things well in hand. My next call went to an old contractor buddy who had grown tired of the construction industry's cycle of boom and bust and had moved from Flagstaff to Vegas to drive a cab. He now had his own limo business.

He answered on the third ring. "JG's Diamond Limos."

"Want to go fishing?" I asked.

It took a couple of seconds for his auditory Rolodex to kick in. "Jake! How the fuck are you?"

"In Vegas, standing in front of the MGM without a ride."

I heard his chuckle. "Give me fifteen minutes to drop off this Saudi prince at the Bellagio. In the meantime, go play your machines."

I didn't need any encouragement. I headed back inside.

I wandered up and down an aisle of Sizzling Sevens dollar slots before I settled on one. It wasn't because of any psychic energy. It was the fact that it was the end machine closest to the main traffic aisle. That meant it got played a lot more. Paradoxically, that's good. More play, more pay. The object is to hit it when it's in its paying cycle. You can usually tell after a couple hundred bucks.

SIZZLIN' 7S

Machine 5398-6 had no problem devouring my first c-note. I played the max: three dollars a spin. You have to play the max to get the progressive jackpot displayed in big letters overhead. The amount went up with every pulling. In this case, it was $1,378.

A good sign. The Sevens usually paid out after $1,200, but you never knew. At one penny per dollar added to the progressive pot, that meant that $37,875 had already been pumped into it, trying to get thirteen hundred. I'd seen the progressives get as high as two grand, bankrupting scores who just *knew* that the jackpot would come up on the next spin. Had to. Pavlov was the first to describe the phenomena when he did his dog experiments back in the early 1900s.

Two hundred bucks was my litmus test.

There's something hypnotic about slot machines. Once you start pushing those buttons, you don't think of anything else. Not the mortgage, the utility bills, relationship problems…just you and Lady Luck. If you have the money, it's sort of therapeutic. On the other hand, it can be anything but. It's all about discipline. At three bucks a pull, one pull every three seconds, it took about two minutes for machine 5398-6 to take half of my discipline.

Not to be deterred, I stuck the rest of my discipline into the machine's pie hole.

Three minutes later, all my discipline was gone.

I ignored a voice shouting in my head, *Don't do it, stupid!* I stuck another hundred in the devil's maul. What the hell, I had another ten minutes to kill, I rationalized. At this rate, it was going to cost me another four hundred bucks until JG showed up.

A little ancient gnome of a woman sat down next to me, her rewards card hanging from her neck on a lanyard. A cup of coffee was in one hand and a cigarette in the other.

Carefully placing the cup with a palsied hand in the space between the machines, she placed her rewards card in its slot. Next, she slowly unzipped the purse she had mounted on top on her tits and her navel and pulled out a twenty. I hadn't seen her take a breath so far. Tough old bird.

"Having any luck?" she asked, finally taking a drag of her unfiltered cigarette and blowing it in my direction. She didn't take her eyes off me.

She had probably been watching me since I got here.

I recognized her immediately. She was a casino TOB. The boomers' new bully of the schoolyard, only now the schoolyard was a casino and she was too small and too old to hit. Treacherous old bitch. A veteran with many battles under her belt, obviously, from her demeanor. Every casino had a hundred, and I've learned a lot from them. This one I named Blue, after her hair.

Getting no response from me, she turned to her machine and put a twenty in. She didn't bother to hit any buttons, instead contented herself to waiting to see what I would do.

If she thought that would intimidate me, she had another thing coming.

My third hundred went the way of the first two, and it was time to either give up the machine or plow ahead. I chose to plow ahead, discipline be damned. I knew what Native Americans experienced when European fur traders first showed up with whiskey and cards.

I needed to hit three red sevens to break even and another three of the same to make a profit. Then I needed a jackpot to defeat the TOB next to me.

My first sixty went in twenty spins, lasting one minute at three seconds a spin. Blue had only hit hers once, bidding her time. She was puffing away faster though, so I could tell she was getting excited at the probability of me going down in flames and her grabbing my machine.

The cocktail waitress came by and gave me a reprieve, asking if I wanted anything. I ordered a Coors. When she asked if I needed anything else, I said, "Do you have any ATMs close by?" knowing full well there was one fifty feet away that I'd used numerous times in the past. I did it so that Blue would know she wasn't getting my machine. I also needed to walk away from the machine to reevaluate my thinking.

"There's one right around that corner," the waitress said, pointing to the left. "Would you like me to watch your machine while you use it? I'd be more than happy to."

God bless her soul. She was gonna get a good tip and deserved it. I love good service.

The sweet little old lady—*not*—next to me was less than pleased, though, and took her frustration out on Cinderella. "I want some coffee," she snapped, stubbing out the half inch of her cigarette in an ashtray with a vengeance. I got up and laid a ten on Cinderella's tray.

"Thank you so much. I'll only be a moment," I told her.

Blue played her last card. "I'll be more than happy to watch his machine for you while you get me some coffee, young lady."

I was only a couple of steps away. Cinderella was having none of it. "I'm sorry. I can't do that, but thank you for offering. I'll call another girl to get you some coffee if you can't wait, but I can't leave his machine."

I continued on around the corner, resolving to give her another ten when I got back.

I started to come to my senses when I got to the ATM. Sometimes you have to do that when you're playing the slots. You need to step away and take a breath. Reevaluate your priorities.

I decided to let the old bitch have the machine. I needed some cash anyway, so I pulled out my wallet and stuck my Visa card in. Suddenly, I remembered that I still had the APEX card in my shirt pocket. I'd forgotten to give it to the girls in my hasty departure. I'm sure Kim needed it for her continued research, but I was gone before she realized it. They'd probably been trying to call me, but since cells don't always work in casinos, I was probably out of touch.

I tried to stay a couple of feet away from the ATM as I pulled some cash out of my account, reaching out as far as I could just in case Kim's prototype wallet didn't work. I didn't want the ATM to blow a fuse and debit my account down to zero.

Then a thought occurred to me.

44

Sister Mary Katherine was not totally wrong for hitting me with her ruler every day in class. True, she was a sadistic, mean bitch that needed to get laid, but she wasn't totally to blame. I was pretty much a bad boy every chance I got. I learned in my night law classes that it was called shared culpability. It meant you were both wrong to some extent.

I was still a bad boy. She was pushing sixty when I was in grade school, so hopefully she's in hell where she belongs. If I don't mend my ways one of these days, I'll probably be seeing her and her ruler again.

But today's not that day.

When I got back to my machine, I gave Cinderella another ten and sent her on her way. I could tell from the relief on her face that Blue had been giving her an earful of grief the whole time I was gone.

The old bitch was not happy. I saw from her credit counter that she'd had to put another twenty in what I knew she considered a losing machine.

I needed to stretch out my last forty credits until JG showed up or had me paged. I figured another ten minutes anyway.

Testing a thought that occurred to me on the walk back from the ATM, I took the APEX card out of its DARPA wallet, leaving the card exposed, and then placed the empty wallet in the back pocket of my jeans. *What the hell, it couldn't hurt to see what happens*, I thought. Gotta test a theory, right?

SIZZLIN' 7S

Making sure that I was at least three feet away from Blue's machine, I hit the play button on my machine. Nothing. I leaned a little closer and hit the max play button again. Nothing. Four more times…nothing. Not even bars. Bars gave you back ten bucks. I was leaning closer and closer to my machine with each spin, but that was classic desperate behavior by losing gamblers, so it wouldn't be deemed unusual by the eye-in-the-sky.

I was down to twenty-two bucks. I was concerned that I would run out of credits before JG showed up. I had no desire to throw another hundred away. I needed to drag it out. Cinderella showed up with my Coors and Blue's coffee. I gave her another ten and Blue stiffed her. Cinderella gave me a smile and scurried off. I doubted that the old bag would be getting any more free coffee anytime soon.

"Are you gonna get off that machine?" Blue asked, blowing another gust of carcinogens my way. "You only got six spins left."

"Actually, seven and one third," I corrected her.

"Yeah, but if you only play one on the last spin, you can't get the jackpot. You gotta play the max." She blew another plume of smoke my way.

I was thinking they ought to rescind the law that says you can't spank your kids or punch your grandmother. I ignored her and hit the play button again.

Ka chunk, ka chunk, ka chunk. It came up three red sevens. Three hundred bucks.

"Fuck," Blue muttered. I wasn't surprised she could cuss like a sailor.

Relieved that I now had enough credits and a reason to hang out until JG showed up, I slowed my pace. I started hitting bars, which paid ten or twenty depending, then another three red sevens. I couldn't tell if it was because I was practically hugging the machine or whether it was finally just in its pay cycle. I didn't give a shit. I was up three hundred plus change and ready for JG to show up.

Unlike most others, this bank of machines paid off in coins, so I decided to cash out and put all my coins in racks to take to the cashier. Sometimes the machines needed refilling, and I didn't want to take the chance of that happening just as JG showed up. I heard the sigh of relief from Blue. The jackpot was still intact, and it was finally hers, or so she thought. She pulled her rewards card out of her machine in anticipation, collecting her half-dozen coins.

JG showed up at my elbow as I was filling up the last rack. I had seven racks at a hundred bucks a rack, with three coins left over.

"Damn, Jake! You're cleaning house," he said after we'd quit doing the high fives, hugging and all that male bonding stuff.

"Not really," I replied. "It took me four before I got the seven. I was lucky. I was going down in flames."

JG never had been one for small talk. "Whatever. I'm double parked in front. We need to scoot."

"Okay, let's go," I said, getting really close to my machine as I stuck the extra three dollar coins into the machine just for the hell of it. Blue moved to take my chair as I got ready to leave. I forgot to pull my own rewards card out when I got up.

As I turned to walk off, I heard the familiar chime of the first Sizzling Sevens fall into place, then another, and after what seemed to be an eternity, the third. The machine immediately broke into a rendition of "We're in the money…we're in the money."

Jackpot. Almost fifteen hundred and change.

JG rolled his eyes. He knew it would take ten or fifteen minutes for them to pay me out. "I'll be waiting out front," he said in disgust. "You're paying for the ticket."

I wasn't sure, but I had a hunch that the APEX card had something to do my hitting the jackpot.

Needless to say, Blue was beside herself. Her hopes of hijacking my machine had gone down in flames, literally and figuratively. Whoever's card was in the machine and pushed the button got the jackpot. Didn't matter I wasn't sitting in front of it. "Fuck, fuck, fuck," she said as she slumped back into the middle chair.

I had a feeling this machine was so screwed up it would probably hit again.

"As soon as they pay me out, I'm gonna put a hundred back in. That's yours," I told her as one of the suits showed up to pay me my 1,500 bucks.

"Why should I believe that shit?" she vented, wanting to believe but unable to.

"Trust me. This baby is going to pop again," I told her as I walked off. I wasn't fifty feet away, probably three pulls, before I heard the jackpot chime go off again, followed by a whoop I recognized as coming from Blue.

That was when I finally realized what Tony was really up to.

He'd found a way to beat the slots.

45

5:00/6:00 p.m.

If my suspicions were right, Tony's primary goal with this card and its technology was to steal from the casinos. It was right up his alley. The part about cyber-attacking an opponent's system was a plus that he was probably only just now appreciating.

But he got sloppy. He assumed that, like a good boy, I would do as he said. But I was not a good boy. I used to be better until I met him.

I've been trying to get out from under his patronage for the last month. I just wanted to distance myself from him. I liked Tony and respected him, but another part of me told me he'd stick it to me in a heartbeat. I wasn't family.

The card in my hand could win my freedom from him.

JG was arguing with a security guard when I got outside. I walked up and tapped him on the shoulder. "Let me handle this," I told him and turned to the rent-a-cop.

"This was all my fault. It took longer than I expected to get paid out," I said, handing him a crisp hundred-dollar bill. "My bad."

He smiled, tipped his cap, and walked off.

JG shook his head and got behind the wheel. I climbed in on the passenger side.

"Shit, Jake, a twenty probably would have worked."

I handed him a c-note. "Feel better now?"

"I'm getting there," he replied as he put the beast in gear and pulled out of the portico.

I pulled out my cell and called Mo. He answered on the second ring. "Yes, boss," he said.

"I need you to pick up Arliss and meet me in Vegas," I told him without preamble.

"When?"

"An hour ago. Call me when you get here." I hung up. My next call went to Arliss.

"Monica's escort service. How may we help you?"

"How are Romeo and Juliet?"

"Still haven't come up for air."

"Roust them. I need you in Vegas. Go down and check out, then stick them in a motel in Bullhead City. Pay cash and use a fictitious name. Call Mo. He'll pick you up."

"You cutting 'em loose?"

"Sabbatini's gonna find them sooner or later, and I think they'd be safer with him. But I don't want to give them up just yet. More importantly, I need your services here with me."

"Gotcha. But speaking of services, I gotta tell you, the room service charge here is gonna be a bitch," he said and hung up.

"Want to tell me where I'm supposed to be taking you?" JG asked as he fired up a joint.

"Don't have a clue, but I'll bet you do."

That got me a sideways look. "What do you know about Big Nicky Mosconi?" I asked him as I rolled down my window. I was getting high off the secondhand smoke.

"Ah shit, Jake. The old mob guy? What are getting us into now? Specifically, what are you getting *me* into?"

"His son is trying to kill me for some reason."

That got a laugh out of him. "Well, tell the stupid son of a bitch to get at the end of the line."

"Cute," I replied. "But seriously, the wacko is trying to whack me."

JG was quiet for a couple of puffs. "He owns one of the old casinos out past the strip. Where Las Vegas used to be. Corporations have pretty much taken over from the mob in gambling, building mega-casinos, but the old boy still rakes it in on other shit. Prostitution, loan sharking, fencing, drugs, ID theft. You name it. He doesn't miss a crumb." The part about ID theft caught my attention.

"Take me to his casino," I told him.

"Once more into the breech," he muttered and put out his joint. We drove in companionable silence for about five minutes. That's how long it took to get to the Wild West Casino.

Big Nicky's place.

46

The building had to be sixty years old and looked it. Red and gold, lots of lights, but half of them didn't work. Graffiti adorned one brick wall, and grime darkened the doorway. The green canvas awning was faded and tattered. An old whore showing her age.

The inside wasn't much better. Low ceilings and dark, it smelled even worse than most old bars I've been in. Penny and nickel slots were lined up along both walls, with a quarter slot here and there. They were the only ones unoccupied. Most of the customers were white-hairs surrounded by walkers and clouds of cigarette smoke. There were a few tweekers here and there, standing at their machines, twitching and scratching.

The U-shaped bar was at the back, empty except for a big man sitting at the end. I assumed he was Big Nicky. The bartender was even bigger. An over-the-hill topless dancer was listlessly grinding away to a Frank Sinatra song on a platform in the corner. She was probably somebody's grandmother and hadn't bothered with a boob job.

We sat down a couple of stools away from him. Nicky gave us the once-over because we weren't his usual clientele. JG was dressed in a tux, and my clothes were a couple of cuts above the Walmart duds everyone else was sporting.

Deciding we weren't cops, he went back to reading his *Racing Form*. He had a pencil in his big paw and was obviously handicapping. The TV over the bar was tuned to simulcast horse racing. The third race at Hollywood Park was due to go off in five minutes. When you've watched this stuff for a dozen years, it's easy to read what going on.

I wondered if Nicky was his own bookie or if he laid it off on someone else. As if to answer my question, Nicky seemed to make a decision, whispering something to the bartender, who promptly pulled out his cell phone, punched in one number, and said one sentence into the phone. I read lips because I've been deaf since I was a kid. "One large. Box the tri at Hollywood three…two five seven," meaning he was wagering one thousand dollars on horses 2, 5, and 7 coming in first, second and third in some order to win race three at Hollywood. Depending how many horses were in the race and what the odds were on all the three fastest horses, the payout could be substantial. A two-dollar ticket sometimes brought in five figures. Multiply that by forty.

Not your average pony player.

The bartender came over and took our orders. Chivas for JG and a Coors for me. I stuck a twenty in an ancient video poker machine mounted in the bar in front of me. JG took his drink over to one of the quarter machines. I knew he'd rather be somewhere else.

I wasn't getting any cards, and my twenty was history in under a minute. I stuffed another twenty in and bet the max on the next four hands. Zero. Zip. Nada. Zilch.

"Shit!" I said, only half faking it. Both Nicky and the bartender looked over. "Sorry," I said, making a big deal out getting a hundred-dollar bill out of my pocket.

"Can you break this?" I asked the bartender. "And bring me another beer?"

I watched as he took it over to a high-tech computer register that looked incongruous beneath the old boxy TV monitor above it. Nicky went back to his *Form*.

The bartender came back with my beer and eighty-five bucks—ten short. No free drinks here. That's when the plan popped into my mostly empty head.

SIZZLIN' 7S

I burned through the eighty-five faster than my second beer. I never even hit trips: three of a kind. I suspected Tony's machines were so tight you couldn't drive a sixteen penny nail up their ass.

Acting agitated, I rummaged through my pockets for more money, appearing to find none. "How about another round for me and my buddy?" I asked the Hulk behind the bar, who was eyeing me now. I could tell Nicky was monitoring the whole thing peripherally.

"It'll be ten bucks," he pointed out, buying the out-of-money act.

"Fine. You take credit cards, don't you?" I asked with a slightly slurred voice, which wasn't all that hard. I must have been buzzed to do what I did next.

I got up from my stool, moved away from the poker machine, and got out the DARPA wallet. Removing the APEX card from it, I offered it to Hulk.

Hulk looked at Nicky, who was looking at me like a bear looked at a salmon. According to JG, Nicky was into identity and credit card theft. He nodded to the bartender, who took my card and proceeded to swipe it through the card reader attached to the plasma. Hulk pushed a few more buttons, but nothing helped.

Shaking his head, he returned and tossed the APEX card on the bar. "It's been declined, and our computer's down momentarily," he said with hard stare. Nicky looked disappointed and went back to handicapping.

"No more money, no more booze," Hulk said, crossing his tree-trunk arms.

"Hey, no problem," I told him, scooping up the card and backing away. "I guess we'll be leaving now." I put the card back into its protective covering and headed for the door, motioning to JG that we were done.

He got to the limo before me and had it running before I got in.

"I didn't see any fireworks. What did you do besides lose your ass at video poker?" he asked as we pulled out of the parking lot.

"Started a shitstorm, unless I'm mistaken. I gave Nicky a shot across the bow."

"Well, it was certainly the quietest shot I've ever heard," he said, trying to keep from laughing. "Hopefully, he didn't hear it either. I've got to live here." He pulled out the half-smoked joint and pushed in the cigarette lighter.

If I was right, he'd probably be leaving town with me. Hopefully vertically.

"That was fun." JG was on a roll. "Where to now? Hooters has a new casino. They have video poker there too. Lot better ambiance, meaning you won't see a woman's navel between her tits, like back there." He took another toke. I rolled down my window.

"Keep any Febreze in this rolling felony?"

"Pot is legal in Nevada," he said.

"But you probably should be driving while you do it," I replied.

JG grinned and reached under his seat, tossing me a full can. I used half of it. The limo smelled like someone had been smoking dope in a whorehouse after that. I opened the moon roof while JG tossed the roach.

"Take me back to the MGM," I told him. He looked relieved. When we got to the MGM, I handed JG five c-notes and told him keep a low profile until I called him. "You might consider packing a bag," I said.

He didn't bother to ask why.

47

6:00 p.m.

I ignored the come-hither calls from the Sizzling Sevens slots as I made my way to the elevators and up to our floor.

Lucille was just coming out of our suite when she spied me coming down the hallway. "Where have you been, Jake? I was just going down to look for you. You took the card. We can't get any further without it." She acted like she was a little pissed, but I could tell she was relieved.

"Sorry, baby. I had something I needed to do, and I couldn't do it without the card." I'd actually forgotten all about the card until I needed it, but it sounded plausible. I handed her the DARPA wallet, and we went back into the suite.

The living room looked like something out of NASA Houston Control. Electronic equipment was everywhere, and cables snaked the carpet like roots on a jungle floor. Kim was hunched over a computer facing three monitors. She didn't even look up when we came in.

Lucille walked over to her and handed her the DARPA wallet. Kim smiled at getting the object of her investigation then frowned when she noticed me. If she'd worn a habit, she could have been Sister Mary Katherine's twin. It was obvious she was only doing this for Lucille. I was the devil she had to deal with in the meantime.

I motioned Lucille into the bedroom so we could have some privacy. "How are things going?" I asked her as I closed the door behind her.

"I have no idea what she's doing, but apparently it's fascinating to her. It's really got her psyched. She's already worked with other cards and the reader. From what I gather, she needed the card you had to progress any further. Maybe she'll quit muttering to herself now," she said, giving me a kiss. "What have you been doing?"

"Sticking a red-hot poker up the local mob boss's ass," I replied truthfully.

"That's not exactly what I wanted to hear."

I gave her a kiss back. "Would I lie to you?"

"In a heartbeat. I hope this is one of those times."

"I never lie to my lawyer or my bondsman."

"I'm a lawyer, and my clients lie to me all the time," she said.

"You're right, but I *never* lie to my bondsman."

That got me a laugh and another kiss. "Are you serious?" she asked when we disengaged.

"I'm afraid so. I used that card to corrupt the computer system of Little Nicky's father. I think. If I'm right, all hell is gonna break loose, and we'll all be in danger. You'd better let Kim know." I paused to let that sink in. "The clock is ticking, and I think we've only got a day or so. After that, we'll either be dead or in the clear."

Sweetheart that she was, she just nodded. "Speaking of which, your twenty-four hours are up. I've got to do something with Earl and Susan. I think you need to turn them over to your detective friend." She was trying to reign me in.

"Working on it already," I said as we leaned into each other. Our lips met, and we were just getting started when Kim banged on the bedroom door, interrupting the moment.

"I need to talk to you, Jake!" she yelled through the door. Lucille pulled away and opened the door. Kim was already headed back to the dining table that was her desk. I rearranged my shorts so Woody wouldn't show and followed the two women into Mission Control.

It apparently hadn't taken long once she had the APEX card to reach some conclusions. She began before sitting down, "Remember what I told you about RFIDs? Well, whoever developed these"—she held up the cards and the reader—"could be the next Bill Gates."

Great. And the mob owns him…

"This," she said, raising the APEX card in her right hand, "is a mini-PC. It's powered by micro solar film, the black APEX logo. Clever. This—" she held up the Marlboro pack in her left—"could be the equivalent of a micro CRAY. It's seems to have a huge memory. I don't know what its power source is because I don't dare open it up, even if I knew how. I'm not sure what its transmission distance is either. Could be sat capable." She raised her eyebrows, questioning whether I got the implications.

I was a Luddite, but even I knew what a CRAY was—one of the biggest and most powerful computers in the world. Only governments and big corporations had them. They were the size of closets and were a hell of a lot bigger than a pack of cigarettes. I assumed sat capable meant it was bouncing its transmissions off *satellites*.

"No wonder people are trying to kill you. Hell, our *own* government would," she continued with a shake of her head. I knew she was thinking that they'd kill her too if she didn't bring them in on this. She knew them better than I did. I knew what she was going to do. She didn't have a choice. This had gone beyond a favor to a friend.

Preempting her, I said, "Okay, I agree. But I need a day, at least, to get us some protection. From everybody. Meanwhile, you can have the chance of a lifetime to get in on the ground floor. Learn all you can. It'll probably save our lives."

Kim studied me for thirty seconds. "Deal," she said and dived right in. I could tell she was jazzed. Retirement was probably killing her, and now something had finally come along to give her life meaning. Coming up with a gem like this in post-retirement, like a character out of a Connelly novel, would put her in legendary status with her former peers.

She typed in a command on her keyboard, and a printer sitting on the floor under the table came to life, spitting out page after page of columns and figures. "You're going to love this," she informed me.

I picked up one of the sheets. To me, it was an incomprehensible jumble of figures and letters arranged in columns.

"What you are seeing," she said quietly as if the walls had ears, "is data collected by your card. A lot of data. I imagine it would take a team of forensics *weeks* to go through all this." She looked thoughtfully at the printer. "You better run down to the Office Max and get some more paper. And don't dally."

As much as wanted to get the hell out of that room, I wasn't going to be dismissed that easily. "I may be seeing, but I'm not understanding."

I don't mind being looked down on at as long as I can learn something.

Her need to nurture through teaching overcame her distrust of me. "Okay. We're obviously dealing with major OC figures here. Organized crime," she said to me as if I was an idiot.

I gave her my best idiotic smile.

"What I think we have here is what fifty years ago we would have called a second set of books. A lot of businesses do it. But the books are gone. Everything is electronic now. No paper."

I was standing off to Kim's side, and Lucille was standing behind me. When Kim mentioned organized crime, Lucille moved up behind me and pushed her mini belly against my mini butt. I lost focus for a few seconds.

"Are you paying attention to me?" Kim asked, annoyed. "This is some serious shit."

I pushed Lucille's hands away and gave Kim my full attention.

Kim held up a thumb drive. "Got it all right here." Pulling another one from a port on her computer, she tossed it to me. "There's yours, partner. Now go out there and do what you gotta do." She turned back to her console.

Lucille gently led me back to the bedroom. I didn't resist. I was tired but not that tired. The clothes went hither and yon, and we didn't worry about it. I think we came at the same time.

All too soon, Kim was banging on the door again.

"*Yoo hoo*!" she was yelling. "Yoo hoo. Get your asses up. I think we have company."

I was up like a shot. Paranoia was not necessarily a bad thing. Like my grandmother used to say, "Just because you think somebody's watching you, doesn't mean they aren't." Then again, she was one of thousands that saw UFOs over London one night. She reported it and was sure that MI5 was following her after that. She might have been right.

Lucille had her pants on before I did and got to the door ahead of me.

I went to the suite door and looked through the peephole. That was a no-no. If somebody wanted to kill you, as soon as they see you look at them, they could blow a hole in your belly through the door.

Fortunately, it was somebody I knew. It was Arliss. Mo was fidgeting behind him. They hadn't called me, and I hadn't told them where I was, but here they were. I must be losing my touch.

"You must be losing your touch," Arliss said when I opened the door. I followed the two of them into the entryway. "You didn't answer your phone. And *never* look through the peephole."

I pulled my phone out and realized I'd forgotten to put the battery back in.

"Then how'd you find me?" I asked, but I knew the answer.

"Yours is the only room in town registered under my mama's name, you dipshit," he said as he dumped his suitcase. Lucille and Kim turned their attention to the pair. The big Black guy and the small Turk with a big mustache threw Kim for a minute, but when Lucille didn't blink an eye, she calmed down.

"Leave your stuff here. Let's go somewhere else to talk," I told him. Mo was looking around, all wide-eyed. I gave Lucille and Kim a wave before leading the guys back out the door. We made the walk down the hallway to the elevator in silence.

Once the elevator doors closed, Arliss spoke up. "I gather this is some deeper shit than normal. Otherwise, Mo and I wouldn't be here."

I turned to him, raised my eyebrows, and smiled. Sometimes Arliss could be the king of understatement.

"Let's go down and get you guys a room. Then we'll go have a drink," I said, still looking at him.

"That bad, huh?"

The elevator doors opened to the casino floor before I could say anything more, but he already knew the answer.

48

6:30/7:00 p.m.

After checking them in, I led Arliss and Mo across the casino floor to the bar at the sports betting area. We took a table overlooking a dozen huge plasma monitors, each displaying a different racetrack. A waitress appeared to take our drinks.

I didn't say anything after that. I took in the different races and the odds on the horses in the meantime. Arliss was waiting for me kick it off.

Our drinks arrived, and I drank half of my Coors on the first pull. Then I told them everything that had happened since I last saw them.

They were quite stoic about it. Mo finished his beer before I did. Arliss didn't touch his. I ordered Mo and me another round.

"So basically, Tony left you hanging, Little Nicky wants to kill all of us, and now you've stuck a hot poker in his daddy's ass," Arliss said.

I nodded. "Pretty much."

Nobody said anything, so I refocused my attention on the last race at Aquaduct. Number five—Live Fast—was going off at fifty to one odds and looked good, prancing around like he just couldn't wait to get out and kick ass. The favorite was going off at even odds. Favorites very often fail on the last stretch. Sometimes owners put

SIZZLIN' 7S

their horses in for distances that are too long. This one was eight and a half furlongs, over a mile.

Two more horses, one a gray, caught my attention. Numbers 2 and 7. Both at ten to one odds. I left the boys so they could talk if they wanted to and walked up to the betting window. An old handicapper I knew swore that last races were more prone to have big payouts.

"Aquaduct. Two-dollar tri box, two five seven. One-dollar super, two five seven, two five seven, two five seven, all." The busty babe behind the counter punched in the numbers. Two paper slips popped out of the simulcast machine.

"Thirty-six dollars, please." She smiled as she handed them to me. I gave her two twenties, left the change, and walked away. I didn't go back to the table, though.

I turned and looked out at the casino floor. On my first trip to Vegas, decades ago, all the casinos resembled opulent 1880s whorehouses, resplendent in red and gold. Now it was like something out of a science fiction movie. Sometimes, after a trip here, I would hear the constant electronic ringing of the machines for days afterward, singing, *ching, ching, ching, ching*.

A couple of guys at the bar distracted my thoughts with their hollering. They had apparently bet on Live Fast as well, and he was turning the corner, headed for the stretch with a ten-horse lead. He didn't look like he was going to slow down either. My attention turned to the remaining horses. The favorite, I'm the King, was second; 2 and 7 were running fourth and fifth. It looked like a dead heat to me. I turned away so I couldn't change the results.

I've recently developed a new theory. I read in *Scientific American* that at subatomic levels—quantum physics—just observing a particle can change its position. I have no idea what that means, but I believe it. In the last year, every time I've watched a race that I've bet on, my horse has lost. If I get distracted and miss the race, my horse wins. Go figure.

So for the time being, I'm going with the quantum theory of horse racing. I looked over at Mo and Arliss. They were having a discussion. I'm sure it was about yours truly and whether they wanted to get killed along with me.

I heard another affirmation from the bar. "Two, seven!" one of them yelled. They came in second and third. I had my trifecta. Fifty times ten, times ten, times ten. Five grand. The one-dollar superfecta might pay twice that—ten grand. Total of fifteen thousand, plus or minus.

Anything over twelve hundred is a signer, meaning paperwork from the IRS. I would have to do the requisite paperwork and leave a trail.

Not.

I sauntered over to the boys, giving them time to finish their conversation. They smiled when I joined them, a good sign. I guessed they'd made a decision about whether they were with me or not.

"Anybody want to make a couple grand real fast?" I asked.

Arliss chuckled, and Mo raised his hand real fast. "I do."

"You got a Social Security card?" I inquired.

"You bet, boss," he said proudly.

Arliss had told me that one of Mo's kids was having medical problems and he was hard-pressed to pay for the mounting bills. He didn't have insurance.

I handed him my ticket. "Take this to one of the windows. It's a big winner, and you'll have to pay tax on it. That's why you need a Social Security card. We'll split what's left over. I don't want the tax problems."

Mo didn't hesitate. He grabbed the ticket and headed for the nearest window, leaving Arliss and me alone.

I looked at Arliss. "What's the matter with his kid?"

"MS. It's his youngest. A girl. The rest are boys. The doctor bills are killing them." He paused. "He needs the money. He's on board for anything, short of a felony."

"I think we're already past that, but don't tell him."

Before Arliss could respond, Mo was back, waving a handful of bills.

"Ten thousand and twenty dollars!" he exclaimed. "After taxes."

A cocktail waitress appeared out of nowhere. "Another round?" she asked disingenuously. I grabbed the extra twenty out of Mo's hand and gave it to her. She was off in a flash.

Mo sat down like he was in shock. "Ten thousand," he repeated. He looked like a man that had just been relieved of a burden. A father that had delivered. He was practically vibrating.

He handed me the bills. I counted out five grand and gave it to Mo. He was ecstatic. He'd probably get a tax-return check as well. I counted out two more and gave them to Arliss. He cocked his eyebrows, and I said, "For expenses." I pocketed the remainder. Everybody was happy.

"Okay, guys. Here's my half-assed plan. If you see any flaws in it, I would appreciate your input."

When they both nodded, I laid out my plan. It wasn't perfect, but it was good enough. All three of us were in danger of being killed by Little Nicky or his father. Tony didn't give a shit, so I couldn't expect any protection from him. We were pretty much on our own.

"Does Big Nicky know you've stolen his data yet?" Arliss asked me.

I grimaced. "If he doesn't yet, he will soon."

Arliss accepted that without comment. Mo was quiet.

"You guys go get the cab. I've got to get something from the room. I'll catch you out in front," I said, getting up.

Neither Lucille nor Kim looked up when I reentered the room. They were looking at a computer monitor. *Engrossed* would be a better word.

"Hey," Lucille said when finally noticed me.

"Hey." I smiled back.

"That didn't take long," Kim observed without looking away from the plasma screen.

"I was just leaving actually, but I need something before I go."

Kim finally looked up, knowing I was talking to her.

"I need a copy of that data you printed out earlier."

She thought about it for couple of moments then pointed to the pile of paper next to the printer. "Take it. I can print another copy. There's a manila envelope on the sofa."

I found the envelope and stuck the inch-thick pile into it. Lucille moved over to me, putting her hand on my arm. "How long will you be gone?" Her eyes held concern. And beautiful eyes they were too.

I snapped back to attention before I could lead her back into the bedroom. "A couple hours at most. Don't worry, it's no big deal. I'll call you if I have a problem."

I could tell she didn't believe a word of it, but she just gave me a sweet kiss and said, "Be safe."

I was out the door before she could change my mind.

The boys were waiting out front in Mo's bright green cab. I piled into the back seat, and we were off in a shot. Mo and Arliss both drove alike. I was thrown against the other side door as he executed the first left he could find. He drove like a cab driver in Baghdad.

"Jesus, Mo! Take it easy, will you? What's the deal?"

"Sorry, boss. I was just making sure were not being followed."

I pushed myself back upright, rubbing my head. "I'm pretty sure the following part won't happen for a least another half hour, so just drive normally."

I pulled the wad of hundreds out of my pocket and counted out five. I handed them over to Arliss. He looked at me for a second then stuck it in his jacket pocket.

"After you drop me off, go over to that Avis lot down the block and rent a car. Pay cash." I thought about that then changed my mind. "In fact, stop at Avis first and I'll walk from there. This won't take long, and I'll probably be back before you finish the paperwork. If not, just wait there for me and be ready to move our ass posthaste."

Mo pulled over to the curb just before we got there, and I got out of the cab, taking the envelope with me. I tapped the rooftop when I was clear, and Mo pulled up to the rental office.

Big Nicky's place was only a block and a half away, and it felt good to walk. Rethink this. To give myself one last chance to back out.

Nah.

Little Nicky was hell-bent on killing me and anyone else nearby. Just because I had been suckered by Tony into pulling a cyber Pearl Harbor on him was no reason to go homicidal. I was just the messenger. Tony was his real enemy, but Tony hadn't issued any insurance coverage with the two hundred and fifty grand he gave me. The messenger had to fend for himself.

And that was exactly what I was going to do. The only way I could call Little Nicky off was by blackmailing his old man.

I walked into Big Nicky's place like I owned it.

49

7:00 p.m.

I walked past the same white-hairs playing the penny slots on both walls of the narrow old casino and didn't stop until I got to the bar. The same tired dancer was going through the motions on a pole in the corner.

The bartender looked up, and after a moment of confusion, he placed me as the guy who didn't have any more money. He scowled at me as I sat down.

"What'll it be?" he asked, not nice-like.

"A Coors Original please," I replied with a neutral expression.

He immediately challenged me. "That'll be five bucks."

I took out my roll and peeled off a hundred. "Keep five for yourself." I knew he would anyways. His whole demeanor changed. Instead of a deadbeat, I was now a sucker ripe for picking. His shark smile flashed. "Thank you, sir," he said, emphasis on the *sir*.

I laid the envelope next to the video poker machine in front of me in the bar and stuck a different c-note in its pie hole. I looked around while I waited for my beer. All the penny and nickel machines were busy. The two quarter machines were unoccupied. I didn't see any dollar slots.

The bartender came back with my change. I didn't bother to count it. I could tell it was ten light. I looked down the end of the bar, where Big Nicky usually sat. He wasn't there, but a *Racing Form* was, a pencil lying beside it. He was around. That was good, because otherwise this wasn't going to work.

I played poker for five or so minutes, betting the minimum to stretch it out. When my hundred ran out, I sighed, ordered another beer, and stuffed the remaining bills on the bar into the machine, except for a five.

I could see Hulk was disappointed to see only the five when he got back with my beer, but before he could get pissy again, I said, "Is Big Nicky here?" Not *Mr. Mosconi*. That told him I wasn't John Q. Citizen. I was a player.

He went into his bodyguard mode. "And who the fuck is asking?"

If I didn't give the right password, I was going to wake up, hopefully, in the alley minus my roll and wallet. Fortunately, I knew the password.

"Tony sends his regards. Tell Nicky that I've got a message for him."

Hulk squinted his eyes, studying me. He made a decision and headed for door that might have led into an office, closing the door behind him. It had a mirrored square at eye level, probably one-way.

I started betting the max on the poker slot, figuring I wasn't going to get to spend it no matter what happened. It wasn't like I was going to hang around to collect any kind of a payout.

I was down to my last two hands when the office door finally opened and Big Nicky stormed out, followed by Hulk. He sat down next to me and didn't do anything physical, but he definitely invaded my space.

"Tony from Phoenix?" he said without looking at me.

"Is there any other?" I asked, taking the last pull from my beer and acting like I wasn't scared shitless.

"And what is this *message* from that old fat fuck?" he spat.

I didn't bring up the fact that they grew up together and were the same age and same build. I picked up the manila envelope and placed it in front of him. He eyed it suspiciously, then opened it up and pulled out the bundle of paper. One look at it from him confirmed that he knew what it was. His business records. The ones that only the Commission saw. And another set that only *he* saw.

The veins on the side of his head showed he was enraged. I assumed he was carrying and could very well kill the messenger in a fit of rage, here and now. Hulk would take the rap.

He turned to look at me. "You! I remember you. You came in here before the computer problem started. Your card was denied, and we kicked you out. Was that when you did it." It wasn't a question.

"Yes." I didn't offer that I left before being asked, actually.

He eyed for what seemed to be an eternity. Then he asked the question that I hoped he would. "What does he want?"

I almost fainted from relief. He was going for it, maybe.

"Hands off Laughlin. Your son needs to come home. That's number one. Number two is no retribution to those involved. That means me and my friends, the dog catcher, it doesn't matter who your son is pissed at. It was business. Any vendetta ends here. These demands are nonnegotiable. Any violation will result in both sets of books being released to the Commission."

That came off my tongue so well, I ordered another beer. What the hell.

"So all this came from my son's actions?" he asked disingenuously.

I knew then that he'd called my bluff. Screw the beer. It was time to go. I pushed a bar napkin toward him and said, "Call this number. Tony says you got a day."

I got up and walked as fast as I could without running. I hit the door.

Then I started running.

I used to run the two-mile in high school, but I haven't run anywhere near that far since, so I was pooped by the time I got to the Avis lot. Arliss was just getting into a vanilla Toyota. I hopped into the passenger seat, huffing and puffing.

"You okay?" he asked, not surprised I was there.

"I might survive if we can get the hell out of here," I managed to wheeze.

He wheeled out onto the street and headed away from the casino, keeping one eye on the rearview mirror.

"Where's Mo?" I asked.

"Following us a couple cars back."

Arliss normally waited for me to initiate the conversation, but this time he couldn't help himself.

"And?"

"I dumped the data on him, gave him the ultimatum along with my phone number, and got my ass out of there. He called my bluff. I think we're gonna have to go with plan B."

"Do we have a plan B?" he inquired as if he didn't already know.

"Got any ideas?"

"Now that you ask, actually I do."

"And?" I parodied him.

"I thought we might make him do something stupid, like try to kill us."

That made me laugh. "I think I've just done that, and I've been through that with his son."

He didn't take offense. "I know. But I'm thinking in a public place. Not a casino like how his son tried in Laughlin, but something tougher, with more security than even the Bellagio. Like an airport."

Another piece of the puzzle fell into place. The airport.

It made sense. Big Nicky probably already had my picture from the surveillance cameras and was printing out copies for his headhunters. He would put every man he had on the streets and in the casinos. It was just a matter of time before he tracked me down. I was lucky the first time. I wasn't willing to bet it would work again. Besides, I was in his backyard. I needed to get back to my own turf. I was just the messenger, and I'd delivered the message. Arliss's last word had planted a seed, however.

But now I needed to get the hell out of here, and not just me.

50

"**Take me to** Circus Circus," I said to Arliss. I needed to pick up the Corvette and stash it at the airport. In the short-term lot, so that Big Nicky would think I left in a hurry to someplace far away, which makes sense.

"I don't know. If we're going to punch his ticket, I think we ought to do him someplace more upscale, like the Bellagio," Arliss said misunderstanding me.

"No. We can't fight him here on his own turf. We need to get everybody out of town and reorganize."

He was incredulous. "You mean run away?"

"I prefer to think of it as a strategic retreat."

"It's the woman, isn't it? Now that you've got her neck-deep in alligators, you're having second thoughts and you're going to save her from the shitstorm you created. Is that it?" he said, shaking his head. "Damn, Jake, women are going to be the death of you."

I realized he was right. Now that my plan to blackmail Big Nicky into calling off his psychopathic son had been called for the bluff it was, my first concern now was to get Lucille and Kim out of the line of fire. Usually I only think about myself, but damsels in distress were like a drug to me, even though I was usually the one causing the distress.

"You're right," I told him. "I'll work on it. In the meantime, pull into the RV park behind the casino. I need to pick up my car." He left me alone after that. I called Mo.

"Go to the MGM. Park and go up to the room. The ladies are going to need help moving their stuff. They're checking out."

"You got it, boss," he replied and hung up. I saw his headlights do a U-turn behind us.

A minute later, we pulled into the sprawling vintage casino. It was only a matter of time until it, too, was torn down, replaced by something else over the top, and it struck me as sad that none of the original casinos were going to survive. Land values would guarantee that.

"Take your first right and then a left," I told Arliss as we pulled into the ten acres of bus-sized RVs parked behind the casino.

He spotted my car next to Kim's RV and pulled up next to it.

"Follow me to the airport," I said. "We've going to throw them a curve." I could tell from his look that he was starting to figure out what I was up to. He gave me a nod, and I shut the door.

McCarran Airport was practically in the middle of town, so it didn't take us long to get there. I pulled into short-term lot, found a slot close to a door, and parked. After locking the car, I walked over to Arliss's car behind me and told him to wait for me. I had a phone call to make.

I found a bank of pay phones just inside the terminal. Announcements of departing flights could be heard in the background as I called the Wild West Casino. Hulk answered on the third ring. Apparently, he had many duties.

"Let me talk to Big Nicky," I told him without introducing myself.

He recognized my voice right away. "Let me see if he's available." He was not missing a beat. He put me on hold. I figured I had thirty seconds before I'd have to hang up. Hulk was back in twenty.

"He'll be here in a minute," he informed me.

Right. Like I'm gonna wait.

"Look, I don't have time. Just tell him Tony summoned me and I can't wait around for an answer. Don't call me. I'll call him." Southwest was announcing a departure for Kansas City just before I hung up.

I figured I couldn't make it any more obvious than that, but then I noticed there was no line at the Southwest Airlines counter. I hustled my ass over to it and purchased a ticket to Kansas City, leaving in thirty minutes. Kansas City had a thriving Italian community.

Fortunately, I had no luggage, so the young woman with a tireless smile went for it. Obviously, I was a man in a hurry. I tipped her twenty bucks so she'd remember me if anybody flashed a fake badge at her and showed her my picture.

Arliss was just cruising by the door when I got there. He pulled up in front of me and I hopped in.

"Okay, what's the plan, chief?" he asked as we headed for the toll booth.

It was time to lay it out for him.

"We need to get Lucille and Kim out of town. Mo will take them to Kim's RV. Then they'll head for Laughlin, with Mo watching their six. You and I will hang back to make sure they slip away okay. We can cause a distraction or two if that'll make you feel any better."

I could tell from his grin he was feeling better about the whole thing.

Just when I thought I had everybody covered, I remembered someone I'd forgotten about—JG. I pulled up his number and called it.

"Jake, what a coincidence. I was just about to call you," he said, sounding like he was taking a toke off a joint. "You wouldn't happen to know anything about a black Escalade that's been shadowing me for the last half hour, would you?"

Big Nicky wasn't wasting any time. He must have pulled up the parking lot surveillance tapes from my first visit and made JG's plates. Now they were watching him, hoping to find me. Sooner or later, they'd get tired of waiting and resort to more aggressive tactics.

"My apologies, JG. I suspect it's some blowback from the ride you gave me earlier."

"Why am I not surprised?" I could hear "Hotel California" from the Eagles's "When Hell Freezes Over" concert in the background. Everybody loved that song.

"I think it's time for you to go visit your mother in New Mexico. Did you pack a bag like I suggested?"

"It's sitting in the trunk, bro."

"Can you shake those guys?"

"I'll act like it's my one of my girlfriends."

"Call me when you're free," I told him and hung up.

My next call went to Lucille. She answered on the first ring. "Jake, where have you been? I've been worried sick. Are you all right?" I could hear the concern in her voice. A warm feeling washed over me. I could get used to this.

"Sorry, baby. I'm fine, but things are happening fast. I need you and Kim to pack up and check out. Mo's on his way up to help you. He'll load everything up and carry it down to his cab. Tell Kim to hang on to the cards and the reader. Everything else goes into the duffle bags. He'll take you to Kim's RV." I waited for a response. Not getting one, I asked, "Are you getting this?"

Her concern as a lover evaporated into that of a lawyer. "What's going on, Jake?"

"I think I've just kicked a tiger in the ass, and I need to get you and Kim out of town as quickly as possible. Get your stuff together. Let Mo haul it downstairs. If you can't do it quickly, just abandon it and get out of there. In fact, don't even bother to check out. I'll take care of it. I'll meet you at Kim's. Do you understand me?"

"I don't think I'll ever understand you," she said, hanging up. I think she was unhappy with me. I guess that made two of us.

51

7:30 p.m.

Arliss was one of the few people that I knew who were not felons and therefore capable of buying enough weapons from any corner gun store in Arizona to equip an army. He had a particular fondness for grenades and rocket launchers.

"Did you bring any goodies with you?" I asked him.

"I just picked up a nice vintage RPG."

That was a rocket propelled grenade. Kind of like a cheap bazooka. Instead of BB guns, every male over the age of ten in the Middle East had one of them, or an AK-47.

"Russian, by way of Afghanistan. Only got two rounds, though. But I *do* have some fresh flash-bangs."

Flash-bangs were ultrasonic and strobe-light grenades that cops used to disorientate hostage takers without killing anybody. Unless you closed your eyes, opened your mouth, and crawled into a fetal position when you saw one coming through the window at you, you were basically fucked. Blind and deaf for an hour or so, if you're lucky.

"I think the flash-bangs will suffice," I told him. "Let's go raise some hell."

He gave me a manic grin. "Now you're talking."

"Do you have one with you?"

He reached under the seat and tossed one in my lap.

"Let's drive by Big Nicky's," I suggested. It took us five minutes to get there.

Like every establishment, there was a back alley where all the employees had to park, smoke, and haul off the trash. It was no different with the Wild West. We pulled into the alley and stopped at the back door. I got out and checked to see if it was unlocked. It was. Without bothering to see who was in the line of fire, I opened the door, pulled the pin on the flash-bang, and threw it inside.

We were two blocks away before the first cop car went screaming by. The poop had definitely hit the fan.

"Why do you always get to have all the fun?" Arliss asked after the third slick-back passed us in the other direction, lights flashing.

"Would you rather I drive?"

He thought about it for a moment then nodded. "You're right. You can't drive for shit."

"Okay, let's go back to Circus Circus and make sure that Mo and the girls are gone." I wouldn't be able to relax until they were on the road.

52

Arliss had us there ten minutes later. We had to detour a couple of times for traffic and emergency vehicles. As we turned the last corner, I saw that Mo was throwing something in the trunk of his cab. It looked like another duffel bag.

We pulled up behind him. Lucille was just coming out of Kim's door. The rental car was unfamiliar to her, but she recognized me as I got out. She smiled at first then frowned, obviously conflicted by being both happy to see me but pissed off. The pissed-off part won.

I avoided the conflict by going over to Mo and explaining what I needed him to do while pulling out a brick of hundreds from the wheel well next to the taillight. I could tell that at first he was surprised that it had been there all along, and then he laughed. I used a key on my ring to break the plastic wrap. It popped open like a bundle of insulation.

I pulled two banded bundles out and handed one to him as Lucille approached. "Follow them and make sure they get home safely. Leave your cell on." He nodded and got out of the line of fire. I stuffed the remainder of the bills back into the bag before my lawyer and lover got to me.

"What's the deal, Jake?" It was the lawyer talking.

I handed her a bundle of hundreds. "Things are getting out of hand. You and Kim need to go back to Laughlin, where I can protect you better."

Like any lawyer or woman, she picked up the money and tossed into her purse like it was an inconvenience then said, "Does that mean I'm not going to get laid tonight?"

I decided I was going to hit the pawnshops on the Strip as soon as I could to see if I could find a four-carat flawless canary yellow marquise-cut diamond ring for half price. Maybe I could get one overnighted from one of Arliss's fence buddies.

"I'm afraid so, baby. I'm going to have to stay here for a little bit longer. Mo is going to follow you back home, and I'll be a couple hours behind you. In the meantime, I want you to call Detective Sabbatini and turn over Susan and Earl over to him. Tell him where they're at. That way, you'll be protected. Tell him to personally take care of their protection because his department may have been infiltrated, jeopardizing their safety as witnesses."

"Infiltrated by whom?" she asked.

Whom. Wow, I wondered if four carats were considered obscene or just ostentatious. It didn't matter. She was getting a big ring for Christmas.

For some reason, that thing about the old Nazi floated to the surface again. I remembered how deferential the cops had been to him.

"I think Little Nicky may have somebody in his department on the payroll. He needs to take care of this personally."

I don't think she was pleased with my answer, but I was acquiescing to her demand that I be up front with her, so she couldn't call me on it.

"Also, I want you to find out who owns that half-finished casino past Harrah's," I said before she could ask more questions than I had answers for.

Not only was she a woman but she was a lawyer, so she couldn't help herself. "Why?"

"I think the old boy that owns the trailer park and half of Bullhead City is one of the players. He and Little Nicky have a connection. It's the only thing that makes sense."

She looked dubious.

"Think about it. Big Nicky wants to move on Laughlin. There's a half-finished casino down the road from Harrah's. If somebody has the juice to finish and open it, they'll score big time. I think that somebody is Big Nicky. He can use it for some serious drug distribution. That's where the real money is, and he knows it. The casino would be the perfect drug money-laundering facility. He throws a million a day into the take, he pays the taxes, who's to know?"

I had her there. She saw how it could all come together. After a minute of silence, she said, "How bad is it?"

"As bad as it gets. I'll meet you in Laughlin. Might be a couple hours after you get there. I'll call if I have a problem."

I wrapped her in my arms and gave her my best "I love you" kiss before she could start grilling me and walked away. Humphrey Bogart with Lauren Bacall at the airport. Classic move, and it worked. I was in the car with Arliss before she came to her senses, and by then it was too late.

"That was good," he said as we drove off.

"Guy stuff."

"Yeah, but one of these days, one of those girlfriends of yours is gonna miss and shoot you in a place that can't be fixed. Like your nuts."

"I'm concentrating on the ones that are farsighted," I told him, hoping he'd get off his high horse. I suspected he was gay, but I didn't know how to bring that up to my best friend, a guy that was half a foot taller than me and had the body of Mr. Universe. I'd have to shoot him if he turned on me, and I never carried.

"You want to have some more fun?" I asked.

"What did you have in mind?"

"How many rounds do you have for that RPG?"

"Two. I already told you." I could tell that just the thought of firing one of those babies was getting him off.

"Let me see what I can do." I called JG. He was hot to trot and answered on the first ring.

"Where are you?" I asked him.

"Fixin' to pull into Bellagio's. I was going to dump the limo here and scoot out the back door."

"Change of plans," I said to him. "There's an industrial park a couple miles west on I-95. AAA Storage just before Exit 231. Big sign, you can't miss it. Let him follow you and bring him there in fifteen minutes. Park in front of the gate. We'll be waiting."

"You got it, pal. The towing fee was gonna kill me, not to mention my license suspension. This is much better."

"Trust me, you're going to be on I-40 to see your mama within the hour," I said before I hung up.

We headed up the freeway to get there ahead of JG. It took five minutes. The storage complex was surrounded by acres of flat, bulldozed predevelopment property. Five years from, now there'll be apartment complexes cheek to jowl surrounding it.

Arliss was beside himself with the expectation of blowing up a car, with or without occupants. I have a problem with killing people, even when they're trying to kill *me*. Arliss doesn't.

We parked about twenty yards away from the security gate of the storage complex. Nine minutes later, JG showed up. He pulled up to the gate and waited. He didn't get out. He just waited.

Two minutes later, a black Escalade pulled up across the street and parked. Arliss had the RPG ready. He stepped out, put it on his shoulder, and pointed it. Hell, he couldn't miss from this distance.

I got out on my side, picked up a discarded beer bottle, and heaved it at the Escalade, bouncing it off the hood. The driver stepped out and looked around just in time to see Arliss fire the RPG off. He dove to the side. It was spectacular. The gas tank on the Escalade must have been full because it exploded in a mushroom cloud.

JG didn't need any instructions. He exited the area in a cloud of dust, headed for Albuquerque. Hopefully there was no one else in the burning wreckage, but at least it would send Big Nicky a message.

Once JG was gone, I told Arliss to take us home. We hit the interstate ten minutes later and were in Laughlin ninety minutes after that. Along the way, I called Lucille to tell her that we were behind her.

"I called the detective. He wasn't happy, but I think he's going to let most of the legalities slide for the time being. You know, kidnapping, assault, obstruction of justice. Stuff like that. You need to call him and do some male bonding," she said. "I don't want to have to bail you out when you get to town."

I didn't think it was a good time to bring up the possible federal weapons and explosive charges we'd just incurred. I was wondering if four carats were going to be enough.

53

7:30/9:00 p.m.

As we approached the lights of Laughlin, I called Detective Sabbatini. Lucille was right; he was not a happy camper.

"Your lawyer called," he said instead of hello. My cell number must have come up as PIMA. As in *pain in my ass*. "These witnesses better be good or I'm turning you over to the Feds for a RICO violation, or worse."

RICO was the catch-all federal law meant for gangsters, before the Patriot Act that got anybody *else* thrown in jail without due process for as long as they wanted, the Constitution be damned. I don't generally give a shit as long as the government or any law enforcement body doesn't target me, but that sounded like a threat.

"I guess we have nothing to talk about. You'll read about it in the *Las Vegas Journal*."

That got his attention. "All right, all right. Speak your piece."

"I'm coming back into town, and I don't want to be hassled until you get a chance to debrief the witnesses. I've got other problems to deal with," I told him. "You'll understand why after you talk to them. Needless to say, you need to protect them somewhere that only you know about, because I think the killer may have connections in your department."

I expected some kind of protest from him, but he said nothing, which spoke volumes, so I continued, "The guy behind the killings is Nicky Mosconi, who I think you're familiar with. And I think the old German is involved somehow."

That got me a grunt, which I assumed was an acknowledgment. I could almost hear him smiling on the other end. I knew he had a hard-on for both of them.

"Did you get anything out the hitter from the Aquarius?" I asked while he was chewing on that.

"We will when I parade his boss past his cooked ass. Ballistics should be back today. I guess I owe you for that."

I was curious about something. "Any jurisdiction problems?" Meaning: *You went to another state to grab him?*

He didn't miss a beat. "My kid brother is the chief over there."

That worked. Before he could start in on me, I said, "I'll call you when I hit town." He didn't know we were already there, so I disconnected before he could say anything in rebuttal. I figured that was as much male bonding was going to happen for now.

We were pulling into the Riverside Casino when I hung up. I told Arliss to pull into the north lot, where only the locals parked. It was perfect for staying out of sight and slipping in the back door.

We made our way into the casino without anybody hassling us, cops or goons. Arliss could have taken care of the latter without any problem if need be, but as much as he'd like to, he couldn't beat up any cops.

"What do we need?" he asked as we approached the elevators.

"I need to pack up and check out."

"Why don't you give me the key and I'll clear everything out? Then meet you at the Sizzling Sevens on the way out," he said with a wink. He knew my vices.

I turned around and headed for my three girlfriends—machines SS6200, SS6201, and SS6203. To my dismay, they were all busy, and it didn't look like anybody was going to get off them soon. These were, by far, the three most favorite slots in the house, and I wasn't surprised. I hung around for a little bit just for the hell of it, but nobody was hitting anything, not even triple sevens. That was a good sign. The jackpots were up to $1,300 and above. They were

SIZZLIN' 7S

all primed. I'd drift around and hope that somebody got off their machine.

About a hundred feet away were a bank of quarter machines. I decided to play the Lucky Sevens, which could pay up to four grand on a three quarter play if you hit the jackpot. It also gave me a good view of the Sizzling Sevens, in case anybody bailed.

I put a hundred into the middle machine, which gave me four hundred credits at a quarter. I started playing the max, which was seventy-five cents a pop. At three seconds a spin, that worked out to be fifteen dollars a minute, which gave me about six and a half minutes if I didn't hit anything.

The eighty-year-old white-hair beside me was muttering and swearing like a hooker. Her grandchildren would probably be surprised those words could come out of her mouth.

I hit a hundred-dollar payoff right away, which got me my money back. It also got me a sideways glance from Granny. At least she wasn't smoking. "You from here?" she asked.

"Flagstaff," I replied. I don't usually like to engage in conversation when I'm playing, so I kept it short.

She was not to be denied. "Me too. My kids and grandkids live there too, and they're driving me crazy. Think I'm a goddamned free babysitter on call. Screw that shit. I left town and didn't tell anybody. I may never go back. They're probably crapping bricks about right now."

That got a laugh out of me.

I happened to look over at the Sizzling Sevens and saw one of Little Nicky's thugs walk by, acting like he wasn't looking for me. Daddy must have put out the word to find me after screwing with him in Vegas, not to mention blowing up one of his Escalades. He probably had somebody waiting in the airport in Kansas City just in case I actually used that ticket.

I guess I wasn't going to get to play with my girlfriends—machines 6201, 02, and 03.

I had a feeling my machine was going to hit, so I decided to give it to Granny. I pulled my payout ticket out from the machine then stuck a twenty in.

"I'm outta here," I told her. "I'm leaving eighty credits in there 'cause I think it's gonna pop. We'll split it if it does, and you can pay me if I run into you in Flag."

She looked at me like I was nuts but didn't hesitate to push the max play button. "Thanks, sonny," she said as I walked off. I didn't get a dozen yards before I heard her whoop.

I hope she hit the big one. I didn't look back.

I got to the elevators just as Arliss was coming out, lugging my suitcase. "We need to scoot," I told him quietly as I took the luggage. "I spied one of Little Nicky's boys casing the floor. Go get the car started."

He nodded and took off for the north door. I followed leisurely so as not to attract attention. To my luck, I found an abandoned baseball cap on one of the penny machines I passed by, jamming it down low on my head. Nobody stuck a gun in my back before I made it out the door.

Arliss had the car waiting and didn't waste any time getting out of the parking lot. "Take us to Bullhead City," I told him as I tried to find the strap to my seat belt. Arliss did everything fast.

Traffic was light on Casino Road and across the bridge to Arizona, then thickened as we headed south on 95 into Bullhead City, giving me time to think.

Things didn't look good. Two bunches of mobsters and the cops from at least two states were probably looking for me as a person of interest, as they called suspects that just hadn't been arrested yet. Or snuffed. I wondered if I'd left anybody out. Tony, another mobster who orchestrated this whole thing, was going to be of no help. All the bullshit about me being the son he never had aside, he'd paid me well and I wasn't family. Unless I pulled a rabbit out of the hat, the least I could expect if I survived the next twenty=four hours was twenty years in the joint and no nookie, unless the warden was a woman.

The upside was, I had a shitload of hundreds an enthusiastic associate who loved to play with weapons, a kamikaze cab driver, a lawyer/girlfriend, and a rental car. Somewhere in that combination was a plan. As we drove past the trailer park, a part of it came to me.

SIZZLIN' 7S

"Where's your VW?" I asked Arliss as I looked out my window at the forlorn row of single-wides that constituted the Riverview Trailer Park.

"Parked behind the Tiki Lounge. Ruby said she'd watch out for it," he replied, eyeing the rearview mirror. I wondered if he was just being cautious or had seen something. Before I could ask, a Bullhead City Police cruiser pulled alongside in the outer lane.

Arliss was nothing if not good under pressure. He thrived on it. I, on the other hand, could do without the stress.

When the cop turned his head to us for a look-see, he saw a Black man that wasn't the least bit intimidated by the cop and was, in fact, smiling and talking to his Caucasian companion. The cruiser pulled ahead and went in hunt of other prey. I finally took a breath. At least Sabbatini hadn't put out a physical description of us or we'd have had to make a run for it. There was no way I was going to be taken into custody willingly, and Arliss loved a good car chase.

"Let's go get it," I told him, and for the next five minutes, we sat in companionable silence while I fleshed out my new half-baked plan.

54

10:00 p.m.

The parking lot was practically empty when we pulled around to the back of the Tiki Lounge. The ancient green and white VW van was parked nose out in the corner between the fence and a dumpster, no plates visible. Ruby had parked her pickup in front of it, further obscuring it.

Ruby was working the bar. There were only a couple of rummies nodding off at the far end and a soccer match from God knows where on the muted TV. If she was surprised to see me and Arliss come in the back door, she didn't show it. She merely put up a Coors and a Bud Lite on the counter in front of us and went back to cleaning bottles behind the bar.

Being a longtime student of human behavior, she sensed that we weren't her to ask about her grandkids, so she left us alone. That was good. I needed to talk to Arliss in private. We took our beers to the other end of the bar.

"Okay, here's the deal," I said as we sat down. "I think that old fart Nazi is a player. He's been snooping around Willows, and I think he's tight with some of the cops. He owns half the town, and I wouldn't be surprised if he holds the paper on that half-finished casino across the river from his trailer park. That and Little Nicky's involvement adds up to a conspiracy between those two to move into Laughlin's gambling, using it as a front for the dope money."

Arliss was smiling. He could see where I was going with this. "The only way to find out is to bait the old bastard," he said before I could finish. "With me being the bait."

"You got it, old buddy," I said with a smile.

Arliss's laugh persuaded Ruby that it was safe to approach, and she glided our way. "Howdy, Jake."

"How's it shaking, Ruby?"

"Not as well as it used to, but I still get a bite every now and then," she said with a twinkle in her eye. "Interested?"

Ruby was a hoot. I wasn't sure she wasn't serious.

"I don't think I could handle you," I told her truthfully. "And I've got enough problems already."

She cackled and patted me on the cheek. "I believe it. Since the last time I saw you, there's been a parade of cops, gangsters, and government black suits passing through here, scaring all my customers away. I think that damn van in the back is like a dead deer attracting vultures. What the hell are you up to?"

I couldn't fault her on that. "You don't want to know." I laid three hundreds on the counter. "Here, let me make it up to you. We're taking the van out of your hair. And thanks."

The c-notes disappeared; her hand moved so fast it was blur, her other hand patting me on the cheek again. "Any time, handsome," she said before gliding away. I'd have bet a hundred bucks she had skates on under her full-length tie-dyed skirt.

From what she'd just told me, I figured this place had to be under surveillance, and the sooner we got the hell out of there the better. We didn't bother finishing our beers. We just went out the back door. I had no idea how Ruby had managed to move her truck so quickly, but it was gone.

I waited until Arliss was back on the road before I followed. The old van smoked like a steam locomotive, so it wasn't hard to keep track of it even in the dead of night. I hung way back. Traffic was moderate, but I didn't see anything obvious in the way of tails.

As we planned, he pulled into the trailer park and slowly made a circuit of the two rows, passing by the dark office twice. Just past the office, he stopped for a couple of minutes and then got back on 95 and headed north. I waited on 95 then followed. It wasn't long before an unmarked slick backcop unit passed by me and got on his tail, but not doing his flashing light thing. Just following. It confirmed what I thought: the old Nazi was tied into the cops. At least *some* cops.

Arliss led them across the river to another state and obviously out of their jurisdiction, but that didn't seem to matter to them. They followed him all the way to the Aquarius Hotel.

The cop car hung back as Arliss parked near the front door and walked the hundred feet to the entrance. I parked in the Edgewater's lot in direct sight of both. Only when Arliss walked through the front door did the two cops venture out of their vehicle to approach and break into the van to do a search. One of them scooted under the chassis to plant what I suspected was a GPS tag. Then they went back to their slick-back and waited. All the parts were in place.

Ten minutes later, Arliss climbed into the passenger side of my car, having come by way of the River Walk.

"Well?" he asked.

"Just like we figured. Some of Sabbatini's guys are on Nicky's payroll." I handed him the binoculars. "Not only are they in the wrong town, they're in the wrong state."

I pulled out my cell phone, put the battery back in, and dialed Sabbatini.

"About time you checked in, Jake," he said instead of hello.

Before he could give me any crap, I dug right in. "Two of your boys are hanging out in the Aquarius parking lot, in the next state, surveilling my associate's personal vehicle. I think they're dirty and working for Mr. Mosconi. I suggest you do something about it." I disconnected before he could say zip.

Arliss chuckled. "Ouch. That must have hurt."

"Yeah. Tough love," I replied as I pulled the rental out of the lot onto Casino Road, headed for Lucille's.

55

11:00 p.m.

We made it to Lucille's house on wheels without incident. I had Arliss park near the office just for the hell of it and walked the block to her RV. She answered the door on my first knock and looked relieved to see me. She also looked like she had a buzz going.

My suspicions were confirmed by the empty wine bottles sprinkled among the electronic equipment stacked on every horizontal surface.

"Are we having fun yet?" I asked as she hugged me.

"Now that you're here, we will be. I was so worried about you," she said, giving me a really deep kiss. When we came up for air, Arliss had tired of waiting and gone over to greet Kim. To my surprise, she had a lip-lock on him too. Apparently, he'd been doing some sowing that I had missed. And there I was, thinking he was gay.

Lucille ignored them and started gushing. "Jake, you won't believe what Kim has discovered about the card and the reader." She grabbed my hand and dragged me over to one of the monitors.

To me, the lines of numbers and letters scrolling up the screen were gibberish.

"It's the card's computer code," Kim said, coming up behind me. "It tells other computers what it wants. Instructions."

"How can that be? It's so damned small."

"No shit, Ollie." She smiled. She was lit too. It looked like the girls had started the party without us.

She must subscribe to periodicals that far surpass my *National Geographic* because she continued, "I read recently that an IBM lab was able to store and retrieve digital ones and zeros from an array of only twelve atoms. Until now, that has taken about a million atoms."

"Hmm," I said, trying to look intelligent. I don't know how big a million atoms of anything is, but twelve has got to be *really* tiny.

"The really interesting part is that the IBM people needed to do it at close to absolute zero, not room temperature," she said, holding the card between two fingers. "Whoever made this is pushing the boundaries of the quantum mechanical properties of antiferromagnetic materials at molecular levels."

I didn't understand a word of what she was saying, but it sounded pretty damn impressive to me. "Holy shit!" I said.

"I know. But that's nothing compared to *this* baby." She picked up the Marlboro pack. "Remember the movie *Independence Day* starring Will Smith?"

I nodded. I didn't know where this was going, but I was game.

She held up the APEX card in one hand. "If you think of this as the huge alien spacecraft that hovered over the White House and blew it to hell, then *this* mama," she said, holding up the Marlboro box, "is the mother ship."

Whoa. Finally, she was talking in terms I could understand. *Now* I was impressed.

"And this mother ship has storage capabilities that rival the largest computers known at a fraction of the size. I suspect it may even have satellite transmitting capabilities, but I haven't gotten that far yet."

Lucille squeezed my arm, conveying her excitement. She was excited because her friend was so jazzed, plus talk like that aroused her. Me, I felt like I was going to throw up.

The ramifications of what Kim had just told me struck home, but I asked just to make sure I wasn't wrong, "So you don't think that this came out of the IBM lab?"

"Oh, no. No way," she said, looking at me with a mad scientist's gleam in her eyes. "Somebody beat them to it."

And I knew who that somebody is.

The downside was that, besides that somebody, I was the *only* one that did. And I wasn't family.

The thing Ruby had said about guys in dark suits had been bothering me. I thought at the time that maybe Kim had jumped the gun and spilled her guts to her former employer, the NSA. But I was wrong.

The guys in the dark suits were Tony's undertakers.

This was too big for Tony to let me live. No wonder he wasn't worried about getting the card and the reader back. His undertakers would take them off my dead body and bring them back to him, along with his money.

Lucille overcame my queasiness by sucking on my earlobe. She definitely had a buzz going. The possibility of some imminent wild sex, though, distracted me from worrying about how long I had to live, and I let her lead me into her bedroom.

56

6:00 a.m.

I was up at the crack of dawn, in more ways than one. Ratso didn't help by trying to sleep on his mistress's ample bosom where I had first claim. The thought that this might be my last day on earth motivated me to make the most of it, so I got my ass up and in gear.

After a quick shower, I dressed then pushed Ratso aside and gave my lawyer a kiss, saying I'd I be right back. She nodded and mumbled something about aspirin. If I made it back, I'd bring her some.

Arliss was sitting in the kitchen with two cups of coffee when I walked out. "Where'd you stay last night?" I asked him.

"Harrah's."

"What about Kim?"

"She's still there." He grinned, not giving anything away.

I resisted the urge to snoop. "We're going to have a busy day. Let's get the hell out of here."

Arliss had the rental right outside the door, and we were back on Casino Road in a minute. I told him to take me to the Edgewater. "We need to collect the van. It's at the Aquarius, but we'll scope it out first from where we were last night. If everything looks kosher, we'll grab it. I want to get that GPS tracker and use it, but we can't do it there."

SIZZLIN' 7S

We were parked one casino away with a clean line of sight for the area around the VW. It was early, so there weren't many cars. The Bullhead City undercover car was gone. I wished we could have hung around to see how *that* had unfolded. Cops arresting cops. Probably wasn't pretty.

I gave it about five minutes with the binocs before determining it safe. "Follow me to the Auto Zone by Lowe's," I said to Arliss as I got out of the car.

I wasn't intercepted when I approached the van, nor when I climbed in, fired it up, and pulled out onto Casino Road. I took that as a good omen for the remainder of the day.

Sabbatini knew it was there and could have staked it out, but he apparently hadn't because so far, I hadn't spotted a tail. That didn't mean he wasn't using the GPS tracker that I suspected was hanging off the muffler, but I couldn't do anything about that for the next five minutes.

Arliss was about a dozen cars back and seemed relaxed, so I figured we were clear for now. The Auto Zone store was the perfect place to crawl under a vehicle without attracting attention. Short of dismantling a car, you could probably do anything in the parking lot.

The stores opened early in Bullhead City because 90 percent of the population was over sixty-five, and they all got up at four in the morning, looking for something to do.

I parked beside a pickup truck with a homemade plywood camper top and sauntered into the parts store while Arliss parked two slots down. While I bought a couple of roadside emergency flares, a roll of duct tape, and a small piece of sheet lead, he slid under the VW and found the nine-volt battery-sized transmitter. He had it disabled and was back in the rental before I came out of the store with my purchase.

"Quality stuff," he said, holding up the tracker and a small square battery. "Not your everyday small-town police equipment. Homeland Security maybe. Your tax dollars at work."

"Can you reactivate it?"

He nodded. "Just hook it back up to its power source, and if anybody's listening, they'll know exactly where we are."

I corrected him. "No. They'll know exactly where the tracker is."

"Ahh," he said, sensing some fun.

There was a RadioShack next to the Auto Zone. I grabbed the tracker from Arliss and got out of the car. Ten minutes later, I walked out of the RadioShack with another purchase.

"Okay. We need to skedaddle," I said when I got back into the car. "Once whoever is monitoring this thing sees that it's been disabled, they might move on us, so let's get the hell outta here." I reached for my seat belt. He didn't need any encouragement, and we shot out of the parking lot, abandoning the VW van.

After I managed to get my buckle snapped, I told Arliss to head south on 95, then pulled out my cell and put the battery back in. It crossed my mind that somebody ought to invent something so I didn't have to do this all the time. Then again, there were probably not enough paranoid people out there yet to make it profitable.

I hit speed dial for Sabbatini. He answered on the first ring and had his grouchy pants on.

"Where the hell are you?" he snarled. Not "Good morning, Jake. How are you doing?" He sounded like he'd been up all night thanks to yours truly.

"Never mind where I am. Are the witnesses safe?"

He didn't answer immediately. I could tell he was making an effort to bring himself under control. "Yes. And before you ask, they're being guarded at a location that only I know about."

"Guarded by whom?"

"Two of my best men that I brought with me when I retired here." I could tell he didn't like having to explain anything to me.

That was probably as good as I could hope for. "Have you finished interviewing them?"

"Not yet, but I've got enough to get indictments."

The way he said it told me that one of those indicted could be me if I didn't start playing ball with him. The negotiations had begun.

"Are you going to pick up Little Nicky?" I asked.

"Oh yeah, and a few others."

The few others being you and your two buddies, he didn't say.

This conversation was beginning to remind me of liar's poker.

"How would you like his daddy and the old Nazi too?" I offered.

He thought about it for a minute then came back with "And what's in it for you?"

"Immunity from state and local charges."

He didn't have to think about it for long. It was a no-brainer. He'd interviewed Earl and Susan, so he knew that most of the felonies I'd committed were in Laughlin, Nevada, and Needles, California. I had transported a kidnapped victim through his town, but that was a federal crime and he knew it. He wasn't giving anything up, so he went for it.

"I think I can do that," he said, trying not to laugh. He figured the feds were going to lower the boom on me, so what the hey.

"Plus I want freedom from arrest and unfettered freedom of movement for me and my associates for the next twenty-four hours."

He wasn't expecting that but didn't see the harm in it. Besides, he was probably up to his ass now in paperwork that I had brought about and I'd been put on the back burner. I mean, how much more trouble could I cause?

"Okay, but I want you to answer the phone if I call you. Now how are you going to give me the two old men?" he replied, moving on to new business.

I ignored his question and asked one of my own. "What happened to the two officers at the Aquarius?"

"I cleaned it up. They're in the county lockup, in segregation. No visitors, no calls. I guess I owe you on that one too."

My chips were building up.

"When are you planning on picking up Little Nicky?" I asked so he wouldn't clam up on me. Having to arrest two of his own men on corruption charges must have been humiliating for everyone involved.

"The warrant is in front of the judge now. Any time after that."

"I'd appreciate it if you'd hold off on arresting him until I call you. It'll give me time to put my play in motion."

Sabbatini was skeptical. One in the hand was better than three in the bush to him.

"How long?"

"Give me a couple hours. I'll leave my cell on." That was the best I could give him.

"Two hours. Not a minute more, Jake," he said before disconnecting.

"Drive us to the trailer park," I told Arliss as I pocketed my phone. Regardless of what I told Sabbatini, I took the battery out.

57

8:00 a.m.

When we got there, I had Arliss drive slowly past the office. I wrote down the telephone number next to the office door as we cruised by. I spied a late model Mercedes parked way back in the driveway on the side of the building. It was just what I was looking for.

We made the loop of the park in under a minute and got back on 95, headed south. There was a greasy spoon a half block away, and I had Arliss pull in there and park. We needed some cover.

"Go get us a couple cups of coffee to go," I said as I got out of the car. I had the tracker, its tiny battery, and the roll of duct tape that I'd picked up at the Auto Zone.

I took the sidewalk back north until I was just past the trailer park, then followed the dilapidated wooden fence that bordered the property to the west, toward the river. The tumbleweeds that choked the adjoining property and rocky terrain made it tough going, but I made to the rear of the office without any rattlesnakes biting me in the ass.

Once there, I pried one of the fence boards off and took a peek through. No dog in sight. I picked up a stick and knocked it against the wood just to make sure. Cujo didn't come snarling around the corner and attack the fence. I pulled off two more boards and slipped through.

The Mercedes was only a dozen yards away, and I was under it in a minute. It took me another couple of minutes to tape the tracker and the battery to the frame, splicing a remote switch between the two. I was back through the fence a minute later, pushing the three boards back into position the best I could.

On the way back to the car, I pulled a pound of burrs and goat's head thorns from my clothes. I marveled how everything in this part of the country stabbed, bit, or stung.

Arliss was chowing down on a breakfast burrito when I got back to the car. He handed me a cup of coffee but didn't offer to share the burrito.

"How'd it go?" he asked with, his mouth full.

"So far so good. And thanks for bringing me one too." I was a little peeved that I was doing all the work. Irrational, because I was making all the money too, but I couldn't help myself.

"Hey, you said coffee. You got coffee."

I've been trying to keep my Russian girlish figure, so not scarfing down two pounds of eggs, potatoes, and sausage wrapped in a tortilla the size of a Frisbee was probably a good thing. I let it slide.

He stuffed the last quarter pound into his mouth. "Okay, what's the latest plan?"

There was a beat-up pay phone next the restaurant door. Hopefully it worked, so I didn't have use my cell. "I'm going to make a call, then we wait." I got out of the car.

I was shooting from the hip here, so I didn't know if this was going to work. I suspected Little Nicky and the old Nazi had a connection. I thought that connection was the half-finished casino. If I was wrong, my half-baked plan was going to fizzle, and my ass was probably headed for the slammer.

When I got to the phone, I pulled the number of the office out of my pocket, along with a couple of quarters. To my relief, I got a dial tone when I dropped the quarters in. I dialed the number.

"Yah," the old man answered. His accent was still prominent after more than sixty years in Arizona. "Vhat can I do for you?"

I tried to use my most thuggish voice. "Nicky's got a problem and needs to meet with you. The cops are on to him." Then I hung up.

I peeled some more quarters out my roll and called long distance to the Wild West Casino. Hulk answered the phone. I did my best rendition of Sgt. Shultz of *Hogan's Heroes* fame.

"I must talk vith Nicky."

It was apparently good enough because Big Nicky was on the phone in a heartbeat. "Who is this?" he asked, agitated.

"You know who zis is. Ve haf un problem. Itz your boy. You vil meet me at our building in zwei hours."

"What the fuck is zwei?" Nicky was now even more agitated. He'd obviously had a rough night.

"Two, dumkoff. Bring vhat I need and don't fuck vith me. I'm tired auf dealing vith your incompetent spawn," I spat back before disconnecting.

I wasn't sure if I'd just overplayed my hand, but I'd know in a couple of hours. I walked back to the car, wondering if I shouldn't go grab a good steak somewhere real fast. I might not be seeing one for a while. I was pretty sure they didn't serve them in jail.

If Big Nicky bought that load of bull, two hours gave him plenty of time to make it from Vegas to Laughlin if he didn't fuck around.

"Now what?" Arliss asked when I climbed back into the car.

"Now we wait," I replied, knowing this was going to be the longest two hours of my life.

We didn't have to wait that long. The Mercedes pulled out of the trailer park thirty minutes later. Much to my surprise, the old man did not head across the river to Laughlin and the half-finished casino. I was sure that any meeting would go down on the other side of the river, in Nevada, which would cause major jurisdiction problems with my new best buddy Sabbatini. Instead, Heinrich headed north to Golden Valley.

Golden Valley served as a reasonably priced place for all the service people that worked in Laughlin to live without bankrupting them. It looked like any rural desert valley community with one- to five-acre lots and that didn't have a lot of HOAs. None, in fact, as far as I could determine.

No restrictive covenants, so single and double-wides, half-finished stick-built houses, and Quonset huts competed with half-million-dollar stucco estates. It was the kind of place where nobody stuck their nose where it didn't belong. I realized it was the perfect place to do a bunch of hanky-panky, and no one would pay any attention.

Fifteen minutes later, we were rolling down a dirt road a mile off the highway. The dust was so thick Heinrich wouldn't have seen the Goodyear blimp following him.

The old German finally pulled into an open gate at a barbed wire fenced compound. A large metal-sided building sat in the middle of the five-acre lot. It looked to be a couple thousand square feet with a two eight-foot doors, one of which slid open as he pulled up and then into the building. The door shut behind him. We pulled up a hundred yards short and stopped on the side of the road.

"What do you think?" Arliss asked me.

"Looks like a stash house to me."

"I think you're right."

"A half hour away from a major railroad terminal, ten minutes from one of the country's major east-west interstates, and twenty minutes away from a gambling mecca," I said, running the scenario by myself as much to him. "If I was into a bunch of illicit shit, this is where I would do it."

Arliss nodded. He could see it. He wasn't exactly an angel himself.

I stuck my battery back in and called Lucille. She was awake but didn't sound like she was feeling too good. I probably should have gotten some aspirin for her before I split.

"You were right, Jake," she said without preamble. "The building is owned by an offshore corporation called Berghof LLC, which is owned by a shell company in Switzerland. It took some hacking, but the sole stockholder is Heinrich von Statten, the owner of River View Trailer Park. Berghof. Ironic, don't you think?"

I shouldn't have been surprised that she knew that that was the name of Hitler's mountain redoubt. The Eagle's Lair. I guess the old

Nazi planned on taking over the penthouse on the new casino as his own eagle's lair.

That was all I needed to know. "Thanks, baby. I gotta go. Things are moving fast now. I love you. Bye." I hung up. Lawyer's bill in one-minute increments.

While we were waiting to see what happened next, I got a wild hair up my ass and called Sabbatini.

"Already you're lying to me," he said in way of a greeting.

"Old habits die hard."

"The way things are going, I think you're going to die hard too."

I knew he was pissed, but the only way this was going to work was if I played him, and I figured the timing was going to be crucial.

"I think there's something going down, but I'm not sure what. If you want to take down Little Nicky, go ahead. I'm out in the middle of nowhere waiting on his daddy." I paused dramatically. "I gotta sign off 'cause I think something's happening," I said, shutting off the cell.

"Ain't nothing happening," Arliss said, screwing with me.

"You want to handle the management part of this?" I asked him, not friendly-like.

When he just laughed and turned his attention back to the Nazi's stash place, I pulled out one of the goodies I'd picked up at the RadioShack—the remote to turn the tracker back on. I pushed the button. It immediately started blinking green.

Then I pulled out a receiver for the tracker that had cost me six bills. It took me a minute or two to follow the instructions that the kid at counter had given me. The two-inch screen on the cell phone-sized receiver came to life with a blinking red light in the middle of it. It wasn't state of the art, but it tracked north, south, east, and west within a quarter mile. At least it put me on a level playing field with the trackers. I laid it on the console.

I turned to Arliss. "Okay, buddy. I've just dropped our drawers. If you've got anything incriminating, I suggest you toss it into the scrub brush on the side of the road."

Arliss liked smoking some herb from time to time, and I didn't give him a hard time about it, but now would *not* be a good time for him to be carrying.

"I'm good. I ran out yesterday."

58

9:00 a.m.

We sat in companionable silence for about ten minutes before I couldn't stand it anymore. I opened the door. "I gotta get out of this car before I go nuts."

"Ahh, man. You're not gonna go snoopin', are you?"

"I'm just going to poke around a little bit."

"Just make sure you don't poke too hard," he told me, clearly not happy with me getting out of his sight and out of communication.

I got out and walked into the scrub that took over anything that wasn't a driveway. I liked snooping around because it came naturally to me. I probably would have made a good police detective, but a poor career choice when I was young ruled that out.

You have to be careful when you're walking through desert brush, even in daytime. Snakes are a problem. They hide under the brush, along with scorpions, cacti, and red ants. I moved slowly around the fence perimeter, watching where I stepped. Good thing too.

I was only a dozen yards in before I spotted the first trip wire. Your basic tin can network. No explosives but a low-tech solution to security in an area that abounded with wildlife. It was set high enough so that coyotes and javelinas wouldn't hit it. I scooted under it and got the metal-sided building without running into anything else.

There was a window about halfway down the back side of the building, and I managed to get there without being stung, bitten, or stabbed. I carefully took a peek, and what I saw wasn't what I was expecting.

Two dozen young Asian women were huddled against one wall, apparently having just been unloaded from a van. Almost all of them held a large green trash bag that probably contained all their worldly goods. They looked beaten down and terrified. And they should be.

Standing in front of them, holding a riding crop, was the old Nazi. And he looked pissed.

"Vitch von auf you cows defecated in the truck!" he screamed, slapping the crop against the Luger pistol on his hip in irritation.

The circle of terrified girls contracted, holding onto each other. They recognized evil.

Heinrich started pacing back and forth in front of them, eyeing them like a vulture. All that was missing from the scene was a black uniform along with a cap adorned with skull and bones.

Stopping in midpace, he reached forward and grabbed one of the girls by the hair and forced her to her knees. She was sobbing.

I was pretty hard-hearted, but this was more than even *I* could handle. I knew what he going to do to her as an object lesson to the rest of them. Kill one of them and the rest would follow like sheep. Obviously he'd done it before and was reliving his youthful glory.

If I'd had a gun, I'd have put a bullet right through his demonic skull, then and there. Hell, he wasn't twenty feet away. Even my daughter couldn't miss.

The best I could do was a rock. It lay at my feet, fit in the palm of my hand, and, like David, I hit him hard on the side of the head even after its passage through the one-eighth-inch glass. I think God was on my side.

Not my smartest move.

All hell broke loose. I took off for the corner of the building closest to Arliss, but that was a futile gesture. Two of Heinrich's henchmen intercepted me before I got there, gang-tackling me. Then they proceeded to kick the shit out of me.

Arliss didn't show up to help me out.

SIZZLIN' 7S

When I regained consciousness, I was in the back seat of Heinrich's Mercedes, a thug on either side of me. It looked like we were headed back toward Laughlin. Heinrich was talking on his cell, and whoever he was talking to was getting an earful.

"I don't care vhat you haf to do. Just clean it up!" he screamed into his cell while holding a towel against his temple. Head wounds bled profusely. I'd hit him pretty good. I suspected that there was some glass imbedded in his wound. I was hoping so.

My eyes were swollen, so it wasn't hard to fake that I was still unconscious. Heinrich didn't know I was listening.

"Just do it! Ve're on our vay back. Meet us at zee casino," he said before snapping the cell shut. He was in the front passenger seat. Little Nicky was driving. How the hell Nicky had managed to evade Sabbatini's net was beyond me, but here he was.

"Your father vill meet us. Then vee can resolve our problems."

I assumed I was one of those problems.

"I told you vee should hauf eliminated him at zee beginning. I knew he vas trouble zee first time I saw him and his Negro companion."

Negro? Who says that anymore? Speaking of whom, where was he?

"How do know that zee authorities are snooping around?" he asked Little Nicky.

"I have a guy on the inside. I make his mortgage payments."

"Excellent. Then all vee need to do is conclude our business and dispose auf the trash."

Now I was *sure* he was talking about me. I didn't want to be disposed of.

"What about the girls?" Little Nicky asked, not taking his eyes off the road and the mirror.

"Same price, but leave the von I picked out. I hauf some unfinished business vith her," Heinrich said, looking at his bloody handkerchief. "Vitch I intend to enjoy."

The old Nazi was running a human smuggling operation out of China, probably. Southeast Asia, anyways. Little Nicky was buying them for his dad. The women worked off their debt as sex workers for Big Nicky in Vegas. It all fit.

That was bad enough, but what Heinrich was doing on the side with one unlucky girl out of every batch was beyond my understanding of evil. He'd probably been doing this for three quarters of a century and had never been called to task for it. So many victims.

I decided right then that if I managed to survive somehow, I would kill this man. It was a dirty job, but somebody's got to do it.

We crossed over the bridge between Bullhead City and Laughlin, leaving Arizona behind, along with Sabbatini's jurisdiction. That didn't bode well. The drive on Casino Road to the half-finished casino took about ten minutes, and it gave me time to think.

One thing I didn't have to think about was how deep in shit I was. I knew that when I woke up from my mugging. I guess one of Heinrich's no-necks had put a boot into my already tenderized privates because it felt like I had a couple of cantaloupes down there. At this rate, I wasn't going have worry about a vasectomy.

I didn't move the whole trip. If they suspected I was awake, I knew they would put my lights out again, and I wouldn't have a chance. The next thing I'd see would be Saint Peter, looking eerily like Sister Mary Katherine, condemning me to hell for trying to see if she wore panties under her habit. I knew for a fact she didn't. I think she was diddling Father Richard. At least that took some of the pressure off the altar boys.

When we got there, one of the thugs threw me over his shoulder like I was a two-by-four and carried me across the unfinished parking lot to the only unboarded entrance to the skeletal structure.

I didn't see the cavalry charging into the parking lot to save me.

My porter dumped me in the light of a Coleman lantern. I'd once read that your brain could only register pain from one part of your body at any given time. That's bullshit. My body hurt everywhere.

When my vision cleared, I saw that Big Nicky was waiting for us. He had some more no-necks on either side of him. By my count, it was seven to one. Big and Little Nicky, the Nazi, and four of their entourage. If I got loose, I figured it was a fair fight.

My personal philosophy was that if there was anything better than a good fuck, it was a good fight. Arliss, along with all my girlfriends, told me I was delusional, and I've been getting beat up pretty regularly lately, so maybe I should rethink that.

"Well, well, well," Big Nicky said when he saw I was awake. "If it isn't my pain in the ass, delivered up to me like a good piece of veal. You're going to end up like every other piece of veal I've eaten. In the shitter."

Little Nicky giggled like the psycho he was. Heinrich was silent but had a ghoulish grin. These guys were not my best fans.

Big Nicky nodded to my caregivers, who propped me against the closest steel I-beam and used some electrical 12/2 wire to bind me to it, chest high.

"You've caused us a shitload of problems, Jake. You corrupted my computer and stole all my business data, and God knows what else. My IT guy still can't figure it out. You did the same with my Laughlin operation." He paused to catch his breath.

"You blew up one of my vehicles, almost killed one of my men in the process. And you tried to blow up my casino."

I had to interrupt him there. "It was just a stunner. A little smoke and bang, for Christ's sake."

"Whatever. I had to evacuate the whole casino. The cops showed up. It was a major hassle."

"Normally I'd apologize, but under the circumstances, I've got to say fuck you," I got out before he whacked me. Another tooth came loose.

"And now you've managed to fuck up our entertainment program."

Entertainment program?

"You mean sex slaves?"

That got me another whack. If I kept talking back, I could make a necklace out of my teeth. Heinrich interrupted, "Pull his pants down."

One of Heinrich's boys did so without undoing my belt. I remember my mom's admonishment that I should always wear clean underwear. I should have listened and at least worn *some* underwear.

My nuts were already tender, and I knew they couldn't take much more. I looked down to see if they were still there. They looked like two oranges with a stack on buttons attached.

I took a look at my surroundings. I was tied to a steel beam that held up what would be the atrium in what would be the casino's main room. At this point though, it was rough concrete floors and I-beams and boarded-up with plywood. A piece of marble laid on a pallet of Italian floor tile served as a table. Heinrich was standing behind it, a briefcase in front of him. His wound was still bleeding but less so now, but the veins on either side of his head were pronounced.

He pulled a switchblade out of his coat pocket and came around the table to me. Big Nicky stepped in front of him. "You can have him later. I'm not finished with him," he said, taking the knife from Heinrich. The old man resisted, but it was like a bear and a cub.

Big Nicky took a moment to inspect it. Black bone handle, six inches long with a silver death head SS emblem on the end. He pushed the button, and an evil-looking double-edged blade snapped out, locking into place with a snick.

"Whoa." He held it at arm's length, turning it this way and that. He made sure I got a good look at it too. "Is this what you use on your surgeries, Doc?" he asked the old Nazi but looked at me. Big Nicky must have known something about that or he would not have said anything. I realized Heinrich was even more evil than I imagined.

"Zat is not your concern," he hissed. "But I vill not be denied."

"I'll give you what's left," Big Nicky told him before turning back to me. "Now where was I?" he said, looking back at the stiletto. "Oh, yeah."

He started walking toward me with a grin on his face.

59

11:00 a.m.

If there's anything that I value more than life itself, with the exceptions of my two daughters, it's my cock. When I was kid, one of my father's friends, a young captain in the Army, was fooling around with the daughter of the post commander. When he tried to break it off to save them both a bunch of grief, she cut his dick off after he fell asleep. That woke up him, naturally, and when he realized what she had done to him, he took her into his arms and bled out. She wasn't able to escape his death embrace, and when they found her the next morning, she was a Screaming Mimi.

I understood why he chose not to let her call for help after she realized what she had done. They had insane asylums back then, and I think she did a tour.

I decided to share that story with Big Nicky. I talked fast because he wasn't that far away. By time he got to me, I think he agreed with me, so I went with it. I would have said anything to give the cavalry a little more time to arrive.

Where the hell were they anyways?

"Not make a long story short, so to speak, if you cut my dick off, you'll never know how I can fix this," I told him before he could do any cutting, assuming he could even find my dick at this point. It was acting like a turtle. You couldn't find its head.

He looked disappointed, but in the best tradition of business, he asked, "So what are you proposing?" He figured he could cut my *cojones* off later.

"What the fuck are you doing?" Little Nicky yelled at his father. I'd forgotten all about him, but that wasn't the case with Junior. "Let *me* kill him. That fuck got the cops on me. Without him, they ain't got shit!"

His father gave him a withering look. I didn't think it was the time to get distracted and tell Little Nicky he was screwed whether I was still around or not, so I concentrated on Big Nicky.

"I've got the device that collected your data and jacked up your computer. You won't get it back without me, and you know what that means."

When he stonewalled me, I laid it out for everybody. The Nazi. Little Nicky. Big Nicky most of all.

"The Commission. The feds are the least of your problems."

I could almost see the permutations running through his mind. He'd been cooking the books for years, trusting his numbers were safe in cyberspace. If the Commission, his bosses, had hard evidence or even suspected that he was shimming, he'd better have his affairs in order. Not only that, he was moving into territory that up until now had been deemed out of bounds. I'm sure his move wasn't sanctioned by the Commission.

His next biggest problem was the feds. Convicted under RICO, he'd spend the remaining years of his life in La Tuna, El Reno, or Leavenworth, none of them country clubs. No air-conditioning. No veal parmesan.

Little Nicky started up again, and his father said, "Shut the fuck up!" I figured I had him.

To tip him over the edge, I threw in, "You've got enemies in the organization. Tony wants you gone. That's why I'm here. But I've still got all the cards."

I could tell he was teetering, so I threw out my last card. "You'll have to kill me. You'd be killing yourself too."

"I'll think about it," he said before hitting me so hard I felt like Linda Blare in *The Exorcist*. Normally that would have knocked a man out, but I've found that as I get older, the only thing that gets harder is my head. The big one.

My eyes were slits, so when my head dropped, Big Nicky figured I was out for the count and turned backed to the other two. "While he's taking a nap, why don't we take care of our business?" he said to Heinrich.

The old Nazi didn't look appeased, but like a true businessman, he turned to the task at hand. "I haf zee documents here, if you haf zee money," he said, opening the briefcase and pulling out a manila file. "Zee property vill be sold to von auf your offshore companies for twenty million dollars, hidden by our other corporations. Vee both own fifty percent. Vee are equal partners. Do you haf zee earnest money?"

I was wishing I had a voice activated recorder, but I couldn't imagine where I could have hidden it.

I watched as another figure materialized out of the gloom. Hulk, Big Nicky's bartender. He laid an identical briefcase on the slab of granite and snapped it open, then stepped back with his right hand comfortably resting on the .9 mm under his left lapel. So much for trust among thieves.

I'm no expert in these matters, but it looked like there was about ten pounds of vacuum-packed hundreds in Big Nicky's case. A half million bucks, give or take an ounce.

"As vee agreed, you vill give me zee other half after the building is completed."

"That's fine as long as you stay the fuck out of the way. You get the permit and let my crews take care of the rest. Are we clear?" Big Nicky said, turning his attention to the paperwork.

"Just remember, my people do all the operations," he continued, flipping through the attorney-generated bullshit. He had no intention of fulfilling any of it. He'd give the old man his million, then off him. Heinrich would be dead of natural—or unnatural—causes within a year. The old fuck was sick in more ways than one, and he'd be doing the world a favor.

Normally I'd agree with him, but I wanted to kill the sick old fuck myself.

Big Nicky signed the papers with a flourish and handed them back to Heinrich, who placed them on top of the half mil and snapped the case shut.

"Remember, I get zee penthouse. Now, vhat about your son? I understand zee authorities are looking for him."

The mobster turned his baleful gaze upon his screwup son for a full minute before he spoke. Little Nicky wasn't so cocky anymore. His Adam's apple was bobbing spasmodically, and sweat popped out on his forehead. He kept his eyes down.

I knew that mob guys sometimes eliminated brothers, cousins, and uncles, but I thought killing your own kid crossed the line even for them. But Little Nicky had brought all this down on them, so he was walking a fine line.

"He'll be going away for a while, until this all blows over," Big Nicky pronounced.

Patagonia, probably. Antarctica would be better.

Little Nicky looked like he was about to lose his legs. They were trembling so bad. "Look, I didn't think it was a big thing, the cards. I thought since they were Tony's, you could do something with them," he whined.

Big Nicky nodded. "You're right. You didn't think."

Then he turned to Heinrich. "Okay, let's clean this up. I need this guy to recover that device, so let me handle this and don't say a goddamned word. When that's done, you can have him. Are we clear?"

The old Nazi had no choice and gave a sharp nod before turning his black eyes on me. It was all I could do to keep from flinching, but that would have betrayed that I'd heard everything.

Big Nicky walked over to me and patted me on the cheek. I acted like that was all I needed to come out of my peaceful slumber. Then I puked on him.

It wasn't hard. I'd been wanting to do it for the last five minutes.

"Ahh, shit!" he yelled as he backpedaled.

Spittle was running down into my beard, but that was the least of my problems. "Aww, sorry. Why'd you hit me?" I asked him after I finished gagging.

SIZZLIN' 7S

"You looked like you needed a nap," Big Nicky said, stripping off his jacket and his shirt. He was willing to put up with anything to get what I had. One of my caretakers shed his shirt and coat for him without being asked.

"Okay, here's the deal. I let you live if you give me the device and all copies of the data."

Right. I must look really stupid.

"And don't tell me you haven't done that, because the negotiations will be over. Are you with me here?"

Of course I'd made copies. Unfortunately, two women that I barely knew, and only one that I'd seen naked, had possession of them at the moment. I didn't want to bring that up.

I was pretty good at acting stupid, so I said, "Okay, cut me loose and we can resolve this without any more violence."

I could tell from Little Nicky and Heinrich's body language that they felt otherwise. They weren't going to let me live.

Big Nicky motioned to his muscle to untie me. I was ecstatic when they unpinned me. At least I could pull my own pants up, gently.

"So where is this device?" he asked.

I knew I couldn't tell him the truth, so I lied.

"Stashed at Tres Palms." I guessed I had about twenty minutes left to live, so I figured since my fishing partner, Shane, had been complicit in this entire affair. I should leave some of the doo-doo on his door. At least he'd have some explaining to do.

I couldn't lead them back to the ladies. I was going to be dead before the sun came up, so I was shooting from the hip here. I concentrated on getting the circulation back into my arms, and especially my legs. You need legs to run, and that was the only option I could see. When I got outside, I was gonna run like hell. Better to die running than kneeling, I figured.

I could tell that neither Little Nicky nor Heinrich were happy, but they preceded me out the plywood door that one of the bodyguards held open. I was next to last out, with one of the hired hands bringing up the rear.

The parking lot was the last place I was going to get a chance to hotfoot it, and it was dark. They might miss if I zigzagged some. I was too old and slow to do anything else. We got about halfway to the cars before I decided it was now or never.

I spun and kicked Heinrich's no-neck behind me square in the nuts. I figured since he'd already done it to me, turnabout was fair play. He went down like he'd been tasered.

I lit out for the desert.

I made it about twenty yards before all hell broke loose. Little Nicky was the first to turn and pull his weapon, yelling at me to stop.

Like that *was gonna work.*

He opened fire a second later with a three-shot volley. I heard one go by my good ear. That was followed another couple of rounds from another gun, probably the Nazi's Luger.

Then the sun came out in the form of a half dozen spotlights. Night became day. "Police! Drop your weapons and lay on the ground!" It came from a bullhorn behind the lights.

I kept running.

Apparently, Big Nicky and everyone else decided they would rather just shoot it out. It sounded like a war.

The firing went on about five minutes before dying out. By that time, I'd almost made it to the river, and as far as I could tell, other than brush burns from the creosote bushes, I wasn't leaking significant amounts of life-sustaining fluids from bullet holes.

If anybody was chasing me, they had to be suffering a little too. When I got to the river, I immediately waded in until I got chest high, then I started swimming for the other side.

60

1:00 p.m.

The Colorado River, at that point, maintained an average temperature of forty-eight degrees. Not exactly warm. I was frozen solid by the time I managed to get to the other side. Fortunately, I had a lot more fat than I needed, and that helped with the hypothermia. I figured I was a mile downstream by the time I staggered onto dry land.

I was on a stretch of million-dollar homes with docks on the river. I walked down the river's edge until I found a concrete drainage easement that led to street. I knew more or less where I was, because I had looked at homes here last year. I knew that I was about a mile west of Highway 95 and four miles south of Lucille and Kim. And I was only two miles from the Tiki Lounge.

I headed that way. It took me about thirty minutes to get there. By that time, my clothes were half-assed dry. Fortunately, I had managed to keep my sneakers on during my cruise down the river, but they were still making a squishing sound when I walked into the Tiki.

Ruby took one look at me as I came in the back door and shook her head. She placed a long-neck Coors on the seat closest to the door, along with a shot of whiskey.

"You know I don't drink the hard stuff," I said as I took a long pull on my beer.

"Trust me." She laughed. "I think you need it. You look like something somebody dragged out of the river."

Finally, I had something to laugh about too. I slammed the shot and pulled my water-soaked cell and wallet out of my pants. The phone was down for the count, but I still had a list of phone numbers written in pencil on one of my business cards. Pencil didn't bleed. The hundred-dollar bills held up well too. At least one government agency, the Mint, did something right.

I put one on the bar and asked Ruby for some quarters.

"I don't think I have that many rolls," she said, still smiling.

"Four quarters will do just fine, smart-ass," I replied, which I knew would please her immensely.

Ruby had a fifties-style phone booth in the corner that actually worked. Rotary dial and everything. It took two quarters, and that was all I needed to get through to Lucille. She answered on the first ring.

"Jake. Thank God. Where are you? I've been worried sick!" Her words were like honey. At this stage in my life, I'd come to value people that truly cared for my well-being. There weren't that many. I'd alienated scores. Probably hundreds.

"Safe for the time being," I assured her. "But I need you ladies to move to another place until I call you again. Things are happening at warp drive, and I'd feel a lot more comfortable if you were on the move."

She knew I meant putting her tour bus on the road. "Where do you want me to go?"

"Head south on 95, toward Needles."

"Okay, baby," she said and hung up. No questions. I liked that. I'd pretty much decided she was a keeper. I could overlook the lawyer thing.

My next two quarters went to Arliss. He let it ring for a while, and when he answered, it sounded like he was out of breath.

"Goodwill Industries, how can I help you?"

"Why are you breathing so hard?" I asked just for the hell of it.

"It's a long trek through the brush to Harrah's, asshole. I thought you'd head for the hills instead of the river. I waited too long for you and had to abandon the car when they put a cordon around the area.

I should have known you'd head for water." We'd done this before, at Lee's Ferry on the Colorado River.

"I need you to pick me up."

"Mo's already on his way."

I was surprised. "How'd you know?"

"It was the only the other possibility, given all the variables," he replied, mimicking Spock's voice. I was impressed until he said, "Not really. Ruby called me as soon as you hit the door. He should be pulling up to the back door any minute."

"Thanks, buddy. Are you near the ladies?"

"Right behind them. They're pulling out now, onto Casino Road."

"Stay with them." I watched Mo slip in the back door and look anxiously around. He couldn't see me 'cause I was in the phone booth. "I gotta go. Mo's here. I'll call you back."

"Gotcha."

I hung up and walked back to where Mo could see me. He motioned more with his bushy eyebrows than any overt arm gestures. I didn't bother to collect my beer or my change and followed him out the back door.

The taxi was running and ready to roll. We both piled in and took off. I had him turn south as we hit the main road.

"You got a phone?"

"Doesn't anybody in America?" He grinned as he handed me his.

I could remember a time, not so long ago, that that meant a landline to an answering machine that you checked when you got home after work. Now everybody was attached at the hip. In this case, that was good. I called Arliss straight off. He answered on the first ring. "Triple A, how can we help you?"

"You can meet me at Walmart in ten minutes." It was about two miles south on 95, on the outskirts of town. He knew where it was. It was the first thing he'd looked for when he got to Laughlin. I was more into Lowe's or Home Depot.

"Gotcha."

Now I had a couple of minutes to think about all the shit that had come down. Because of a firefight that my kidnappers initiated with the cops, I escaped with my life. I had always nurtured the thought that everybody was here for a purpose. I was hoping I hadn't already achieved mine yet.

I didn't have a clue what had happened to Big Nicky, his son, the old Nazi, or the Strong Arms. Actually, I was hoping they were all dead. What kind of a dumbass opened fire on a superior police force?

My best guess it was the old Nazi, blasting away with his Luger. I mean, what did he have to lose?

My priority at this point was recovering the reader and the card. Tony was going to be a problem if I didn't. His whole scheme of planting the cards into Little Nicky's computer data had worked, with catastrophic consequences. Two people had died. You could assume more would follow on the mob side. And not only that, yours truly and all my associates were in jeopardy, not counting the women. Speaking of which, I realized I'd better call her.

She answered right away.

She had her lawyer hat on. "So what's the deal, Jake?" Not "Are you okay, baby?" The ring went down to three carats.

"Thank you for moving so quickly," I replied. It was intentional. I wanted her to know that she had eyes on her and that would make her more comfortable, more willing to trust me.

"You're fixing to cross the bridge now."

A little change in her breath pattern told me I'd scored a hit.

Since she was still in her lawyer mode, I knew I had to lay it out on the line. "I just fled the scene of a multiagency arrest attempt that probably led to multiple deaths. Are you with me?"

"Actually, I don't think I have much choice."

"Can I double down, give you another dollar, and get double service?"

"I don't think so, Jake."

I had to give her credit for not knuckling under. "Anyways, I think Sabbatini, and who knows how many other agencies, busted Big Nicky and his son, along with another bunch of shady characters. There was a shoot-out, and I fled the scene." This was the kind of bread-and-butter facts that lawyers loved. Some girlfriends liked it too.

She lapped it up. "I think we're past the point of worrying about small stuff like that," she said. That sentence probably constituted a one-minute billing of fifty bucks. Plus tax.

Since we were on the meter and she was probably taping this with Kim's help, I continued, "I was kidnapped. I escaped and I'm safe for the moment."

That was met with silence. Lawyers and cops know that silence is the great confessor. The other person eventually says something that gives them power. I let her have a little power, along with some adrenaline.

"You and Kim are in danger. The sooner you leave the area, the better. I suggest you head for Needles. There's an RV park just before you get into town. Stop there for the night if you don't hear from me before you get there. I'll call you as soon as I can. I'm behind you, but I've got a few things to take care of first."

I could almost hear the protests that died on her lips. She wasn't in control and didn't like that. "You've got two hours," she said, her lawyer hat firmly in place. She terminated the call before I could to show her irritation.

"How well do you know this area?" I asked Mo.

His white teeth flashed. "I started as a driver in Istanbul when I was a kid. It is twice the size of New York, and I knew all the streets. This is child's play. Where do you want to go?"

61

2:00 p.m.

While we sat in the Walmart parking lot waiting on Arliss, I considered my options. Cops from a number of federal, state, and local agencies were probably looking for me. I didn't have enough fingers and toes to count the number of felonies I was facing.

The only way I was going to be able to shower by myself for the next twenty years was to get the reader back and use it for leverage. Kim probably knew that, and I suspected she was not going to be exactly forth giving of something that would earn her a gold star on the wall at NSA lobby at Fort Meade. I called Sabbatini.

I got a snarled "Where the fuck are you?"

"Floating down the Colorado, trying to keep my cell high enough so it doesn't short out."

"Bullshit. We're tracking your GPS now, and this is not your phone."

"What happened at the casino?" I asked him, not wanting to chitchat and ready to hang up.

"Three officers down, two critically."

He knew I wasn't asking about that, and he was trying to drag the conversation out to get a triangulation.

"I'm hanging up now," I said.

"Okay, okay. Little Nicky was DOA along with one of his goons. Heinrich is being airlifted to Kingman with life-threatening gunshot wounds. Two others sustained wounds. One guy only has ruptured testicles. Fortunately for him, he was on the ground when the crazy old fuck started blasting away with his antique Luger. We're still trying to figure that out."

What he didn't say bothered me. "What about Big Nicky?"

He took too long before saying, "We don't have a clue."

I hung up and took the battery out. I knew that would piss off my NBFF to no end, but I couldn't let him find me yet. I didn't think Mo's phone had a backup reserve.

Arliss showed up right on time. I walked over to the late-model silver Honda as he rolled down the window. Some things you can't discuss over the phone, and nowadays that covers a lot of territory.

I smiled at him. "Where'd you find the ride?"

"Parking garage at Harrah's. This happens to be the most stolen car in the country because it's more common, and the parts don't change much from year to year. Bread and butter for chop shops. Cruise any big box store parking lot and you can swap plates with an identical vehicle. It would take weeks for any database to pick it up. Piece of cake."

Learn something new every day. I quickly told him my plan. It took all of a minute. Wasn't much of a plan. I reached into the back seat and grabbed the plastic bag from Auto Zone then told him to get gone. He nodded and took off out of the parking lot to catch up with Lucille and Kim.

I climbed back into the cab with Mo. "Take me to Little Nicky's restaurant." He could bail at any time at this point and I wouldn't blame him. "Or you can drop me off anywhere," I added to give him an out. He had a family, after all, unlike me.

But I really needed him, and if I pulled this off somehow, I would reward him well. From what Arliss had told me, he could use it, what with the medical bills and all.

He didn't miss my unsaid question: *Are you with me?* And he didn't disappoint me.

"Yes, sir, boss."

"Quit calling me boss."

"Okay, boss," he replied with a straight face.

"It could be dangerous." I had to make sure he understood.

"I sent my wife and kids to see her sister in Los Angeles. I did that the first night I met you. I used the money you gave me. I knew that wasn't going to be the end of it. Now that they're safe, I'm with you," he said as if that was the end of the matter.

We rode in companionable silence until we got to Little Nicky's restaurant. Mo pulled into a defunct car lot across the street without me saying anything, turning off the ignition. Nicky's was closed, his parking lot deserted.

"Big Nicky got away from the cops, and he might be headed here," I told Mo. "He's on foot probably and hopefully out of resources, so he might show up here." It was a long shot, but the only one I had.

After we sat there for another thirty seconds, I asked, "Arliss says that your daughter has some medical problems. Is she going to be okay?" I was genuinely concerned because my first daughter almost died days after birth, and I knew what it was like to think you might have to bury a child.

"She has MS. We are trying get help, but it is difficult with my immigration status. It will be two more years before my wife and I become naturalized citizens, and it is causing problems even though the children are citizens by birth. The doctor bills are taking all our money, but what can we do? She should be on the playground instead of a wheelchair. There are things we can do to slow it down, but we don't have the money."

I could hear the helplessness in his voice. His little girl was dying a slow death, and there was nothing he could do about it.

I patted him on the arm. "Maybe something will turn up," I said. "Sometimes life turns on a dime."

He smiled bravely. "I would like to believe that."

I couldn't guarantee anything if I got killed or arrested in the next day, so I changed the subject.

"By the way, why'd you call yourself Guaranteed Cab?"

He smiled hugely and pulled a book of matches from his visor. "I give one of these to all my customers." He handed it to me. It was red lacquered with raised gold print. "Guaranteed Cab," it read, with the phone number beneath. I turned it over, and the backside read, "If we can't pick you up within five minutes of our promised time, the ride is free!"

I had to give him credit. He was doing all the right things.

"You keep an eye out here. I'm going to sneak around and watch the back door. If you see any cops or something bad, honk twice." I stuck the matches into my shirt pocket and grabbed a flare from the floorboard. It was the only weapon I had available.

He nodded, and I slipped out the door, closing it quietly. It didn't take me long to run across Highway 95 and then Nicky's parking lot. I got to the dumpster across from the back door and set up my surveillance there.

It stunk to the high heavens, but I didn't have a date later on, so it didn't matter. Kind of reminded me my college days when I was a dishwasher at the Italian restaurant down the block from my boarding house. They only opened after dark and used candles so you couldn't see the cockroaches. I got paid fifty cents an hour and all the bread I could eat. Pasta came out of your check.

It occurred to me that even though I was making more money now, my working conditions hadn't improved significantly.

I took in the aroma of rotting pasta, salad, and rancid grease for about ten minutes before I heard two honks. A black SUV pulled around by the back door.

Apparently, Nicky had more resources than I figured. It looked like he'd picked up two more bodyguards, both sitting in front and looking big. They both got out and checked the perimeter, one of them walking to the back door and opening it with a key, then slipping inside. Two minutes passed before he came back out and gave a thumb's up. He turned and reentered the building.

The other thug opened the SUV's back door, and Big Nicky emerged, looking rode hard and put up wet. His clothes, however, looked new. K-Mart, but clean. He and his second minion slipped into the back door.

I was expecting Big Nicky to show up on foot, limping and looking like a drowned rat. Then I could grab him, turn him over to

Sabbatini, and maybe walk away from all this with the minimum of jail time. I didn't know what I was thinking.

I'd just about decided to boogey my ass out of there when I spied an oil-soaked rag hanging half out the dumpster, and a thought came to me. If I could isolate him here on foot then call it in to Sabbatini, it might mollify him temporarily and, more importantly, give me some breathing room, some time to collect my chips and cash them in.

My only option was to do something I'd always wanted to do, but I hadn't ever had a vehicle that I could blatantly trash. I grabbed the rag, crouch-ran to the SUV, and popped the lid to the gas tank. I stuffed the rag into the port and lit it with one of Mo's matches. For good measure, I popped the flare and tossed it under the gas tank.

I thought I was clear until one of Nicky's boys came around the corner and saw me. I guess he was doing perimeter duty. He must have come out the front door.

He was only fifty feet away and pulling his gun. "Hey! What the fuck are you doing?" he yelled while running at me. I took off like a bat out of hell.

I almost made it to the road when he capped off three rounds at me. One of them put a hole in my flapping jacket. The other two went over my head. Recoil probably put them high. A few seconds later, I heard a loud *whoomp*, and a fireball climbed a hundred feet into the sky.

That must have distracted him because I was able to dodge a pickup and a semi, getting across the highway without any more shots being fired. I barely got the door to the cab closed as Mo peeled out of the auto lot, jumping the curb, tires squealing as he executed a sharp right onto the highway.

"Holy shit!" Mo said as I strapped myself in. He was doing real well at picking up American idioms. "What happened?"

"That was Nicky, and he had backup. Thank God he keeps his gas tanks full."

"Which way?" Mo asked, looking in the rearview.

"The way you're headed. South," I said as I pulled out his cell and put the battery back in. When I'd get the time, I was going to ask one of my daughters if she could do the Internet thing and find me a gadget that didn't make me have go through this all the time.

I called Sabbatini.

He was fit to be tied. "You're dog meat" was his greeting.

I was too far gone to be intimidated at this point. "Big Nicky's at the restaurant. If you hurry, you might catch him. He's probably on foot, but I'd consider him armed and dangerous."

"I don't suppose this has anything to do with the explosion report that just came in at that address, would it?" he snarled. He didn't wait for an answer as I heard him barking instructions to someone, something about roadblocks. He was too late. Up to this point, I hadn't shit in his backyard, but I'd crossed that line a couple of minutes ago, and he wasn't going to let it slide no matter what I said.

"Wouldn't know anything about that," I replied then asked a question of my own. "How'd you know where I was?"

"We put a tracker on you, but the funny thing is, it ended up on Heinrich's Mercedes. I'm not stupid, Jake. I know what you did, but that's okay. Just turn yourself in and go quietly. I'll do what I can for you." He was acting like he was my brother.

I didn't think that was a ringing endorsement to my innocence. "How's the old Nazi doing?"

"He's at Kingman, in surgery now. It doesn't look good. An old fart like that probably won't survive a couple of chest shots. Doesn't matter. We did, however, recover considerable evidence of racketeering, among other things."

Like lots of cash?

"Well, this is your lucky day," I told him before he could get back to the peaceful surrendering thing. "If you go this warehouse I'm fixin' to tell you about, you'll find a shitload of female Asian illegal aliens destined for the sex trade in Vegas. That ought to be another feather in your cap, not to mention in your jurisdiction."

I was trying to cash in some of my chips, and he knew it.

"Where is it?" he acquiesced after a moment's hesitation. I gave him the directions to the warehouse in Golden Valley and hung up before he could triangulate me. I figured I had another twelve to twenty-four hours, depending on how busy I could keep him.

When I pulled the battery back out, we were a good ten miles out of town, past any chance of roadblocks. Mo had the hammer down and one eye glued to the rearview mirror.

"You can relax a little bit. I think they've got bigger fish to fry." It was the best I could do to calm him down. I needed him upbeat if I was going to pull this off.

He slowed to the speed limit. "Where are we headed, boss?"

"Are you familiar with Needles?"

Mo laughed. "What do you need to know?"

62

3:00 p.m.

We got to the RV park just outside of Needles without incident, and I had no trouble finding Lucille's ride. It was parked next to Kim's. I didn't see the rental, so I put the battery back in and buzzed Arliss.

"Acme Recovery Agency, how can we help you?" he answered.

"Where are you?"

"You went by me a hundred yards back. You must be losing your touch."

"I think you're just getting better." I paused to let him gloat. "Anything happening?"

"The ladies got settled in without any problems. They're both in Lucille's unit. I didn't see anything hinky on the way in except for a lime green cab a minute ago." He was on a roll. "This place is as quiet as your mom's place."

"Arliss, you know my mom's been dead ten years."

"That's what I'm telling you. It's like a graveyard here." I could tell he was having a good time, but that was all right. I'm glad somebody was.

"Turn around," I told Mo.

I spotted Arliss a hundred yards down a side dirt road, facing us. I had Mo pull up beside him. We talked through rolled-down windows. "Yo," he said, sipping on a can of Red Bull.

We didn't do chitchat, so I replied, "I don't know where Tony's staying, but I'd bet it's the Beverly Hilton. I'll call you when I know. You better get going. You've only got a half-hour head start."

He nodded and pulled away.

"Pull up to that gold and silver bus over there," I said to Mo, pointing it out as he made a U-turn.

When we got there, I walked the half dozen yards to her door, knocked, and tried the handle. It was open. Both of the women looked up as I entered. One looked relieved, the other one was definitely pissed off.

"You're late," Lucille said, her arms crossed and her lawyer hat on. Kim jumped up and hugged me. Go figure.

"Is Arliss with you?" Kim asked breathlessly.

This was good. I was trying to figure out how to pry the reader and the cards from her clutches, and all I had to do was pimp Arliss out. Piece of cake.

"He's close by, watching over you," I whispered into her ear. I actually heard a kind of "Ohhhh" from her. Whatever Arliss was doing to her, it was working.

While she was vulnerable, I shamelessly took advantage of it. "We need the reader and the cards as leverage on a deal to avoid him and I being killed." I paused to let that sink in. "And I promise I'll bring him back," I said truthfully.

Her heart won out over her brain. She turned and walked over to the kitchen island where I recognized the red and white Marlboro pack lying next to a yellow legal pad and a sat phone. She grabbed the reader and an envelope then tossed them to me.

"Bring him back soon."

I turned to Lucille, who didn't know what to think about all that, and said, "Since you're my lawyer, I have to tell you that I've committed a few more felonies since the last time I saw you. Do you need a couple more bucks?"

I think that defused the situation momentarily. Her mouth opened up to give me some shit, but then she started laughing. I walked over and took her in my arms. She didn't resist. We stayed that way for quite a while, not saying anything, before she pulled away.

"How much more of this do we have to go through?" she asked quietly.

Any answer I gave was sheer speculation because I didn't know. What I said was "If everything goes well, another few hours. I'm going to have to go to LA to see Tony. You can negotiate a surrender for me when I get back." *If I get back.*

I was talking to my lawyer now, not my lover. "If you don't hear from me in eight hours, contact Sabbatini. Tell him where I went and who I went to see. He'll take it from there."

She seemed to accept that. Everything was pinned on Tony's reaction. I suspected he already had a hit out on me, so I was walking into the lion's den. I wanted her to know who was responsible if I didn't return.

She gave me a kiss and patted me on the butt. "Well, then, I guess you'd better get going then so you can hurry back."

I turned to walk away but stopped as I passed Kim. "Call some of your contacts at NSA. I think we're going to need their help."

Arliss must have really done a number on her heart because her look of worry turned to one of hope. "I think you're right, Jake. And I know just the right people," she said.

I headed for the door and almost made it before Lucille, ever the lawyer, said, "Just for the record, Jake, what felonies were you talking about?"

I turned and gave her my best smile. "Arson, I suspect. Fleeing the scene, maybe. No murders."

She shook her head, and I scooted out the door before she could give me a ration of you-know-what.

63

I climbed into Mo's cab, and we made our way back to the highway.

I let him do the driving and as we crossed over the Colorado River into Needles, California, and onto the interstate headed west. I concentrated on how to approach Tony. A surprise attack seemed the best way. Call and set up a meet. He wasn't expecting that, so I might have an advantage. It wouldn't give him much time to call back his undertakers. I was an hour ahead of them if they were still sniffing around Laughlin. That didn't mean he wouldn't just have his butler, Leo, do the job though.

I decided I'd wait until we got closer before I talked to him, so he'd have less time to figure out how to kill me. I leaned the seat back and took a nap.

Mo woke me when we about an hour away from LA. "What time is it?" I asked.

"Almost six, but we gained an hour when we entered California, so it's really five here."

I think he was just trying to confuse me, which wasn't difficult. I'd been dreaming, and in my dream, my grandmother was saying, "Jake, you've always been a difficult boy. If you don't straighten up, your headed for perdition."

My grandmother died when I was five. I wasn't sure what perdition was, but from the sound of her voice, it was not good.

Mo looked at me with concern. "Are you okay, boss?"

I opened my window to get some fresh air to clear my head. Boy, was that a mistake. When I was younger, I'd lived downwind from a smelting plant, and that's what it reminded me of.

I rolled the window back up and turned on the air-conditioning. After a couple of minutes, I felt better. Having lived in northern Arizona's good quality air for a decade, LA's pollution came as a shock to my system.

"Jesus," I said, more or less to myself.

"Hah. This is nothing. You should be in Istanbul." Mo laughed.

I couldn't imagine. I pulled out Mo's cell then thought the better of it. I spied a convenience store with a pay phone. "Pull over into that store," I told him.

I always kept a roll of quarters on hand for pay phones. I slipped four quarters into the antique phone and dialed Tony's number. By now, I knew it by heart.

Leo answered. "Who is this?" he said, not nice-like. There was no caller ID number on his end, just an 800 number, and he didn't like that.

"Just tell him it's the son he never had."

I could tell Leo recognized my voice and went into protection mode.

"Hold on," he said but continued to talk as he walked. "Where are you?"

Right, Leo. Nice try.

"Las Vegas, but that doesn't matter. I'm fixing to fly in. I need to talk to him. I've got what he wants." I didn't have a problem sounding really stupid.

"Here he is," Leo said, handing me off to Tony. There was a ten-second silence while Leo held his hand over the phone and told Tony what an idiot I was. I could see Tony nodding sadly, as if he gave a shit.

"Jake, Jake, Jake. You've always been a good boy. Leo says you've got my stuff?"

"Of course, Tony. Haven't I always come through for you? But I've had a couple blips along the way, and I think you need to give me some advice."

I could tell he immediately became guarded. It was subtle, but it was there. "Good. We need to talk anyways. How long before you'll be here?"

"A couple hours. I'll rent a car. Where do you want to meet me?" I asked.

He didn't hesitate. "Beverly Hills Hilton. Call me when you land."

He didn't know it, but I'd already landed.

64

I walked into the convenience store to get something for my growing headache and was surprised to find an overpriced Ace bandage next to the overpriced aspirin. Only in LA. I got a brain fart and bought both. I also bought a pack of Marlboros, three nine-volt batteries, red nail polish, and key chain LED light that was next to the register. The latter was an impulse-buy pitch to women probably, but it worked for me.

When I climbed back into the cab, I asked Mo, "Do you think you can find the Beverly Hilton?"

"I can find anything," he replied as he merged back into the madhouse of LA traffic, perfectly at home. I put my seat belt on.

As Mo merged in and out of lanes and exits, I pulled the reader and the envelope out of my jacket pocket and laid them on the dash. Then I went through my purchases. First, I emptied out the cigarettes from the pack and carefully placed the three batteries in their place. Then I stuck the little LED light, lens up and button on the bottom, off to one side. I closed the lid and hefted it in my hand. The weight was light, and the nine-volts rattled around a bit. That wasn't good. I opened the lid and, taking the small piece of lead out of the Auto Zone bag, folded it in half then cloaked it around the batteries. I closed it and shook it. Much better. The weight was good.

Then I took Mo's Sharpie from his visor and drew two black dots on the lid, using the reader as a guide. When I was finished, I held them up next to each other. The LED lined up nicely with one of the holes, so I punched a hole there. Looked good enough if you didn't look too close, but it was the best I could do on the fly. I pushed up on the bottom of the pack, and the light came on. I dabbed a bit of nail polish on the lens and blew on it. It glowed red. It would have to do.

I placed the reader under my seat and opened up the envelope, spilling the cards out into my lap. I picked out the APEX card, placed the rest back into the envelope, and put them under the seat too. Opening up the Ace bandage, I placed the APEX card on my palm and used the Ace to wrap up my hand and wrist, leaving only the fingers free. Lastly, I pulled my personal Chase debit card out of my wallet and put it in my shirt pocket. If I lost it, it was no big deal. I rarely kept more than a hundred bucks in the account.

By the time I'd finished doing that, we were pulling up in front of the famous hotel. The lime green cab didn't even get a blink from the valets and security guys. I got out without saying anything to Mo. He knew what to do.

I walked into the place like you would walk into a casino, like you belonged there. I didn't make it halfway across the lobby before Tony, Leo, and some nerdy looking guy exited the elevator next to the front desk. They looked like they were in a hurry.

If Tony was surprised to see me when we met close to the entrance to the bar, he hid it well. His eyes registered confusion and then resignation. Only Leo tripped up by instinctively reaching with his right arm into his left lapel. Tony stayed his hand with a sharp glance at him, but it told me volumes.

He was booking because somebody was waiting on me at the airport. When I got whacked, he could truthfully claim he was out of town at the time. He'd get his cards and reader back, and the problem would be taken care of.

And now here I was, fucking everything up by showing up early.

The nerdy looking guy was holding a state-of-the-art brushed aluminum laptop case with all the bells and whistles, and he didn't have a clue what was going on. I figured he was Tony's wonder boy and had developed the reader. Tony was keeping him close.

"Jake! We were just going to a meeting. Why didn't you tell me you were going to be early?"

"Time change," I said to confuse him. It worked. "This will only take a minute, and I could use a drink. Why don't we step in here?" I was already walking into the crowded bar. He had no choice; if he wanted his shit back, he'd have to follow me.

Fortunately, there was a corner booth available with a good line of sight of the entrance. I parked my ass on the end seat closest to the door and waited until they all filed in and sat down. A waitress was there like a shot, and I ordered a bottle of Cristal before anybody could say zip. She patted me on the knee and ran off. When you only have minutes to live maybe, why not go for the best?

I could tell Tony was pissed, and Leo was in the stratosphere. The IT guy couldn't believe he was actually going to get some three-hundred-dollar champagne. He was sitting next to me with Leo taking up the other quick exit position on the other end of the horseshoe-shaped booth. The brushed aluminum Swiss laptop case was lying next to my right hand, closer than I had hoped.

Tony didn't waste any time. "You got my stuff?"

"Yeah," I said, taking the bogus pack of Marlboros with my left hand and brought it down with a satisfying clunk on the glass table. It was heavy and had the desired effect. Tony's eyes went to it with only the slightest tell, but I could see he was going for it.

"But I got a few things I need to clear up first." I pulled out my Chase debit card while pushing on the bottom of the cigarette pack. I laid the card on top of it, my hand over it and out of his reach.

I could see it took an effort for him not to have Leo just shoot me right there. He tore his look from the box and concentrated on how to get it out of my hands. *Then* he could have Leo whack me.

He was all concern. "What's the problem, Jake?" This guy missed his call as an actor. He had Marlon Brando beat all to hell. I pushed the bottom again to turn off the LED, still keeping my hand over the Chase card. All he could see was its blue color.

"Just a few minor things, and I really hate to bother you about them."

He waved it away and waited. Leo looked like he was on a short leash and was watching me with dead eyes. The waitress chose that time to show up with the champagne. I let the IT guy do the taste test.

She bent over to give him a good cleavage shot while she poured. He looked like he was in seventh heaven and wasn't paying any attention when I helpfully used my bandaged right hand to move the computer case out of the way for him so he could get a better shot at her hooters. I had my hand on it for about five seconds. I hoped it was enough.

Only Tony looked alarmed but didn't interfere when I moved my hand back.

When the waitress moved off, Tony repeated, "What problems?" There was a touch of suppressed menace in his voice.

"I did what you paid me to do," I said, moving the fake reader back and forth with my left hand like a nervous tic. I could tell it was distracting him.

"I knocked Big Nicky out as a player, and I'm getting a lot of flak. He's trying to kill me as a result." I held up my bandaged hand like it was a bullet wound. "I'd like to know why, exactly." Tony considered me for so long, I thought maybe he hadn't heard me. Then I guess he decided I was more like the stepson that he'd never had, and since I was going to die anyways, at least I deserved the truth.

"My associate here in LA and I are going to do a sort of *merger*."

I never thought Tony was here because Francine wanted to go shopping and see the grandkids. The last piece fell into place. The Phoenix and LA families were coming together, controlling the entire southwest.

The only problem was Little Nicky, working point for his old man who wanted into Laughlin, which up until now had resisted mob influence.

"If Big Nicky succeeded in reviving the unfinished casino, he would cut into our business by a third. He was trying to claim what was previously agreed by the Commission to be untouchable. It woulda started a war. Therefore, he had to be stopped." He gave me a grim smile. "That's where you came in. You were there, you've done work for me before, so you got the job."

Lucky me.

"We have also branched out into new businesses, moving into the twenty-first century," he added, glancing at the brushed aluminum case.

Yeah. Computer fraud, identification theft, not to mention ripping off every casino on the planet.

"How did you know your card would be lifted?" I asked.

He gave me a grim smile. "Let's just say we been keeping an eye on him and his associates for some time."

He waited for me to ask. So I did.

"You set him up." It wasn't a question.

His smile disappeared. "Does the Commission know about your new enterprises?" I was stalling, and he knew it.

"That's none of your business." He held out his hand. "And it's time to conclude ours."

I saw the two guys as they walked into the bar from the lobby. A Black and a Hispanic with buzz cuts and dark suits, white shirts, and spit shines. One of them pulled out a badge and flashed it at me. "FBI, Mr. Leggs. I'm Special Agent Hernandez. You're under arrest. Please stand up and turn around."

The only thing I could think to say was "What the hell for?"

The Black agent did the honors. "Where do you want me to begin? How about we start with kidnapping, interstate flight to avoid prosecution, weapons violations…tell me when to stop."

I was facing Tony and still had the Marlboro pack in my hand until Agent Hernandez cuffed me and I dropped it, along with the card. He "accidentally" stepped on the Marlboros, and it made a satisfying crunch, unlike fresh tobacco. Then he made a display of picking them both up and putting them into his jacket pocket. "Oops. Sorry, Jake. But that's okay, you won't be needing them," he said with a smile. "Where you're going, there's no smoking allowed, and they don't take credit cards."

I only got one quick look at Tony. He looked mortified. The IT guy looked like he was going to throw up. Then the two agents frog-hopped me out of the bar, through the lobby, out onto the sidewalk, and around the corner. Very embarrassing.

It wasn't until they stuffed me between them in the back seat of the lime green cab that I dared to believe that Arliss had pulled it off. He and Mo were sitting in the front seat.

"These are my cousins, Tito and JT," Arliss said as Tito undid my cuffs and put them back on his belt. Mo did a U-turn and hauled ass out of the area.

"Holy shit, Arliss. I gotta tell you, I was pretty convinced they *were* FBI."

"Actually, they're both are in law enforcement. Military, CID, and they just happened to be home on leave from Iraq. Big family reunion this weekend." He was grinning from ear to ear.

I shook hands with both of them. "You guys were very impressive, and I can't thank you enough."

JT waved it off. "Our aunt, Mama Rose, is in town and said to take care of you."

"And you know Mama Rose," Tito added, handing back my debit card.

Arliss's mom. A formidable woman who made the meanest donut in Flagstaff. Curious, I asked, "Where are you guys based?"

"Right down the road, Twenty-Nine Palms," Tito said. "That's why it happened to fall into place. Logistics and timing just happened to be right."

Now I knew where Arliss was getting his toys from.

Twenty-Nine Palms was the massive Marine training base halfway between LA and Laughlin. Arliss must have picked them up on his way to LA. When I'd told Arliss that I'd planned to meet with Tony, the only thing I asked was for him to somehow extradite me from that meeting, hopefully not bleeding from too many holes. I didn't care how he did it—that was up to him. Hooking up with his cousins was nothing short of a miracle. I normally didn't believe in miracles.

I must have nodded off from the aftereffects of so much adrenaline, because the next thing I knew, we were pulling up next to a plain brown late model Ford parked in a deserted strip mall in Twenty-Nine Palms.

After Tito, JT, and I exchanged the required fist bangs, they hopped out and went through a complicated ritual with Arliss, who had gotten out to see them off. Nothing like family when it comes down the nut-crunching.

I noticed as we drove off that the Ford had government plates and a security barrier between the front seat and back. A little antenna protruded from the trunk lid. Definitely not a rental.

I let that sink in while Arliss filled me in on all the details of calling ahead to his aunt's house to see if any of his fifty streetwise cousins were hanging around and hit the jackpot. His aunt gave him JT's cell number, and one thing led to another. The cousins were bored, itching for some action, and readily agreed, helped along by their mom's sister, Mama Rose. Plus, Arliss promised them some weed.

Arliss picked them up, and they cooked up the plan on their way into LA. They were dressed in their suits and used their own creds, but with Tito putting a finger over the seal that identified their agency. It wouldn't hold up under scrutiny, but it was just for flash before the wham, bam, thank you, ma'am, and out the door.

I must be getting too old for this shit because I nodded off again. Next thing I knew, Arliss was poking me in the shoulder.

"Wake up, Jake. We're getting close to Needles. How do you want to play this?"

"Give me a minute here," I said, trying to get wool out of my brain. My grandmother had been giving me another talking-to while I was asleep, but damned if I can remember what she was trying to impress upon me in the dream. I did, however, remember the one word she kept repeating. I felt unsettled. That's the problem with dreams. Most of them don't imprint, but they leave you with the ghost of a feeling.

"What's the definition of *perdition*?" I asked no one in particular. That was the one word I could recall from the dream, and I was pretty sure it meant something unpleasant.

Mo looked at me in the rearview mirror. "It is said to be the capital of hell, boss."

Great.

I decided to call Lucille and let her know I was alive. It was getting close to the eight hours. She answered on the second ring and sounded relieved when I said hi. Also slightly annoyed. Only women had that talent.

"Where are you?" she asked after she took a breath.

"On my way back." I tried to keep it brief and businesslike, since I assumed that somebody was out there somewhere, listening. By now, I had to be on *everybody's* radar.

Sensing that nothing more was forthcoming from my end, she dived right in. "Kim got a hold of some of her *friends*. They are currently en route."

This was not good. "How soon?"

She hesitated for a moment. "Could be here any time." Her lawyer voice was firmly in place.

"Thanks, baby," I said to my lover and disconnected. I didn't have much time, and information was power, so I called Sabbatini.

"Well, well, well. Speak of the devil" I got instead of hello.

When I didn't rise to the bait, he continued, "I just got a visit from some spook agency suits that told me I can't have your ass. They were going to take you into *protective custody*. A matter of *national security*, they said. My brother got a visit too. What a crock of shit."

I let him vent because he'd already given me some good information. Kim's NSA protégées were already inbound. The question was, how far away were they?

"Did you find Big Nicky?" I asked to sidetrack him.

He took a moment to respond. "We busted him and one of his associates trying to boost a car a couple blocks away from the fire. We found another associate concussed and burned near the scene of the fire."

I naturally assumed he meant the SUV. That was why he had quit shooting. He'd gotten blown out of his shoes when the gas tank went up. Tony and his remaining bodyguard had then abandoned him and gotten busted trying to steal another car. Good, that took care of Nicky.

"Damned shame about the building, though."

Building?

"Seems the gas tank from the vehicle landed on the roof and spilled its contents everywhere."

Jesus. "The building was totally engulfed when the first fire units responded. Damned shame. The only decent Italian place in town." He waited a couple of beats to give me the coup de grâce. "But I think we got some good video from the ATM across the street. I'll get to the bottom of it, you can bet your ass." I could almost see him smiling at the other end.

I guess I wouldn't be picking up my winnings from Jimmy anytime soon.

Well, shit.

"In the meantime, until you come clean with me, I better not see your ass in my town or I'll bury you so deep in county jails, even your mama won't find you."

"My mom's dead," I told him.

"Well, there you go," he said. "Stick a fork in you."

"Call me when I can come back. Just for the hell of it, how long ago did they leave?"

I guess the gold stars he was getting out of this whole relationship outweighed the pain in the ass I was giving him, so he said, "They just walked out of my office. Do us both a favor and go somewhere else for a while."

He didn't say goodbye.

65

We were already across the river and into Arizona, approaching the road to the RV park. The realization that we were back in Sabbatini's jurisdiction wasn't lost on me.

I had Mo pull up the dirt road that led to Lucille's RV. As Arliss and I got out, I told him to pop the trunk, and I retrieved the canvas sack from the wheel well while Arliss grabbed some of his prized possessions. I pulled out two vacuum-packed bundles of hundreds and handed them to an astounded Mo through the driver's side window.

"Use this to take care of your kid. I would strongly suggest a month-long vacation somewhere for the whole family as well, starting as soon as you can get them in the cab." I told him before he could start blubbering. "I'll call you next time I'm in town. Now get out of here." I banged my hand on the roof of the car.

He smiled through his tears, nodded, and wasted no time doing a U-turn, boogying down the highway back to his sister-in-law's place in LA, where his family was hiding out.

Arliss and I hoofed it the hundred yards to Lucille's front door in silence. Just before we got there, Kim came tearing out the door, down the steps, and threw herself into his arms. It was like one of those sappy movies where a couple rushed into a lip-locked embrace. Apparently, Kim wasn't just a hit-and-run for Arliss.

I headed for the open door and almost made it up the two steps when Lucille appeared in the doorway. A gamete of expressions played across her face. Relief, then love, followed by anger.

Nevertheless, she grabbed my head and stuffed it between her tits, kissing the top of my head. When she wrapped her legs around my waist, we both fell into RV and onto the carpeted floor in front of the door. I managed to fight my way up to her lips and the missionary position. We played with each other's tongue until we had to breathe.

Kim cleared her voice behind us and said, "For God's sake, woman, try to have a little dignity."

Lucille burst out laughing and tossed me off her with a practiced maneuver. I think there was some cowgirl in her. I helped her up while she finger-combed her hair.

Kim walked through the now open door, dragging Arliss. He looked pussy-whipped too.

"My contacts from my previous employer should be here anytime," she said, going to the kitchen island and depositing Arliss in one of the stools. "So if there's anything you want to do, you better do it now."

"There're one or two things I need," I responded as Lucille came up from behind and hugged me. I pulled the reader out of the canvas bag, turned to her, and put it in her hand. "As my lawyer, I'm entrusting this to you."

I turned back to Kim, unwrapping my Ace bandage. The APEX card dropped out of my palm and onto the countertop. I pushed it across to her and asked, "Can you access the data on this card without using the reader?"

"Sure. The reader is a storage and transmitting unit, but the card can access any computer independently," she said, picking up the card and taking it over to one of her laptops set up on the range top. A printer and a ream of paper sat next to it.

"What about the reader?" she asked as she booted up the laptop. "They're going to want it."

"They can have it. It's been nothing but a pain in the ass so far. I'll leave it up to my lawyer to negotiate an amicable solution." We were negotiating, so I wanted her to know that her friends could *have* the damned thing, but I needed some tit-for-tat here.

"What do you want?" she asked.

I thought she was talking long-term. "Immunity from prosecution. State and federal," I said confidently.

She looked at me. "No, dummy. What do you want me to do with *this*?" she said, holding up the APEX card. That was punctuated by my lawyer cuffing me on the back of my head.

"Print me a copy of whatever the card retrieved, if anything, and do a flash drive," I told her. "And hurry, please. I don't think we have much time."

I turned back to Lucille and took her in my arms. "Use all your legal skills to get me the best deal you can. I'd prefer not to do any time. It wasn't pleasant the first go-around, but I'm all in for community service," I whispered in her ear. "They can have the reader, but I can't testify about anything or anybody involved. That's nonnegotiable."

She nodded. At that moment, she was both lover and lawyer. I was leaning toward a five-carat canary yellow flawless presented at sunset on some Mexican beach.

A minute later, the upload was complete, and the printer was methodically spitting out sheets. I went over and picked up my card and the thumb drive.

Arliss finally came out of his daze and asked, "What do you want me to do when they show up?"

"Not be here when they show up," Kim jumped in before I could reply. She walked over to him and handed him her keys. "They don't know about you, and let's keep it that way. You're mine alone," she said with a smile. "Go to my place and wait. Leave your cell on. I love you."

Arliss was a big dude, but he looked like a puppy as she pushed away from him. I took that as a good time to get my own licks in. I picked up the canvas bag and handed it to him, along with the keys to my 'vette.

"Hang on to this for me, will you?" I said as I guided him to the door. The sooner he was out of there the better.

The printer quit doing its thing by the time I got back to the kitchen. Kim was at the front door, watching to make sure Arliss made it to her RV, and Lucille said all this excitement made her want to go pee, so she was in the john. Nobody was looking. There were about thirty pages or so in the hopper when I pulled them out. I didn't know if the five seconds had been enough, but it looked like it had been long enough to pull a shitload of stuff out.

It was all encrypted, which was to be expected, but I knew what it would say decrypted. It was Tony's books. Not only that, information about his *merger*. Devastating information in the wrong hands, the top two being the Commission and the feds, in that order.

What I had in my hands was radioactive. And I needed to get as far away from it as I could.

So I stuck it in the oven. The broiler part. I put the card and the thumb drive in my jockey strap. It was excruciating, but a man's got to do what a man's got to do.

66

Good thing too, because there was a serious knock on the front door, and the two men didn't wait for Kim to open the door for them.

They were both older men in suits and looking formidable. Kim obviously recognized them and shook their hands. Neither of them showed IDs.

"Good to see you again, Kim," the older of the two said. He looked to be in his seventies, but fit.

"You too, Mr. Director." She had the demeanor of a schoolgirl. Whoever he was, he had her respect. She turned her attention to the other man, extending her hand to him. "It's been a long time, Abel."

"Too long, Kim. We miss you at the institute." He paused while holding her hand a tad too long, and that tensed her up. She didn't like the pause. She didn't like him. It struck me that at one time, they had been more than friends.

Abel turned his attention to me. "Is this the gentleman you spoke to me about?" he asked. The way he said *gentleman* didn't exactly sound complimentary, but I let it go. He gave me a bureaucratic smile. I disliked him right off the git-go. Besides, if Arliss's main squeeze didn't like him, I didn't like him either.

When she didn't respond—we all knew it was rhetorical—he continued like this was a board meeting. "I understand you are in possession of some revolutionary computer hardware. I, for one, am skeptical of Ms. Chan's claims, but given her long and innovative career with our agency, we decided to take a closer look." He ended that sentence with both his palms up like *your move now.*

I didn't like dealing with underlings, so I turned to the man Kim had called Mr. Director. That, and the way she deferred to him, told me he was Mr. Big. The head nacho. The top dog.

"What my lawyer has in her possession is a computer light-years ahead of what even DARPA can come up with."

I saw that I had the director's attention. I must have hit a nerve because from Abel's body language, I figured he must be somewhere high on DARPA's chain of command.

"Funny you should say that," the director said, uttering his first words and glancing at his associate. It wasn't a nice look, more like *Okay, stupid. I'm taking over now.*

His smile was a lot more sincere than Abel's when he turned to me. "Kim said it had broken the barriers existing technology by a factor of ten."

I shrugged. "She knows more about it than I do. My problem is that I'm trapped between a rock and a hard spot," I said so he would know that I had problems other than technological ones. "You can have the device. I don't want to go into witness protection. I'll take my chances after you and my lawyer come to terms." Lucille stepped up beside me and took over.

"I'll handle it from here," she said, placing a hand on my arm.

I was more than happy to let her do her thing. Now it was up to her to keep my ass out of jail, so I walked over and looked out the front window. A black Navigator was parked there. A guy that looked like a young Clint Eastwood was leaning against the passenger side door, staring back at me. We stared at each other for a couple of minutes before I blinked.

I had a sudden urge to relieve my bladder. I glanced across the street to Kim's RV. The lights were off. Clint didn't know he was probably on Arliss's sniper night scope.

When I walked back into the kitchen, all four of them were huddled around a pair of monitors set up of the island countertop. What they were watching looked like gibberish to me, but they seemed enthralled.

I was pretty much a Luddite, having only recently been dragged into this century by my last ex-wife. She bought me a top-of-the-line laptop last year, with all the bells and whistles. I still couldn't get my e-mail without assistance.

"So your client is willing to sign a nondisclosure agreement in return for immunity?" the director was saying.

"For him and all of his associates. He won't go to the newspapers if you let him slide. Most of the charges are state and local. The kidnapping charge is bullshit. I'm sure you can handle that. But he won't testify to anything, period. He'd rather go to jail, and you know where that will lead. And he doesn't want witness protection," Lucille said to the director, ignoring Abel.

"How about we just kill him?" Abel suggested to the director. "Or throw him into one of our black holes. He'll disappear, and so will the problem."

Lucille reached over and grabbed him by the lapels. "Then you better kill me too, you pompous prick," she said with her face inches from his. I think she was capable of kicking his ass.

Kim leaned into his ear. "And me too, shit-wad. And you know that'll be considerably harder." Ratso suddenly shot out from under the table and took a chunk out of Abel's ankle. He tried to act like he didn't notice.

If the director was alarmed by this display of female and canine solidarity, he didn't show it. He merely said, "Abel, shut the fuck up and go sit in the car."

The look on Abel's face was priceless. Nobody talked to him like that, you could tell. Except maybe the man who could make *his* ass disappear with just a word. Red-faced, Abel limped out the door with as much dignity as he could muster.

The director ignored him and turned to Kim, who was calmer now and sitting down. Ratso had disappeared back under the table. "Is this device capable of all you've told me?" He was holding up the Marlboro box.

"I don't think I've even scratched the surface of its capabilities, sir," she replied, all business.

"I understand there are some cards too."

"I'm afraid they were lost during an altercation earlier this evening," I interrupted before Kim could answer. She raised her eyebrow at me but otherwise said nothing.

The director studied me for a minute, apparently deciding he could pursue that later, and turned his attention back to Kim.

"Would you be willing to return to the institute and supervise the inspection of its capabilities?" he asked. When she hesitated, he added, "There's going to be some changes in the institute's management." He glanced to the door. "You'll be given carte blanche."

It took about a millisecond for her to make a decision. "I'll need a week to get my affairs in order."

I thought that was pretty funny. Arliss was one of her affairs.

"That'll work," the director agreed, turning to Lucille. "In that case, councilor, I think we have a deal. We keep this"—he held up the reader—"your client keeps his mouth shut upon penalty of death, and I don't want to read about this in the *New York Times*. Otherwise, he'll vanish. Does that about cover it?"

"Eloquently put," Lucille replied, putting out her hand. I liked that. It reminded me of the days when a handshake was all that was needed to seal a deal. When you're dealing with people that could have you killed with a wink and a nod, paperwork is superfluous.

He shook her hand, put the reader in his coat pocket, nodded to Kim, and walked out the door. He didn't say goodbye to me. Anybody else, it would have hurt my feelings.

67

All three of us breathed a sigh of relief when the door shut. Both of the women slumped down onto their stools like they'd just run a 5k. Me, I still needed to go to the bathroom.

When I finally came out of the john, it reminded me of when I was a kid and I'd come home from school to see the contents of the house boxed up and ready for yet another move. As an Army brat, I'd gotten used to it.

"I'm getting the hell of here," Kim said as she stuffed electronics into a duffel bag. Lucille was busy putting monitors back into the boxes they came in when we bought them yesterday. Kim looked up and said, "Well, don't just stand there. Start boxing up some of this shit."

Sheesh. Grabbing the box that one of the printers came in, I headed for the kitchen. "What's the hurry? They're gone."

Kim stopped what she was doing. "The director will be on a plane within the hour. I'd bet a thousand dollars that he'll fire Abel on the way back to the airport. Abel will come right back here looking for a little payback, but by then I'll be gone."

"He'd actually kill you because you got him fired? Who is this guy?"

"The head of DARPA and my former boss for a while. We had a short relationship, which I broke off. Workplace romances don't work out. Besides, he's a control freak. He took it badly, to say the least. The abuse started at work, then he started stalking me. When I obtained a restraining order against him, he had me fired. I sued for sexual harassment and wrongful termination, and won."

She didn't say how much. It was a wonder the stupid bastard still had his job after all that, but tonight was probably the proverbial straw. And not only that, she'd apparently taken his job now.

Yeah, that might drive a man to kill. I could just imagine this guy sticking a gun in her face and screaming, "Die, bitch!"

"Why did you invite him in the first place?" I asked her. It didn't make sense.

"I didn't. I thought the director, my mentor and the head of the NSA, was bringing the head of the FBI's computer lab, but I guess he was cleaning house instead. Regardless of what he put me through, this was a failure on Abel's watch. This technology had to have come from somewhere in DARPA. Probably one of the hundreds of research scientists they employ or contract. But access to facilities and the equipment is vital, and there are very few places that meet those parameters. I'd bet one of Tony's associates snared an overlooked genius on gambling debts, Tony bought his paper, and made him an offer he couldn't refuse."

Yeah, I could see it. That was why Tony's IT guy was crapping in his pants when Agent Hernandez confiscated his baby. He knew that it would eventually be traced back to him through the equipment needed to create it.

"Why did you lie about the card?" Kim asked, resuming her packing. Lucille stopped and looked at me, as if *she* had asked the question.

"I don't know why, actually," I replied truthfully. "But I've always had this belief that you never show all your cards, no pun intended. I just felt that I needed to hang onto to it for a while longer. A gut feeling."

"You can't keep it, Jake. He *knows*, and if I'm to get his agreement on paper, which I'm obliged to do, he'll want it eventually," Lucille said.

"How about I turn it over to you in a week or two, and you can return it to the proper authorities," I replied, nodding in Kim's direction. "It'll be her baby anyways."

Kim looked at her friend and said, "That'll work."

Lucille smiled at me like I'd done a good thing. I called Arliss and told him to get his ass across the street and bring a handcart.

He was there in two minutes, but no handcart. Kim met him at the door, and they did their love thing again for what seemed like an eternity. I went over and started rubbing on Lucille. She rubbed back. It was a love fest.

Once everybody was happy, we got down to business.

"You men start taking all these boxes over to my place." Kim was obviously comfortable ordering men around, and Arliss, for one, didn't seem to mind. "Lucille, you and I will make sure we didn't miss anything. I want to be out of here in fifteen minutes, girl."

They got to work while Arliss and I hustled duffel bags and boxes from one land cruiser to the other. When we got to Kim's with our first load, I said to Arliss, "Where's the bag I gave you?"

"Right here," he replied, pulling the canvas sack from the closet next to the door.

I set the bag on the floor and pulled out the broken bundle of hundreds. I split it in half and handed one to Arliss.

"Should be close to twenty grand there." I handed him the keys to my 'vette that was parked at the Las Vegas Airport. "Keep an eye on Kim, and pick up my car when you get to Vegas. I'm gonna be gone for a while, but I'll call you when I can. Thanks for everything."

Arliss put the twenty grand in one of Kim's kitchen drawers before saying, "My momma would have my ass if I didn't keep you safe. Besides, I kind of like the excitement."

Excitement? I pulled the APEX card out from the bottom of the bag. I hadn't been sure I wouldn't be strip searched by whoever showed up, so I had dropped it into the sack when nobody was looking. I knew it would be safe with Arliss. I stuck it in my back pocket.

It took ten more minutes and three more trips before we had everything in Kim's RV. Kim followed us with the last load, having said goodbye to Lucille. Once inside her bus, she wasted no time climbing into the driver's seat. "Arliss. Get over here in the copilot's seat and strap your ass in. We're out of here."

I'd never seen Arliss in love, and I thought it was pretty funny. Here he was, a six-foot-four mulatto tough guy, and some little wisp of a woman was ordering him around, and he was loving it. He handed me his RPG. "Here. You might need this."

"Good luck, buddy," I told him as I hit the door. The train was leaving the station, with or without me. I had to give it to her, she had her shit together, and she was a perfect match for Arliss.

I barely got the door before it closed and she pulled away.

Two minutes later, I was back with Lucille in her kitchen. We shared a long, deep kiss before saying anything. I think we were both relieved that everybody was gone, I wasn't dead or in jail, and we finally had some time alone.

I remembered the papers in the broiler and went to pull them out before Murphy's law kicked in. "What are you going to do with those?" she asked.

"Tony thinks I'm in federal custody now, along with the reader and cards. He'll be sweating bullets wondering if I'm talking. He'll also be covering his ass with his associates. They won't be happy if they find out, so he'll just wait until he knows something before he tells them. In the meantime, he'll be beating the bushes to find where the feds are holding me."

"But isn't that data already in the reader?"

"Just Little and Big Nicky's stuff. Laughlin and Vegas. Tony's stuff was never transferred to the reader." I held up the sheath of paper. "This is the only copy. And I still have the card."

And the thumb drive.

"What are you going to do?" The lawyer was coming out.

"I'm going to wait a month and send him a copy of this, along with a note telling him that as long as I keep breathing, this shit will never see the light of day."

"Where do you want to go?" She was my lover now.

I brought her back to the lawyer part. "I think Mexico would be a good idea. For a month, at least. It'll take that long for the smoke to clear and for you to get everything on paper. I've got some enemies down there too, but nothing like here. It would be a good place to send my package to Tony from on our last day there. That ought to throw him off. We can go from there."

I reached into my canvas bag and pulled out the last two vacuum-packed bundles of hundreds and handed them to her. The twenty grand left at the bottom looked pretty sad. Amazing how fast you can blow a quarter million bucks.

"Here's ninety-six grand, give or take. Use it for the battered woman's shelter that you're sponsoring. God knows you been underpaid so far."

Nothing like a hundred grand to make a woman all teary-eyed.

"I think Mexico can wait for a couple hours," she said, taking my hand and leading me and my RPG down the hallway to her bedroom. I decided I would use the remaining twenty grand to get me a five-carat canary yellow flawless diamond ring from one Arliss's associates. He could overnight it to me in Puerto Peñasco.

A half hour later, she was snoring softly, and I was staring out the window, waiting for Abel to show up and wondering if they had casinos in Mexico with slot machines.

Sizzling Seven slots in particular.

I had a couple of credit cards burning a hole in my pocket.

Aces & Eights

PROLOGUE

Funny how a simple text message can turn your life on a dime. Mine read, "Mr. Jones, my husband is out of town this weekend. I'll be in Phoenix this afternoon, and I have your money. Please contact me."

This woman obviously had the wrong number, but my curiosity was aroused. I thought about it for a moment, then texted her back: "I'll be in room 1472 at the Tapatillo Cliffs Hilton. Meet me @ 5PM. Don't talk 2 anyone else. Don't be late."

I was going to be there anyways, so what the hell.

1

The woman next to me was giving me the hairy eyeball. Me being Jake Leggs, pushing fifty, erstwhile finder, sometimes contractor, most times fixer. My job description is a little vague. I do what I do. I don't have a résumé. I don't carry a gun, but I have friends that do. People that need my services know where to find me. Lately, I didn't want to be found.

I was in Phoenix after spending a month in Mexico. The Mexico thing was the result of a misadventure I'd had in Laughlin, Nevada. I was in Laughlin because Flagstaff's police chief had told me to go away and not come back for a while.

A month ago, my new best friend, Detective Sabbatini of Bullhead City's finest, had told me the same thing.

I was starting to see a pattern here.

After four weeks of beaches and margaritas, I was going stir-crazy. I needed to go back to work and have a real life. I needed a job.

Yesterday, I checked out of my beachside casita and flew back to Arizona with my lawyer. Phoenix was the closest I could get to Flagstaff without being arrested. I settled in at one of Hilton's finest, the Cliffs, that had seven pools, balconies with a view, and a superb bar. I wasn't rich, but I had a few bucks thanks to a couple of DARPA credit cards.

"Who was that?" Lucille asked. Lucille was my lawyer and my lover. At the moment, we were both laying naked on the room's California king-size bed.

"Wrong number."

That was always a red flag for women. "Then why'd you text her back?" my lover asked.

It was a trick question. I never said anything about gender. She was a lot smarter than me, so I had to be careful here.

I handed her my cell phone. "I think I just found a job." She was much more proficient, technologically, than I am, and it only took her a second to pull up all my Inbox and Sent. After reading *all* my messages, she rolled on her side to face me.

"What are you up to?" my lawyer asked.

You can lie to your lover but not your lawyer. "I think this woman is being blackmailed." I paused to lay it out for her. "She didn't use his first name. Mr. Jones? Hello? It isn't an assignation. It's a payoff."

Lucille studied the display for a few moments then said, "I think you're right." The lawyer in her had taken over. She had at least two personalities that I know of. Three, if she had more than three shots of tequila. Four, if she had more than six.

With that, I went for it. "I think I should delve into this a little deeper. Just one of those things that drops out of the blue, you know?"

She grabbed my face with both hands and made me look her in the eye until she was satisfied I wasn't scamming her before saying, "Okay, but we're attached at the hip. You're not getting out of my sight."

That was fine with me, so I gave her a lip-lock and rolled her over.

2

After our early morning delight, she went off to visit her battered woman's shelter that she sponsored, and I headed for the pool that had the biggest Jacuzzi.

Life was good.

In the last two months, I'd run into drug kingpins, Nazis, mobsters, and every law enforcement agency in the alphabet. I was still walking on eggs after a month south of the border. Fortunately, I'd kept my lawyer *real* close to me. Now I felt like I was home.

When I got to the pool, I laid my towel on the chaise lounge, settled in with my beer and my paperback, but never got a chance to crack either one.

My cell phone sang out "Desperado" by the Eagles. A little joke from my tech-savvy lawyer. I didn't recognize the number displayed. I thought my phone was new enough that nobody knew about it, but I was wrong.

"Hello?" I said cautiously.

"Tony wants to see you," Leo said. Leo was Tony's butler.

Tony was the head of the Phoenix mob.

My misadventure in Laughlin had been initiated by Tony. What started out as a stolen wallet turned into a mob turf war. The job Tony hired me for didn't come with health insurance, so I had to create some of my own. Something he didn't know about.

Up until last week, he thought the feds had me on a myriad of felony charges. He'd gone to great pains to try to locate what prison I was in. He had to assume I was spilling my guts, and that could not happen.

What he didn't know was I had parked my ass in Mexico to give everybody time to cool down.

Now I was going to see if he still wanted to kill me. I didn't want to have to hide anymore.

A week ago, I'd sent an envelope to his sister from Puerto Peñasco that contained a hard copy that had all his business numbers on it. His books.

I doubted the feds were checking her mail, so I thought it might get through. Even if it was intercepted, they wouldn't know what they were looking at.

The problem for him was that he was hiding numbers not only from the IRS but also his superiors. The Commission.

Along with the file was my proposition. As long as I kept breathing, that information would never see the light of day.

Now I was going to see if we had a deal. Whether I would live or die. I hoped he would look at this like everything else, just a business deal. Nothing personal.

Tony had a sprawling estate in Scottsdale, so it didn't take me long to get there. The gate opened as I pulled up in my twenty-year-old Corvette. He obviously knew I wasn't far away. My passport must have been flagged when I reentered the US. Tony had guys everywhere. So much for trying to slip in the back door.

Leo, his butler of a half century, met me at the door and, without saying a word, led me into the living room that was bigger than most houses I'd grown up in. Francine, his long-suffering wife of sixty years, was sitting beside him on the couch, watching a cooking show on the six-foot plasma screen.

I suspected the only reason Tony was watching was because the show's host was an anorexic blond with augmented tits. Personally, I don't trust a skinny cook.

When Francine saw me, she waved and got up and headed for the kitchen. She knew it was men's talk. Tony muted the TV as I sat down next to him.

I waited for Tony to start the dance while Francine started banging pots and pans around in the kitchen.

After a minute of not-so companionable silence, he spoke. "That wasn't nice, what you did, Jake."

I had to be careful here. "It was just business, Tony. You were going to whack me, so you can see I had to do something to prevent that."

He nodded but didn't smile. "You're right. It was just business, Jake. Nothing personal." I could tell he was starting to relax, so I made my proposal. I decided to be straight with him.

Tony had managed to corrupt a guy from DARPA, the super-secret government research agency who provided him with cybertechnology to use against his rival, Big Nicky Mosconi of Vegas, with my unwitting help.

"Little Nicky's dead." He probably knew that. "Big Nicky is in a super-max." He probably *didn't* know that. "The feds have the reader and the Visa card. The only data they have access to are the Mosconi's, so they have nothing on you. I had your info deleted. I haven't been questioned. What's in my head and my safety deposit box will be our secret as long as my head stays in one piece."

I think Benjamin Franklin said, "Two people can keep a secret as long as one of them is dead."

"I assume you've got your IT guy well hidden, and you can create more of the devices," I said, hoping he would accept my analysis of our situation.

He waved his hand in dismissal. "Why should I trust you?" he asked.

"I've always been straight with you, Tony."

He nodded again. "You know I've always thought of you as the son I never had."

Right. A month ago, you put a hit out on me.

"So I'm going to trust you. But if I hear even a whisper of the feds sniffing around, I'm going to assume the worst. And you know what that means."

Yeah, you'll kill me and everybody I know.

"So do we have a deal?" I asked. I was either walking out the door in the next minute or seeing my fifth-grade teacher, Sister Mary Katherine, in hell.

Tony leaned over and patted me on the knee. "Do us both a favor and try to stay out of trouble. Remember, no feds."

I didn't wait for Leo to show me to the door. Francine waved goodbye from the kitchen as I went by. If you know any Italian women, you would know who was really wearing the pants in this family.

3

I really didn't expect to walk out of Tony's house alive, but I was glad we had the talk. I didn't want to be looking over my shoulder for Tony's undertakers for the next twenty years, and I wanted to stay in Arizona. I knew he would double-check the information I gave him to be sure. Tony was into the details.

He knew I wasn't bluffing about having the goods on him, so as long as I didn't cooperate with the feds, I could go about my business. It was to his benefit that I kept breathing until he could find my safety deposit box.

Right now, my only business was getting back to the pool at the resort.

I almost made it. I had a cold can of Coors in my hand, a beach-sized towel over my arm, and I spied a chaise lounge close to the Jacuzzi. As I sat down, the damned phone went off again. I should have left it in the room, and I damned sure shouldn't have answered it.

"Yes?"

"Mr. Jones, I'm at the airport. I know I'm early, but I wish to conclude our business sooner than later."

I liked a woman that came early. "I have no problem with that. What do you propose?"

"That you come get me. I think someone is following me," she said in a whisper. "I'll be at the Baja Cantina concession in terminal four. I'm in a black pantsuit and a blond wig. Please hurry."

Well, I was looking for a job. Now I had one, and it was shaping up to be a doozy. I slammed my beer, left my towel, threw my T-shirt on, and hauled ass to my car. I was at the airport in fifteen minutes.

I parked close to the door in short-term and took a couple minutes to change from my bathing suit to a pair jeans. There was nothing I could do about the flip-flops.

I was almost to the Cantina when I saw the two guys. One of them was pretending to read a freebie real estate brochure. The other one was studying the arrival/departure board like it was porno film.

They didn't look like law enforcement. More like the dark side.

I definitely had the look of a local, so I charged right ahead. Entering the bar, I picked her out right away. Her black Chanel business skirt and Jimmy Choo shoes probably cost more than I made in a month. Her blond wig only emphasized her beauty. She was drinking a martini, two olives and a twist.

I sat down across from her like I was her husband. If she was surprised, she didn't show it.

"Mr. Jones, I presume," she said, looking at me like I was a zoo specimen. Taking another pull on her martini and killing it, she motioned to the waitress for another.

I didn't mind being looked down upon as long as I could learn something. "We need to go," I told her. I saw a spark of rage in her eyes before she overcame it.

"Fine," she said, getting up and leaving a fifty on the table. I knew she did it so that her waitress would remember her and yours truly. I continued to act like the pussy-whipped husband until we got out of the airport. When we got to the car, I grabbed her elbow and spun her around.

"Are we going to get along or not?"

I could tell she wanted to hit me, but she held her anger in check. "Let's just get this over with," she said, but her lips didn't move.

Letting go of her, I walked the twenty feet to my car. I knew Huey and Dewey wouldn't be far behind. I didn't open her door for her, and she barely got it closed before I peeled out and down the exit ramp. I heard more screaming rubber behind me.

When I pulled up to the pay booth, I noticed the attendant was a Navajo. He was probably related to someone I knew. "There's a couple of skin-walkers following us. Do you think you could slow them down?" I said, handing him a hundred.

"You got it, chief," he replied with a smile, raising the barrier. The watchers were three cars back. The attendant took plenty of time processing each car in front of them before opening the barrier. The two guys were going nuts, waving their arms out the windows in frustration.

I was on I-10 before they got past my new Navajo friend.

When I got to I-17, I headed north then took 101 east. The top was down, so that precluded conversation. That was fine with me. I kept one eye on the mirror for a tail.

When we got to Seventh Street, I headed south to the Hilton. By then, I was sure we hadn't been followed.

4

When we pulled into the Hilton, I knew I needed to call my lawyer. Whatever was going on, I needed some support. At least some documentation.

What I got was voice mail.

"Call me," I said. "It's important."

Pulling up in front of my unit, I got out and headed for my room. I didn't open her door. Corvettes were hard for women to get out of without showing some beaver. She was already pissed to begin with, and I didn't see the point in exacerbating the situation. I had enough on my plate already.

I was already sitting down when she followed me through the door. She had her hand in her purse, and I was pretty sure she would normally have a little peashooter in it. Then again, we just came from the airport, so maybe not. There was another chair on the other side of the table, and she took it.

Without preamble, she pulled ten bundles of hundred-dollar bills out of her purse and placed them in front of me.

"There it is. One hundred thousand dollars."

I didn't make a move on the money.

"When are you going to do it?" she asked. When I didn't respond, she said, "I want the son of a bitch dead."

I furrowed my eyebrows. "Which one?" I was feigning confusion, like I had a list.

"My husband."

Whoa. What the hell have I gotten myself into?

"Take your clothes off," I told her as I grabbed her purse and dumped its contents on the table. Her eyes got wide, and her mouth dropped open. I pulled her driver's license out of her wallet. She was Della Myers with a million-dollar address in Santa Fe, New Mexico.

"That's not part of the deal," she said after regaining her composure.

I already had more than I could handle—not that she wasn't a knockout.

"You can keep your bra and panties on, lady. I'm just checking for a wire."

It turned out she wasn't wearing any of them.

She didn't seem to be the least embarrassed standing butt naked in front of me, but I was. I kept forgetting that nowadays, a lot of women forgo those items, especially if they've got great tits and don't want panty lines.

That's when Lucille walked in the door.